# The Bloody Cloud
# Descends . . .

Marcel bounded away from the car and Holland scrambled frantically over the seat to pull the door shut.

The tattoo increased to a frenzy and the road itself appeared to be alive as the locusts landed, exhausted and hungry from their flight.

Holland slammed the door. Stephanie screamed and pointed through the glass at Marcel, frantically slapping at his shoulders and face as he fought to stop the locusts from shredding his skin.

Holland started the Fiat and slipped it into gear. He drove straight toward Marcel, and leapt from the car— scattering insects from the body. Marcel was still breathing, but Holland felt sickened by the sight of the man's torn and bloody face; an eye socket gaped emptily at him . . .

# THE PREDICTION

## JOHN HYDE

PUBLISHED BY POCKET BOOKS NEW YORK

POCKET BOOKS, a division of Simon & Schuster, Inc.
1230 Avenue of the Americas, New York, N.Y. 10020

Copyright © John Hyde 1980

Published by arrangement with Futura Publications Limited

ISBN: 0-671-83338-3

First Pocket Books printing November, 1983

10 9 8 7 6 5 4 3 2 1

*For John Crisp,*
*who took the trouble with Katie,*
*and for Katie,*
*who took the trouble with me*

# Book One

# GENESIS

*The land is as the Garden of Eden before
them and behind them a desolate wilderness;
yea, and nothing shall escape them.*

*Before their face the people shall be
much pained: All faces shall gather blackness.*

*They shall run to and fro in the city;
they shall run upon the wall, they shall
climb up upon the houses; they shall enter
in at the windows like a thief.*

*The earth shall quake before them;
the heavens shall tremble; the sun and
the moon shall be dark, and the stars shall
withdraw their shining.*

*Then when they saw the portent advancing
towards their valleys in the shape of a cloud,
they said: Here is a cloud bringing us rain.
Indeed not! This is that which you asked to be
hastened: a wind carrying a grievous punishment.
It will destroy everything by the command of its
Lord. When morning arrived there was nothing
to be seen except their dwellings.
Thus do we requite a guilty people.*

The Book of Al-Ahqaf
in the Holy Koran

# PROLOGUE

*It stretched and felt the earth beneath its mass, drew energy from the air around it.*

*Long dormant memories of the past were summoned, but it could not recognize this place. It seemed to be so similar in so many ways, but not quite the hunting ground it had known.*

*It grew in strength with each hour that passed and lifted toward the life-giving rays of the sun. There was greater heat here than in the Other Place, in the Other Time. But that mattered little. It would be better now for the growth.*

*And something else was different. It felt, but couldn't comprehend, the change. It was stronger, yes, but that was not all. It hungered, but that was ever so, that had always been.*

*It could not place the greater need, and so ignored the difference and concentrated on the growth, checking and supervising, replenishing and taking nourishment from the fruits of the soil and atmosphere.*

*Feeling along its flanks, it understood well the weakness that still existed, knew it would need to wait until the power returned. For it would return.*

*The mass would multiply, and then the time would come.*

*It had already strayed from here, and enjoyed once more the sensations that for so long had been denied.*

*It moved again. From the sprawling tail, this time, a part detached and eased itself away, slowly at first and then with gathering momentum.*

*The mass understood the exhilaration of the detached portion and was conscious of all it experienced as it moved, examining what lay below.*

*Soon, very soon, it would be time for all to experience these things together.*

# CHAPTER ONE

MARK HOLLAND HATED AIRPORTS.

They brought back memories of a time he tried to forget, tried to bury in the darker recesses of his mind. All too often, Holland couldn't help thinking of another airfield—a military airfield in Korea.

The tall American spat a wad of phlegm and desert dust through the ineffective screen that covered the open window—a half-hearted attempt at keeping the dust and insect life out of the Quonset hut which served as the terminal building.

Holland stared at an old bitch of a Dakota taxiing slowly and with obvious effort across the apron, getting ready for take-off. Its engines whined and screeched in abject protest as the pilot took the dependable old workhorse through its pre-flight check list.

The whirring, sun-bright blades gathered ever more speed until they appeared to the eye to be spinning in reverse, and as he watched this all too familiar bird lumber from the ground, he experienced again the things that haunted him. His mind turned the clock back to 1951.

\* \* \*

"Captain Holland, I don't give a shit for your feelings. Your job is to get your wing mobile and back into this fucked-up war—or do you really want to finish in the stockade for refusing to obey an order?"

Colonel Gaines glared at Holland and waited for the immediate salute and about turn which indicated an end to the argument. It always worked. These glory boys had a lot of balls when it came to shooting at the enemy from behind the relative safety of their modern jet fighters, but when it came to a few years in the pen, with a dishonorable discharge to boot, they always backed down.

"All I'm trying to say, Colonel," persisted the pilot, "is I think Intelligence has fucked up again. I'm damn sure I drove through that village and I sure as hell didn't see any gook buildings, or even any preparation for defenses. It looked just like an ordinary, peaceful place to me . . . just, you know, peaceful as hell."

The colonel chewed the stump of his cigar and studied the young captain wearily. "When did you say you drove through that area, Captain?"

"Four months ago, but—"

"Four *months* ago? Shit, those yellow bastards could build themselves a fuckin' town in four *weeks*."

Colonel George Gaines sighed and cast tired eyes around the hilly countryside that surrounded the small airfield. He knew that sooner or later pilots and air crew started to lose that touch. The fine edge. They started to unwind the dedication a little. Usually it was because they were coming to the end of their tour of duty and wanted to make sure that they stayed in one piece for the time when they would walk down Main Street with the welcoming hometown band strutting out in front while the local hero sat in the back of a convertible and waved to all his old friends and neighbors. They all wanted that brief feeling of glory.

And now his best wing leader was going soft in the head. Another opening salvo in the familiar struggle to evade a mission. Gaines shook his head sadly. He'd seen a lot of other good pilots go the same way.

But Holland was something else. A contradiction to the normal pattern of battle fatigue. Holland, Gaines knew, was a tough battle-hardened man who didn't seem to care about getting back to the States. But maybe, just maybe, it was getting to be too much even for Holland.

Gaines turned from the doorway and fired his lighter into life, bending to suck the flames toward the cigar end. After satisfying himself that it would draw sufficiently, he raised his head to stare icily at the younger man.

"Request to abort the mission denied, Captain. Now get going, your wing is waiting for you to get this war goin' again."

Holland nodded slightly and snapped off a cursory salute as he brushed past the colonel. He walked steadily toward his own plane at the front of the line of five parked and ready, conscious that Gaines was staring after him. The colonel's eyes seemed to burn into his back. The man didn't understand the Feeling, and how could Holland explain that he knew, just *knew* it was wrong to fly this mission?

The Dakota rose from the single, shimmering concrete runway and into the clear desert sky. Mark Holland shook himself free of the memory and turned back into the overcrowded waiting room. Today of all days should not be spent thinking morbid thoughts.

The small provincial airport was as untidy and as dusty inside as it was out. Saudi Arabia was not at the top of the international jet set list for the "must be" place in June, but for Holland it offered some solitude and escape. Not quite home, perhaps, but then home for him had never been in one particular place.

He glanced around the hot room at the mixture of faces: Saudi nationals too poor to be in London buying up Oxford Street, salesmen, construction workers, oilmen, a few Western women who looked as though they were secretaries with one of the large oil companies, and a group of nurses returning to Riyadh after a field trip into some of the more remote settlements and construction sites.

The oilmen dreamed of cold beer, the salesmen thought of

that new house in the country they would buy with their commission checks—or a new compact car if they hadn't had such a good trip. It made no difference what they wanted the money for. They were the new pioneers, suffering abstinence instead of Indian arrows, celibacy instead of stampedes, scorpions instead of rattlesnakes.

The big difference was that if it really got to be too much for you, and if you weren't under contract to a company, you could get on a plane and be back in civilization in no time flat—though Holland didn't know what in hell civilization meant.

The heat outside the terminal swept across the tarmac in visible, suffocating waves as he kicked the ancient Coca-Cola machine in a vain attempt to get it to surrender something, anything, for the coin he had inserted.

He caught sight of his reflection in the cracked, worn mirror of the machine. The face, a little on the rugged side with a strong, square-cut jaw, stared back. Were it not for the sun-bleached hair, cropped short to accommodate the searing heat, his tan could almost have allowed him to pass for an Arab.

He turned from the machine and studied the wall clock. If it could be trusted he had a little under an hour to wait for the Trans-Global flight from Addis Ababa.

Holland walked the length of the terminal, past small, frustrated gatherings, half listening to the snatches of complaining conversation that came in pulses through the heat.

"Another month and I'da brung that well in. Another month is all . . ."

". . . diamond as big as your . . ."

". . . coldest beer in the whole damn wor . . ."

". . . if she's taken another friggin' lodger in I'll kill the pair of them. So help me, this time . . ."

". . . not looking forward to that screaming brat. Still ain't sure it's mine . . ."

Human flotsam with human problems. Holland smiled inwardly at his fellow sufferers and walked toward the rickety bookstand that boasted two-day-old copies of the world's major newspapers.

Human flotsam, he thought to himself as he leafed idly through an old copy of *Newsweek*. He himself had been just that. Flotsam. Until Kate.

They had met just over a year ago while he was flying construction crews and equipment into the interior. The Saudis had decided to build another airport, one of several the country boasted and yet another which would never be used.

He had been attracted to her immediately. She had moved with a grace and assurance which made men's heads snap around in approval. Holland recalled the first time he had seen her, her blouse pulled taut across her magnificent breasts, then parting as she reached around for a large portable typewriter. He had admired the brief glimpse of flesh and the way in which she coolly rebuttoned the blouse.

Deep brown eyes had flashed around the room in silent warning to the grinning males that it would be dangerous to carry any lustful thoughts to their logical conclusion. Holland had been more than appreciative of her manner and ability.

Kate had at that time been working as executive assistant to the head of the construction company and he had had to fly them to the site. She had taken an immediate liking to the surly American, and on discovering he was an aeronautical engineer had expressed amazement that he was flying—"jockying" she had called it—rust-bucket aircraft around the Middle East.

The woman hadn't given him the line about his surliness and curt attitude being a front, a protective shield which he placed around himself. She had respected his reticence in talking about his past. Over the next three months he had flown Kate and her employer around several major development areas from their base in Riyadh, and had found himself warming toward her in a way he had not thought possible.

There had been many women in Mark Holland's life— temporary necessities who floated through his subconscious like offensive reminders of his youth. Kate was younger than he, much younger. Yet at length he had discovered a need for her, a need that had always existed, but that he had learned to do without.

The realization of Kate's importance to his own being had

come slowly, like the gentle wind across the desert. It was not that he had leaned on her or used her for support, although in truth he knew there had been an element of that in the relationship. It was more that she was an extension of his own person.

Mark had found that while they had agreed on so many things, there were, understandably, subjects on which she simply couldn't agree with him. One of those was Mark's seeming inclination to hide himself away in the desert, "escaping from responsibility and purpose," she had said during one particularly heated argument.

Kate finally told Mark she couldn't be the sort of woman who would move heaven and earth to change her man. She would help with her support, her love, and a good measure of guidance, but the initial move back into the human race would have to come from within himself. "I don't intend to just be a soft body to lie next to when the going gets rough," she warned him. "I can and will be an important part of you, but if you want our relationship to grow then you must make up your mind to be more of the man you must have been once."

When the time finally came for her to return to England, she told Mark that she would stay to be near him until his contract expired. He smiled to himself at the memory of that evening as they had walked along the beach talking softly to each other while the warm ocean ran over their bare feet.

Kate was unable to stay in Saudi, as her visa was nonrenewable. Her boss had arranged for her to join Trans-Global Oil in Addis Ababa, again as an executive. It was a long way for courting, he had remarked, "but I'm sure you two will be able to figure a way around the distance."

They had. Whenever Mark's flying took him within easy haul of Addis he would make the detour. She, conversely, found perfectly legitimate and regular reasons for flying to Saudi with a research team. If she couldn't find one, and Mark wasn't scheduled for a route that took him within easy hoppi.g distance of Ethiopia, then she talked one of the Trans-Global pilots on a Saudi shuttle into giving her a free ride.

One way or another, they saw each other at least every two weeks.

Today, however, was different. Mark's contract was at an end and he and Kate were flying to Geneva to get married. From there on to England to see her parents and then back to the States and the small ranch left to him by his father.

He still couldn't believe it. He had found—no, that wasn't quite right—he had *been* found, rescued by her and he wanted to settle down. Kate had made him ready, prepared him for this. It was a long time in coming, but finally it was here. Today was the first day of his life.

He glanced at the clock. Still forty minutes to go.

Kate, he recognized, had taken the shell of a bitter, twisted, cynical bastard, and through her gentle coaxing had helped him to find the way back to—what? Fulfillment? Yes, that was it in part, but not quite enough to describe what he had gained as a result of knowing her.

Kate had nurtured him and helped him to overcome even the nightmares that he had suffered for so long. She had learned of his terrors and guilt, and had never condemned or excused. She had merely understood and guided him back through the darkness. And now they would make that final step. They would return to his home for the first time since the day his mother died, the day his father told Mark he never wanted to see him again.

The sound of an anxious voice cut through his reflections. A small, seedy Arab bustled around from the rear of the line of desks which served as the airline departure counter. He was obviously greatly disturbed and drew a handkerchief across his forehead. Holland's stomach gripped him in a sudden spasm. He became instantly alert. The warning sign couldn't be ignored.

The official stood in the center of the room and swatted anxiously at a persistent fly which had followed him from the other side of the counter. Had it not been for the knot in his belly, Holland would have been amused at his stilted, awkward English.

"Gentlemens and ladies please to listening regarding this announcement. We must wish that those who are awaiting the flight of Trans-Global Oil from Ethiopia to please joining me in our office at the other side of the departing counter."

The Arab bustled away like a frightened scorpion and Holland crushed his cigarette under the heel of his right boot before pushing himself away from the newspaper stand and striding after the man.

As the Arab reached the door to his office, he felt a heavy hand grip his shoulder, twisting him around.

"What's wrong with that flight?"

"You had someone you waiting for, sir, on this plane?"

Holland squeezed a little harder and the man winced. "What's wrong with that flight, mister?"

The Arab avoided Holland's stare, could sense he already knew something terrible had happened, and that did not make things any easier. He motioned that they should enter the office.

The tall American had been the only person to come forward, other than a small group of curiosity seekers. The Arab indicated that Holland should sit in the wicker chair, then when he refused walked across to the window and looked searchingly into the desert. He had never had to undertake this task and had always dreaded the moment.

"Sir, I am with the airport authority for many years. This day will, without a doubt, be the worst of all those many. The Trans-Global Oil flight has gone down. I am very sorry to have to tell you this."

Holland stared uncomprehendingly at the Arab. The thought had passed swiftly, uneasily, through his mind when he heard the summons out in the lobby, but he had dismissed it. No way. He was aware of an exclamation behind him and he turned. A girl was holding her hand to her mouth in horror at what she had overheard. She turned and looked toward an older man who shook his head sadly. Holland turned back to the airport official. "How? *How did it happen?*"

The Arab shrugged his shoulders and held out the palms of his hands. "They tell me that the airplane was shot down somewhere over Yemen by guerrillas. That is all that is known this time. There was a radio with ground control, many sounds, and nothing. Dead air."

The wing had swept in low, jets screaming a momentary warning to the people on the ground. They came out of the sun to prevent the anti-aircraft gunners from finding them too readily. Holland led the sweep, knowing that to his left and right and slightly behind flew his cover—just in case the MIGs should decide that they wanted to come to the party.

Cloud cover was good and the weather boys said that they would have it down to at least 1,000 feet. When they broke through the overcast they would see the village, and as soon as they saw their target would commence firing. They had to have enough maneuvering room to pull out of the narrow valley.

At 1,500 feet Holland flipped the safety flap off the stick and exposed the firing button for the four synchronized, heavy-caliber machine guns—two on each wing—that would rake across the village and would, perhaps, keep the defense forces' heads down, enabling him to release the bombs slung under his wings and get out before they had a chance to react. That was the theory. Sometimes it worked.

He put the bomb switch to "Ready" and steeled himself for the sudden surge that the aircraft would experience when the bombs were released. Holland didn't mind the bombs so much, but he didn't like the guns. They gave him a headache.

Just under 1,000 feet, the wing broke through the ceiling and he caught a glimpse of Korean huts.

He flipped the bomb switches at the moment of recognition, just as he knew the rest of his squadron would be doing.

He pressed the red button on the joystick and heard the familiar yammering of his guns. The aircraft lurched forward with the sudden release of the bombs and Holland eased back on the stick to put the plane into a climb.

It was more dangerous to fly straight up. The gunners could easily follow his flight path and pick him off. But Holland had gambled that the gunners would be expecting him to fly through the village and take a normal turn either left or right. He placed his chances higher if he did the worst thing possible, on the premise that the enemy wouldn't be expecting it.

His radio crackled to life. "Skipper, this is Fire Watch Two, over."

Holland snapped his transmit button, angry at the break in radio silence by his co-leader. "Go ahead, and fast."

"Skipper, take a look at that village, for Christ's sake. Jesus, I think we made one hell of a mistake."

The knot in his stomach tightened. "What did you see, Bob?"

"Mark, there's nothing down there but old women and kids. I held back and took a look." Then he said quietly, "Intelligence has done it to us again, Skipper."

The flight leader felt the wave of revulsion sweep over him. No gooks, no gun emplacements, no soldiers. Nothing but women, children, and old men. He swung back over the village and saw the devastation that his wing had just inflicted. Well, that was one more village that would, in the future, welcome the North Koreans and spit on their so-called protectors.

"Fire Watch Two, this is Fire Watch Leader. Pass over it again, Bob, and take some tourist-type pictures of our good work in the name of freedom. Fire Watch Wing form up. We're going home to ram some napalm down the throat of the first Intelligence Corps bastard we see."

Holland felt the bile rise in his throat and wondered what would happen if he vomited into his oxygen mask. He felt as though it wouldn't matter if he drowned in his own sick. They were all drowning, only most of them didn't realize it.

He broke radio silence again to call the airbase with the request for medics and helicopter ambulances to be rushed to the village to aid the injured.

The jet landed and Holland could distantly hear the scream of reverse thrust as the thundering metal machine struggled to stop in the available distance. He looked around and for a moment fought with himself to understand what had just been said in the airport office.

Dazed, he had left the small Arab and walked purposelessly around the untidy terminal. One emotion fought with another inside his mind and he brushed away the warm tear that rolled down his cheek.

He leaned against a pillar, ignoring the stern looks which the porters gave him for blocking the access route. His forehead rested against the cool marble of the column, incongruous in an otherwise austere terminal, and gently he started to sob.

Eventually, Holland straightened himself and the first flashes of rational thought started to filter through the heartache. What should he do now? He shook his head from side to side in slow admission that he really didn't know what his next step should or would be. He fished out a cigarette and shakily fired his lighter, drawing the harsh smoke deep into his lungs. He rested against the column for a moment longer and then, instantly, he knew what his course of action would be.

Holland pushed through the small crowd, hearing snatches of conversation about the air crash, and caught the eye of the pretty girl behind the ticket desk. "When's the next flight to Addis?" he demanded brusquely.

"One hour, sir," she replied tartly, annoyed at his manner.

He thrust a wad of Riyals across to her. "Give me a seat."

# CHAPTER TWO

THE PRESS CLUB IN ADDIS ABABA REEKED OF CIGARETTE smoke, spilled whiskey and sweat.

It didn't matter what last night's party had been for. Most people had celebrated different things. Some had not celebrated anything at all.

If nothing else, a Press Club provides a source of warmth when you're cold, alcohol when you're thirsty, of stories—not necessarily reliable—when you're short of copy and your editor's screaming for something, anything, on the latest development from whatever corner of the world you happen to be relegated at the time.

To Mark Holland, the Addis Press Club would, he hoped, be a source of information above all else. He paid off the cab at the corner of Independence Street and dodged traffic and drivers' curses to cross the road.

The doorman officiously demanded a press card but Holland waved him aside. Something about this man's eyes made the Ethiopian withdraw his request and step back to let him pass.

Sandy Howard was just where Holland expected, propped against the corner of the bar waiting for somebody to buy the next round.

Holland moved behind the wreck that passed for *France Soir*'s African correspondent. "Sandy, the last time I saw you, you were in exactly the same spot. That was eight months ago. Have you moved since, or do you still piss in your pants?"

The journalist turned slowly, a smile on his face. "Jesus Christ himself! My God, old boy, I thought it was going to be one of those days I wouldn't see a single friendly face, and now here you are. My Lord, this calls for a drink."

Holland shook his head in amusement as Howard's hands waved frantically to the barman. "Still Scotch, old boy?"

"Bring the bottle," Mark ordered. "With the seal unbroken and a bucket of mineral-water ice cubes."

The two men found a clear table in the already filling room.

"My dear boy," said the Englishman as he poured two hefty shots of Scotch. "I can't tell you how jolly delighted I am to see you again. Now you must tell me where you have been, what you have been doing and who you have been doing it to."

Holland took a careful taste of the Scotch. He knew that as often as not the barmen at this club were inclined to siphon some off and replace it with urine. The last time he had been here he'd thrown a guy through the window for doing just that. He didn't want a repeat performance if he could help it. Now he always made sure that his whiskey came from a sealed bottle.

"Not a lot, Sandy," he said quietly. "I've been flying for a construction company over at Al Qunfidhah in Saudi. Matter of fact, I need some information—that's why I'm here."

Howard eased his backside across the chair seat to get more comfortable, and sighed. "I thought there had to be a reason for you to come in here this early. As I remember, you never touch the old booze until after one o'clock. What is it that I can do for you, Mark?"

"That plane that went down yesterday—what do you know about it?"

Howard thought for a moment before replying. "Trans-Global's? Addis to Sana, on to Abha. Believed to have been shot down by rebels in Yemen. Probably no survivors, but then they still haven't found the wreckage, so there could be. Passenger list comprised mostly of Trans-Global employees, but there were a few Arabs and other foreigners on board: three scientist types from the company; two bankers, Arabs, one doctor, British as I recall. Couple of Trans-Global secretaries; two or three Jerry construction types. No French on board so I didn't get too involved. My paper doesn't like me wasting time on other nationals. Why?"

Holland drank deeply and reached across the table for the bottle. He carefully refilled the two glasses and swirled the ice cubes.

"You never met the girl I was going to marry, did you, Sandy." It was a statement of fact rather than a question to the journalist, who sensed that there might be a human interest story coming up. Howard liked human interest stories. They sold papers, pleased the home office, and didn't require a lot of legwork.

Mark had drained the whiskey without realizing it and gagged on its unaccustomed strength.

"She was called Kate. Kate Carson, one of the passengers."

"She . . . was . . ." Mark stumbled over the unfamiliar tense. "She was working here in Ethiopia as an executive assistant for Trans-Global.

"I met her a couple of years ago when I flew this construction team into the Empty Quarter. We decided last month that it was time we settled down. She was on her way to meet me."

Howard looked through the dirty windows into the equally dirty street below. He'd not thought of this American as ever wanting to have that kind of relationship with anyone. A home, family, mortgage, bills, weekly shopping—that was the sort of routine that men like himself had. Or used to have, once.

"Mark, I can't tell you how sorry I am to hear this," he said. "I had no idea. Is there anything that I can do for you?" Then, as an afterthought, "I know; the biggest bloody wake this town has ever seen." He clapped his hands together in expectation of yet another party at the club.

Mark Holland shifted himself in the chair. Standing over six feet tall, he found it difficult to get comfortable sitting down; now in the company of this Englishman he felt even more uncomfortable. The guy was a loser and everybody knew it. But he could still be a useful loser.

"No thanks, Sandy. Not tonight. I'd like you to do something for me, though. Find out through your contacts whether or not the rebels did shoot her plane down."

"I do have a great many contacts, it's true, old boy," replied the writer self-importantly, "but why on earth do you need to know that? Surely the fact that it's down is enough. Why tear yourself apart finding out the gory details?"

The "gory details." Mark took his turn looking through the window. Ziad had used that phrase a lot. It was one of the first English catch phrases that he'd learned from Mark when they had been roommates at Johns Hopkins.

Mark had arrived fresh from Korea to study aeronautical engineering and Ziad's family had sent their eldest male to learn the ways of the world, albeit the American world. Mark had proved to be a good teacher, for Ziad liked nothing better than going downtown to examine all the "gory details" first-hand. They had graduated at the same time, Mark with his engineering degree, Ziad with a medical degree and a young doctor's hopes and ambitions to return home and wage war on the diseases that ravaged his people.

"I have my reasons, Sandy. Just find out as much as you can, will you? As soon as you can."

Howard sighed and reached for the bottle. "As you will, old boy, but I must warn you that information doesn't come cheap in this dusty metropolis. Sensitive subject I know, but . . ."

Mark reached into his desert jacket and extracted the roll of bills. "Five hundred bucks. Don't spend it all at one time or in one place. I'm staying at the Excelsior. Start digging and let me know what you find out, as soon as you find it out. *Capiche?*"

Howard smiled. "*Si, signor. Capiche.* I'll be in touch this evening. Now, what about the rest of the bottle?"

# CHAPTER THREE

THE WOMAN RAN DOWN THE DUSTY ROAD WITH THE FIRE reaching toward her gaping mouth. Her silent scream engulfed Holland as he ran toward her. Bob Strake walked out of the burning hut with a rifle in his mouth and jets screamed overhead dropping cans of Coca-Cola that turned to napalm as soon as they hit the ground.

Kate walked toward the burning woman, oblivious of her, tinkling a Korean religious bell.

The woman ran into Kate's arms and flames leaped hungrily toward the new source of fuel. Mark screamed and woke up bathed in sweat. He could still hear the bell.

It took several seconds before he realized that the ringing was coming from the telephone by the side of the bed. Wiping sweat from his face with his shirt sleeve, he reached for the instrument.

"Yeah," he said huskily, feeling as though his throat were on fire.

"Hello, old boy. Did I wake you? I'm in the lobby. Perhaps you'd like to come on down so I can fill you in on what I've dug up."

"Meet you in the bar in ten minutes, Sandy." Mark hung

up the telephone and hastily stripped off his soaking clothes. He moved rapidly into the bathroom and turned on the shower.

Ten minutes later he walked into the bar and spotted the now elegantly dressed journalist holding court by the serving counter. Holland smiled to himself. The five hundred dollars didn't look like it would last long.

Howard spotted him, excused himself from his new-found friends and proceeded to steer Mark toward an unoccupied table. "The gist of it is, Mark—though for the life of me I don't see how it can possibly do anything for you—the gist of it is that the Yemeni rebels have spread the word through to their people here that they have had nothing whatever to do with that plane coming down.

"Of course, they haven't been able to get the world press to listen because, you understand, communication with them is very limited. Bit difficult, I should imagine, holding a press conference on the side of a mountain. My contact says the rebels' official line is that this is simply the government's way of further discrediting their just fight for the people and all that rot. Bloody awful things anyway. I can't see why anybody would want to go up in one."

Holland nodded silently. "Where did it come down?"

"In the mountains, apparently. By the way, did you know that it was logged out of the airport half an hour earlier than it was scheduled to leave? I found that out at the airport. Seems that all the passengers had arrived and they figured that it wasn't worth hanging around."

Mark felt the knot in his stomach return. After digesting what the journalist had reported, he leaned back in the chair and signaled to the waiter to bring drinks. "Right, you've done pretty good. Now go back to your contacts and tell them that I want to go into those Yemen mountains and take a look for myself—"

Howard interrupted. "Waste of time, old boy. Those chaps refuse to allow any foreigners into the stronghold. They've sealed the mountains off completely. Without a safe passage they'd shoot you down as soon as they spotted you. Can't be done."

"Yes it can. Tell your contacts to pass the message along and make sure they spell my name correctly. I want to go in there, so start earning that new suit I seem to have bought you."

Howard shrugged. "Can but try, old boy, can but try."

"You do that, old boy, you just do that."

The next evening a breathless and excited Sandy Howard plumped himself down in front of Mark as he ate supper in the garish restaurant at the Excelsior. Mark watched calmly as the man gasped his request for a large Scotch and water to the waiter. Holland realized that there would be no point in hurrying the report. Howard would want to savor every moment of his success. And his Scotch.

"Well, old boy," he said finally, "really don't know how—although I suppose it has something to do with spreading all your money around. Even guerrillas can be bought, it seems. I really am surprised at the extent of my con—"

"Get on with it." Mark snarled the words.

"Of course, sorry, old boy. The nut of it is that the OK has come through for you to pay a visit to bandit country. I had a call this evening and hot-footed it right over. It's really a strange thing though because—"

"When?"

"Eh? Oh yes, of course. I'm rambling, but you see I'd give my eye teeth to be able to go over and do an on-the-spot interview. I'm not as washed up as some people might think, you know," he finished quietly.

Mark looked at the man for a moment and then repeated, in a softer voice, "When?"

"Right away, or at least tomorrow morning. You are going for a trip first, across the Red Sea. We have to rendezvous with our contact just north of Assab, on the coast. There's a small cove there and the boat will be waiting, but it will only wait for twenty minutes, so we can't be late.

"Look, old boy, I feel that I must warn you that you could be facing the most awful risk. You'll be sailing with rebels. If you are stopped by the Ethiopians you'll end up in jail. If you're caught by the Yemenis you'll be shot—and that goes for when you're on land, but more so. Added to all that is the chance that the rebels might decide you're a spy and shoot you themselves."

Howard leaned back in the deep leather comfort of the chair and lit an English cigarette. "Of course," he continued, "there is yet another possibility. They could hold you for ransom. There have been three or four cases in the area over the last couple of years. The French bailed out one of their nationals a couple of years ago, but he was an important man, while . . ."

"While I'm just an American sky jockey without any value," concluded Holland. "I know the risks, Sandy, but I don't think I'm in much danger from the rebels. I have to see for myself if they brought the plane down. I have to begin somewhere, and the crash site is probably the best starting point."

"I have been told to leave Addis at nine in the morning. I assume that's so they can monitor us as we cross the country."

Mark nodded, rose, and strode without further word from the restaurant. In fifteen minutes he was settled into his bed and fell into a deep sleep.


"This court-martial is again in session," intoned the major from Seoul who was acting as judge advocate. "Captain Holland will take the stand, and I remind you, Captain, that you are still under oath."

Captain Mark Holland walked to the front of the mess and saluted the six officers who comprised the board, before again taking the witness chair. The previous day had been a long arduous affair, as he had recounted the events that had led up to the destruction of a "friendly" village.

By the end of the testimony, however, he found that his attitude and voice had hardened to the point where he felt as though he were recounting, not a part of his life that he would never forget, but a bad and distant dream.

The mood in the courtroom was tense as he settled himself, ready to begin his testimony again.

"Captain, at yesterday's close you had just finished relating this altercation you had with Colonel Gaines after you returned from your flight. I must warn you that the Fifth Amendment does not apply in this situation, as you have admitted voluntarily that you assaulted the colonel. I must, therefore, warn you that additional charges may now be pending against you, and caution you to be damn careful about what you say today."

Holland looked at the president for a moment before nodding his head. "Thank you, sir. I understand your caution."

"Let the record show. Captain Holland, do you have anything further to add to your testimony of yesterday?"

"Yes, sir, I do have something to add. When I was told that we were wiping out a friendly village, I ordered photographs to be taken. When these were developed and blown up we all had the opportunity to take a look at our handiwork. I can tell you that I sure as hell didn't feel proud of what we'd done and I know that a couple of the guys got kinda messed up over it.

"Well, my second-in-command was a kid by the name of Bob Strake, from Pittsburgh—"

"Objection. This is irrelevant to the matter under consideration and has already been the subject of a separate court of inquiry."

"Thank you, Mr. Advocate," replied the president, "but this is a court-martial. As such, anything that anybody has to say is of the greatest interest to this court; if it helps us to avoid a repetition of an incident or bears evidence on a man's emotional state prior to the alleged offense, we want to hear it. Clear?"

"As the court wishes, sir."

"Proceed, Captain . . . but I warn you, no gratuitous sensationalism that has no direct, repeat, direct bearing on the issue. Do you understand?"

"Yes, sir. Well, Lieutenant Strake was quite a guy. He did all the things that you'd expect of a pilot stuck in this hellhole, and with a damn fine sense of belonging to a team that was— is—trying to do something worthwhile."

Holland hoped that there wasn't too much irony creeping into his voice. He ran his hand through his hair and thought of Bob Strake. There had been few, if any, other men as close to Holland. There had not been the feeling of competition between them that often resulted in petty envy and jealousy.

Each had been the equal of the other, each providing the other with an important support and source of inspiration. They were two halves of a whole.

"Bob Strake saw those pictures about the same time that I did, and they floored him. I mean, I've known men to break down over things they've seen or done, but Bob went to pieces. What really got him, I think, was the shot of a woman carrying a child, running away from her burning hut. She was screaming in terror. The child was held close to her, as though she could protect it from the napalm. We assumed that it was a kid, but we couldn't be sure. The woman was a mass of flames from the neck down.

"Napalm had been sprayed onto her and the clothing was burning first, but she still had it in her to try to run away, and to scream. Of course, we couldn't hear the scream in the photograph and maybe that made it all the worse. It was like the agony would never stop.

"Bob clammed up right then and there. Couldn't sleep or eat; didn't want to move out of his bunk. He just lay there all day looking at the ceiling.

"Three days after the mission we found him in the bathtub. He'd shoved a rifle into his mouth and blown his head all over the wall.

"Strake was also a casualty of the Fong Lee raid, but he's not included on the casualty list. Suicide while the balance of his mind was disturbed, that's what the inquiry said. But, as sure as God made little apples, it was because he couldn't live with his part in that raid. I honestly don't know how the rest of us can either."

Absolute quiet descended on the courtroom as Holland finished. Spectators avoided looking at each other and several were wiping the corners of their eyes. The president of the court cleared his throat and mentally cursed Captain Mark Holland. It was all right screwing up occasionally, but why the shit did these glory boys insist on spreading the blame around?

"Thank you, Captain," he said at length. "Any questions?"

He looked to the other members of the court, hoping that

nobody would want to prolong the session. Nobody did. "At this point, as Captain Holland was the last witness, this court-martial is adjourned. We shall reconvene once . . ."

The journey across Ethiopia was uneventful. They shared the driving, with Sandy making exaggerated moves in the passenger seat, turning around to make sure that they were not being followed, when Mark drove.

Mark was sure that they had been followed on leaving Addis, but he had taken over the wheel at Dessye and lost the tail by driving backwards and forwards through the endless alleys which seemed to be all that the desert town contained. Mark had then joined a troop convoy which was moving out of the town, probably toward the Somalian border, and from then on he was sure that they had lost that particular shadow. He was not convinced, however, that they would not pick up another.

The old American car, a Pontiac which had seen better days, hurtled across the desert road. They got to Assab just after three in the afternoon. They parked the car off the main road, finding a café nestled under trees, giving them a good view of the road leading back to Addis. For the next two hours the only traffic to come into town were three over-laden donkeys and two trucks straining with farm produce.

Shortly after five, as the shadows lengthened in the square, Howard nodded. "Time to go, Mark, old boy."

"How far now?"

"'Bout ten miles. I figure we have an hour in total to get there, so there's plenty of time."

Mark flipped a handful of coins onto the table and allowed Howard to climb into the driver's seat. His stomach was starting to ache again. Something was wrong.

Howard found the right cove on the third attempt. "I hope that old tub isn't going to sink, old boy," he mused, as they stared at the ancient-looking fishing smack which bobbed lazily just off the shore.

"Back in Addis you forgot to add drowning as a possibility," replied Holland dryly, as he opened the door of the car. He hesitated for a moment and then turned back to the journalist.

He reached into his pocket and took out an envelope which he handed to Howard. "Sandy, if I'm not back in a month I won't be coming back. Take this to the manager at the Excelsior, and he in turn will give you a package. Make use of it in any way you see fit. Thanks for everything."

"You'll be back, old boy. Chaps like you are inclined to survive. I won't take the envelope. I'm afraid that I'd be tempted not to wait the month and when you return you'd probably find I'd pissed the lot up the wall. No, you can hang onto it. You've given me something pretty good in the last couple of days. Perhaps I'll shape up and start really working again. I haven't touched a drop all day, y'know. That's enough, old chap."

Mark smiled and gripped his arm. They both climbed out of the aging Pontiac. As they did, a man emerged from behind a rock and walked hurriedly toward them. He was dressed in the worn clothing fishermen the world over affect, and he looked extremely nervous.

"Hurry. We cannot wait longer. Who comes?"

Mark couldn't place the accent for a moment, but nodded, "Me."

"You are Holland?"

"Yes."

"What university you go to before going to army?" inquired the man cautiously.

"Johns Hopkins, and it was *after* I'd been in the Air Force."

The fisherman smiled, extending a massive hand that rested at the end of what appeared to be a small tree trunk. "Welcome. I am Katsos the Greek. Sorry about questions, but we have to be sure."

Holland turned to Sandy to say good-bye. As he did so the man's chest burst outward and Mark's shirt was splattered with warm blood and fragments of bone. Shock and incomprehension registered briefly on Sandy's face and then he crumpled slowly to the reddening sand. He was nearly down when the loud "crack" reached their ears.

"Run for the boat," shouted the Greek as he pulled a revolver from his belt.

Mark looked quickly at the Englishman and felt a wave of

regret. A second report sounded and a bullet smacked into the ground near his feet. Then Holland was moving in a zigzag run across the beach.

Three more shots penetrated the gloom around them before the fishing boat roared away from the cove on the powerful engines that were hidden beneath the decrepit deck planking. Minutes later they were safe, hurtling across the Red Sea toward Yemen.

"You brought company from the city," admonished the Greek.

"No chance. We were very careful." But the fact was they *had* brought trouble with them. Somehow. After leaving Dessye, they had still watched for the telltale sign of vehicle lights behind them, but had relaxed their vigilance. Mark slumped against the rail and thought of the journalist who now lay dead on the sand behind them.

The surging boat rocked him in his reverie.

"Nothing like a nice sea cruise to get the blood coursing through the veins, eh, Captain?"

"I guess not, Doc, but I still prefer to feel air under my boots. I never could get used to the lazy way of traveling."

The army doctor spat with the breeze and stretched his face toward the sun. It was a long, long way from Korea, and for that he was heartily glad. No more trying to stitch kids' legs back to their crumpled bodies, or dig chunks of metal out of their guts.

They were two days out of Pearl Harbor, steaming ever onwards toward San Francisco and good old American apple pie. No more war, no more grief. "What you going to do now it's over for you, Capt'n?"

Holland looked across the open stretch of water and then back at the close-packed troopship. The stench of human bodies crammed too closely together was nauseating, yet caused little complaint among the soldiers and airmen. They were going home.

Many were doing so because of wounds that were not serious enough to warrant passage by the Air Force. Others were returning to familiar soil as the result of having completed their tours of duty.

Still others, perhaps twenty in all, were under escort to begin a different kind of hell in a military prison, for a list of offenses as long as the Indo-Chinese border. Scuttlebutt even said that one of these unfortunates was being sent back for execution.

Somewhere in this variety of categories fit Mark Holland.

"What *did* you say you were going to do, Captain?" asked the army doctor as he spat again toward the heaving water.

"Take the Air Force scholarship route and study aeronautical engineering I guess, Doc. Flying is all I really know how to do."

"What you do before the war?"

"Crop duster."

"See what you mean!"

They lapsed into silence as the troopship moved toward the horizon and home. The sounds of the wounded men drifted towards Mark's ears, but soon the sounds merged with the slapping of the water against the hull.

# CHAPTER FOUR

"WAKE UP PLEASE. WE ARE THERE."

Holland woke instantly at the rough shaking of his shoulder. He glanced over the side of the ship to see a cove similar to the one they had left—how many hours ago? He couldn't see his watch. He half expected to see the same body lying in the sand.

The Greek pointed to the top of a rise. "Road is up there. Truck come take you inland to Taizz. Then, maybe, you walk rest of the way. Good luck, Yank."

Katsos shook his hand roughly, then added, "I am sorry about your friend. I know what it is to lose such a friend."

Holland nodded, then dropped over the side into the warm water.

There was a truck parked along the road with its hood up. A small ferret-faced man was tinkering with the engine. As Holland crept soundlessly up the embankment, the man dropped the hood and motioned to Mark to hurry.

"I'm Sam," said ferret-face. "I doubt that you could pronounce my real name, and I prefer Sam anyway." He tossed Mark a bundle of smelly clothes, telling him to put them on.

The picture of a Yemeni farm laborer was completed by an old ski hat, which he pulled roughly onto Mark's head after concealing his bloodstained shirt behind a rock.

"Why *Sam?*" Mark asked as the truck started to move.

"Samantha was the name of the girl I shacked up with at Oxford."

That answered what would have been Mark's second question—where had Sam learned English?

"How long will we be driving?" he asked instead, as his skin started to itch.

"Couple of hours," grinned Sam. "Clothes starting to itch? The fleas are hungry, like most of the people in Yemen."

The rest of the journey across the bleak landscape was conducted in relative silence, with Sam offering tepid water or wine every so often, or pointing out places that he thought Mark would be interested in. Mark wasn't.

Just before noon they pulled to a stop in a small grove of trees that might once have offered some shelter from the sun but now looked as sparse as the rest. Half a mile away toward the mountain range that separated civilization from the guerrillas.

"You are to wait here," instructed Sam. "Someone will be along soon to take you the rest of the way. Don't wander off, because they won't bother to come and look for you."

The truck took off back down the rough dirt track in a cloud of dust. Mark was, as far as he could see, quite alone.

With the departure of the truck, the insect life in the area, disturbed by the arriving vehicle, came alive again. Chirps, squeaks and scuttles could be heard all around and it reminded him that the borrowed clothing he still wore was also host to a multitude of vermin. He stripped off the disguise that hadn't been needed and brushed his body down with clumps of scrub brush before donning desert clothing from his canvas air force bag.

From the slight rise, he looked northeast and could see the shimmering heat reflecting off the floor of the Empty Quarter. It seemed like an eternity since he had flown construction materials across it.

The afternoon wore on; still nobody arrived to escort him the rest of the way. He sat beside a withered tree in an attempt to gain some relief from the scorching sun. Ferret-face had given him a small canister of water. Fortunately, he had not drunk it all at the first hint of thirst. Now he wondered just how long he would have to eke out the precious fluid.

If they had brought him here to abandon him, he wouldn't be able to last more than another day in this heat. *Had* they brought him here to leave him? First Howard takes a bullet in the back and then Holland's left in the desert foothills. It made sense. Get rid of the two men who had shown an interest in meeting with the rebels.

A lizard darted quickly from a rock to look for food. Mark watched and wondered, idly, if lizards carried a high water content. If they left him here long enough he might have to put it to the test. Burn up too many calories catching it, though, and he'd get thirstier quicker without any guarantee of success.

Holland watched the lizard for a while as it went about the business of catching its next meal. Suddenly the creature sat up, whipped its head around and looked at Holland.

"Christ, it's going to have a go at *me*," he muttered aloud. The lizard turned its head slowly, first one way and then the other. It dawned on Holland that it had heard something and was trying to locate the source of the sound. The lizard, forgetting its supper, darted off.

Seconds later, Holland heard the sound as well. A helicopter. There was no cover anywhere. If this was a government helicopter, it was all over.

The helicopter flew in, low and fast, circling around the area before dropping stone-like to the ground. A door was pushed open, and a hand indicated frantically that Holland should climb aboard. So far so good.

They were not shooting right away.

Mark ducked under the rotor blades of the McCullough Tri-Star, pulling himself in to face a pistol.

"One question, sir. Answer it wrong and you're dead." The pilot held the Mauser steadily, with the air of a man who was quite prepared to carry out his threat.

Mark nodded. "Ask away."

"Your room number at college, please?"

"I didn't have a room number. I shared an apartment in the town with another guy. Mitre Apartments. Apartment 1601."

The Mauser was lifted away and placed in a holster attached to the pilot's door. "Welcome aboard, sir. Sorry about that, but we—"

"Have to be careful," finished Holland wryly.

The helicopter lifted into the air, speeding toward the mountains that Mark had sat and stared at all afternoon. Back on the ground, as the noise of the helicopter receded the lizard resumed its hunt for supper.

"Careful enough to leave me sweltering in that heat?" asked Mark.

The pilot laughed good-naturedly. "Sam had to get back to Hudaydah safely before we could pick you up. If he hadn't made it, that meant you were probably a spy; but he did. We got the radio call half an hour ago that he was home. Sorry about the delay, but he had trouble with his engine and couldn't drive too fast."

As the helicopter wove its way through the gullies and canyons, Mark wondered what god it was that had led him into a situation where he could have died because of a broken-down engine. He sighed and settled back. The pilot said that the message had been received half an hour ago. That meant they probably had twenty-five minutes' flying time—if they were going to the same base.

They weren't. Two hours later the pilot pointed straight down and Mark saw, for the first time, the encampment that steered the rebel activity against the Republic of Yemen. Tents, shanties, Nissen huts were grouped together in orderly lines, giving the impression of a well-ordered, permanent military encampment.

"Welcome to Sadallah City, Captain," smiled the pilot as he fingered switches to kill the power to the rotor blades. Three men carrying Armalite rifles walked forward, and the pilot nodded toward them. "They will escort you from here. See you again soon."

The pilot then lost all interest in Mark and returned to his gauges. Snapping open the catch on the glass door, Mark swung his feet out of the cockpit and dropped to the ground. The three men had stopped ten feet away, waiting patiently, rifles slung over their shoulders.

As Mark walked toward them they turned, leading the way for him to follow. He felt like a prisoner, despite the fact that his "guards" were ahead and not to the side or behind him. Even if he had wanted to, he could not escape from this eagle's lair.

The pilot had called it Sadallah City. It could just as easily have been Valhallah, or the Home of the Angels. Mark could see cloud cover below them, obscuring lower mountains and valleys, and a cursory glance around told him that the layout for this city had been carefully thought out by a trained military mind.

Russian anti-aircraft guns dotted the perimeter of the large, flat plain that served as a shelf for the base, while American machine guns covered the three approach roads that wound haphazardly up the side of the mountain.

Gasoline drums, bearing Yemeni markings, were stacked behind a wire fence, close against the back wall of the mountain. The position of the fuel dump made a direct hit from the air impossible, even by the most experienced pilots. Iranian fifty-pound bombs were stacked near the fuel—probably, thought Mark, on the theory that if either dump were to be hit it wouldn't matter a shit where the other was located.

A motley-dressed group of men was marching in British close order. The mixture of weapons that these soldiers carried indicated that they were not at all fussy about where they obtained their supplies, the only provision being that the weapons have the capacity to kill.

The three-man escort stopped at a Nissen hut that had been almost completely built into a depression in the hillside. No back door. One of the three indicated the entrance to the hut. "This will be your accommodation while you are with us. Please stay inside until you are given clearance to move around the base. If you should attempt to leave the building before being given clearance, you stand the risk of being shot. Do you understand what I have said or do you require that I repeat these instructions?"

The man looked intently at Mark. Mark looked back and at his companions. There was no doubt the escort was not just an escort.

"I think I catch your drift. Will these men be guarding the door?"

"No, sir. They will, however, be stationed outside it to ensure your safety."

"Thanks a million." Mark opened the door of the hut. It had started to get dark outside with the onrush of the mountain night, but inside it was pitch black—the windows looked out onto solid rock. He searched for a light on the side of the wall, out of habit, before realizing that it was highly unlikely that the Yemen government would lay power cables up the mountain to supply electricity to this band of rebels.

"You will find the switch approximately four-and-one-half feet up from the ground and about two-and-one-half inches in from your right hand side, Captain Holland," said a voice from the darkness.

Holland was momentarily startled, then slid his hand to the position indicated by the disembodied voice. A faint yellow light pushed its way through the blackness. Four army cots lay against one wall, two already made up. At the rear of the hut Mark could make out the shape of a chemical toilet and small washstand. In the center of the room was a large table. Sitting at its head was a slight, handsome man, who looked as though he were carved from ebony.

"That's a great trick," said Mark sarcastically, indicating the doorway. "The commies used it on our boys when they captured them in Korea—used to unsettle them, arriving in a dark room, unable to find the light source. Is that what you were trying with me?"

The man smiled tiredly. "Not at all, Captain. I was merely sitting here waiting to greet you and failed to notice that night was drawing in."

He rose from the table. Dressed in military green, he wore

no insignia, he didn't need any. Everyone in this part of the world knew his face. That was insignia enough. One pistol sat in a well-worn leather holster on his right side. It was an American holster, quick-draw. The Colt .45, complete with pearl handle, was designed for a swift kill at close quarters.

"Mark, my old friend, how are you? It has been a very long time."

"Hello, Ziad," replied the American as he cautiously shook the other's hand. "Yeah, a hell of a long time. But now I need some answers and I need them quick, and I'm going to tell you this straight. If I'm not happy with the answers you give me, you'd better be ready to call in those goons outside damn quick because I'm going to have a hell of a good try at killing you."

Sadallah laughed and held his hands up in mock protest at Holland's verbal assault. "Stop, Mark, I surrender," he laughed. "My God, all these years and the first thing you are saying to me is that you may try to kill me. This is not the way old and good friends should behave when they meet after a long, long time," he admonished. "Come Mark, sit down and relax first. There is plenty of time to tell me what has brought you here— although I think perhaps I already know." He turned toward the door. "Mustapha, bring whiskey."

The guard who had spoken with him outside the hut immediately entered carrying the inevitable bottle of Black Label, three glasses and, incredibly, a glass bowl with ice cubes.

Sadallah saw the look on Mark's face and chuckled good-naturedly—it was a chuckle from deep in the throat which Mark remembered well.

"We are not savages here, Mark," he explained. "We do at least attempt to retain some of the semblances of civilization, and some of the comforts that go with them. It's the bad things we are trying to change."

"In that case, will you tell this big ape to stop glaring at me and pour that damn whisky before I have to teach him some manners?"

Mustapha and Sadallah both broke into a broad grin and

Mustapha put the glasses down, pouring three full measures of the liquid. Ziad beamed at the larger Arab. "Did I not say to you, Mustapha, that my old American friend was scared of no man? Did I not say this to you?"

Mustapha drained his glass and banged it on the table. "Yes, General, you did. But you didn't say he was stupid enough to threaten to kill you when there were three of your own men armed outside the door."

Ziad poured more whiskey into the glasses and laughed. "I shall always wonder who would have been the quicker, my dear Mustapha—the Captain, with his strong hands, or you, with your protective instinct for my worthless neck."

Mustapha laughed too. "To save any later discomfort then, General, perhaps I should shoot him now. Then we never have to find that out!"

He withdrew to leave Sadallah and Mark to talk. Mark was aware that the door to the Nissen hut was left slightly ajar, just enough to make him wonder how far Mustapha had been joking.

After a while, Sadallah stood up from the table. "Mark, I must go and do my rounds of inspection. Please excuse me. We shall dine at my bungalow in one hour." He shook Mark's hand firmly once again, and walked to the door. On the threshold, he stopped and turned. "It *is* good to see you again. I couldn't believe it when I got the message from Addis saying a Mark Holland wanted me. Until later, then. And please, if there is anything you need in the meantime, just ask Mustapha to arrange it. He's very obliging, really."

Fatima was unaware of the situation seventy miles away on the mountain top. Indeed, Fatima was only barely aware that the mountain existed at all. And she knew nothing of the events outside the small desert community in which she and her husband lived.

The woman worked steadily at the mound of horsemeat in the small windowless shed that served as the food preparation area. The kitchen in the house, if indeed it could be called that, allowed only room for the actual cooking and eating of the steamy dishes which took so long to prepare.

Today it was Fatima's turn to prepare food for the whole community while the other women helped with the harvest of dates that had ripened so well this year. Without a doubt, they would enjoy a bountiful crop.

The noise reached her ears and she stopped in mid-slice with a huge knife poised as though on the defensive. She inclined her head toward the direction of the sound.

Through the doorway she could see only an endless stretch of desert with dancing swirls of sand leaping upward in short bursts of activity. She was puzzled. She had never seen the sands act this way before. It was not the way the desert behaved at the approach of a sandstorm, nor the way it told of the approach of a fast rider. And the smell of the meat she prepared was replaced by another, stronger odor.

She put the knife onto the wooden block before stepping out into the bright sunlight. Her eyesight adjusted from the gloom of the shed as she looked rapidly around, and she found the cause of the strangeness.

It swept down toward the settlement as Fatima watched. Trees dipped their top-most branches. A noise like rain resounded in a deafening cacophony as it descended onto the roofs of the huts.

The woman was as yet unafraid, accepting the way of life in the harsh country that was her home. Then, suddenly, complete silence descended over the area and Fatima drew in her breath. She looked carefully around, as though any sudden move would break the stillness that now blanketed the settlement.

She felt alone, wishing that her man was with her to explain such a happening, to reassure her that everything was as it should be, that there was nothing to fear. But there was fear. Fatima could sense, could feel the evil around her as it readied itself to strike.

She edged slightly further out of the doorway of the hut and a sudden sob burst from her throat. She felt a sharp stab of pain in her bare foot and glanced quickly down, screaming as her mind seemed to burst.

The pelting sound began again in earnest and gradually the woman's screams were replaced by a low, animal-like moan. At length, she was still.

It had begun.

# CHAPTER FIVE

ONE HOUR EXACTLY AND MUSTAPHNA RETURNED TO LEAD Mark across the camp to a building that would not have looked out of place in any moderately expensive suburb. The bungalow boasted tastefully laid-out gardens, even a small fountain crowned by a marble statue of a boy holding a jug through which water flowed perpetually.

The bungalow itself had clear white stucco walls, red window frames and trim, and a gray slate roof obviously added to help the structure blend in with the surrounding rock. It would take several passes by an aircraft to identify Sadallah's headquarters and by that time, Mark reflected, there would be no aircraft.

"Jesus," muttered the American.

"You like, eh, Captain?"

The Arab led the way through the front door, which was guarded by two heavily-armed men. He pulled open the insect screen before standing aside to allow Holland to enter.

Sadallah walked toward him with his hands outstretched in greeting. His smile was one of genuine pleasure. "Welcome to my house. All that I have is yours. May you relax and enjoy."

Holland grasped the man's arm. "I remember that greeting well, Ziad, and I thank you for it. I just wish it was another time, another place."

Ziad nodded, then guided Mark through another doorway into the lounge. The American glanced around the room and was surprised to see it furnished and decorated in contemporary American style. The only concession to the life-style of Ziad's ancestors was the low coffee tables adorned with silver platters containing portions of Arab food.

"We managed to capture some furniture," explained Ziad wryly. "Though, to be honest, we thought we were capturing a truck loaded with rifles. Our intelligence network has considerably improved since then, I can assure you. Even so, it was quite a nose-rubbing for the authorities. The furniture was scheduled to go to one of the junta bigwigs."

"I guess if you have to live on top of a mountain, this is the best way to do it."

A fourth man entered the room and solicitously removed and replaced dishes as the need arose.

"You live very well for a bandit, Ziad," Mark observed casually.

"My dear Mark, you are still so abrasive. But no matter. While you are our honored guest you may call us what you like. But let me tell you this, my friend," he added, suddenly serious. "We know who we are and why we must fight. The world outside our strongholds may not give us the credence we think they should, may not help us to rid our country of this corrupt and evil band of killers which calls itself a government, but I assure you that one day they will.

"The day will come when the people of this country will stand together and say, 'enough tyranny, enough disease, enough poverty.' I don't believe that this day is too far away. Soon the peasant in the field who starves because he does not have enough water to irrigate the poor soil will take up his scythe and use it to cut down the oppressors of his land."

Sadallah smiled and shrugged his shoulders. "I'm sorry, Mark, I don't mean to preach at you, but this fight is very important to me and my people."

"I guess I can understand that. But how can you justify living in relative luxury when the people you are supposed to be trying to save live so badly? You talk about insufficient water for poor soil, yet right out front you have a fountain pouring it out like crazy *and* you have grass that's as green as Central Park. That must have cost a fortune."

Sadallah grinned. "Not Central Park. Perhaps Yankee Stadium, but not the park. You see, it's Astroturf—imitation grass. It was scheduled for a soccer stadium in the capital. We thought we could put it to better use. The convoy carrying it was protected by a military escort and so attracted our attention.

"As far as our fountain is concerned, I suppose it would seem unnecessary, but these are symbols."

"Fake grass and recycled water? On that you're going to build the new order?"

"Even Christ needed his miracles. And before you jump in with what I imagine just went through your mind—I am not the Messiah reborn, nor do I intend to be. Now suppose we eat and stop this ideological bullshit. It's bad for the digestion!"

The three ate and it was only after they had finished and relaxed once more into the opulent depths of the cushions that Holland realized just how hungry he had been.

The empty dishes were removed and steaming jugs of coffee were placed on the low table. Holland offered his pack of cigarettes to Ziad and Mustapha and in turn accepted the ubiquitous glass of Johnnie Walker.

Sadallah blew a long stream of smoke toward the ceiling before looking toward the American.

"Mark," began Sadallah carefully, "you have made a long and dangerous journey to this place. Although I am delighted to see you after so long a time, it grieves me. The reason you are here must be a serious one indeed. As I indicated to you earlier, I think I know why, but I should like for you to tell me in your own words what is troubling you and how I can help."

"Trans-Global Oil had a plane go down in these mountains a few days ago. The official view seems to put the wreckage right in your backyard, along with the blame for its coming down—although nobody really knows because they haven't found the pieces yet. I know how easy it is to mistake a company plane for a military one and I'd like to know, first of all, whether you or any of your men brought it down."

Sadallah leaned forward in his seat and looked intently at the American. "I assure you at no time have we brought down an aircraft by mistake. It is true that, on occasion, the government has tried to attack this position by using commercial aircraft and it is equally true we have always rebuffed these Trojan horses. But we have never made a mistake. Never! Now, may I ask why you are so concerned about this particular crash?"

"My fiancée was on board, Ziad. In Addis I heard rumors that your guerrillas had shot the plane down, and I was coming to settle things with you."

Sadallah shook his head sadly and placed his hand on Mark's arm. "You have my deepest sympathy, Mark. I know what it is to lose a loved one. My own wife and children were killed some years ago." He glanced at Mustapha. "I think we can be of help to you in clearing any question of our complicity in this crash. Mustapha, tell him."

"Captain, some of my men came in this afternoon and said they had spotted wreckage of a plane about forty miles from here."

Sadallah refilled the glasses. "And I had ordered some of my men to the site tomorrow. Now I think perhaps you and I shall go with them."

"What about survivors?"

"No sign."

"Are you *sure?*"

"Captain, my men are used to looking for signs of life. There are no survivors."

"What time do we leave?"

"Just after dawn."

"There, by that outcrop!"

The English-speaking pilot pointed eagerly down to the left as he wheeled the Tri-Star around to take them closer to the crash site.

They had left the mountain base shortly after dawn that morning in three helicopters, two of which had been brought in during the night from other bases. Ziad, Mustapha, Mark, and the silent bodyguard had flown in the lead helicopter. Ten men had flown in the second and third, together with a miscellany of equipment they might need during the search.

Ziad had told Mark they would stay out for two days if necessary, but he hoped they would be able to complete their search in one. It wasn't wise to linger this far from their nearest base, some ten miles further back along the mountain range. Now, with the pilot finding the site as quickly as he had, there was every likelihood they would not need to.

The pilot maintained radio silence and indicated the other two helicopters should follow him down by rocking the Tri-Star from side to side.

He selected a wide, flat expanse some sixty feet above the main concentration of the scattered wreckage and landed. The four passengers dropped from the helicopter, and with a wave from Ziad the pilot took it back into the air and sped away to the northwest. He noticed the surprise on Holland's face. "The helicopters are more important than we, Mark. When we are ready to leave, we shall send a one word message that will bring them back. If there are any government forces in the area they may well have spotted us flying in.

"One jet from the capital could wipe out our entire air force if it caught those three helicopters in one place on the ground."

The other two craft landed as rapidly as the first, disgorged their cargo and also flew away. Holland assumed without asking that if they did not receive the call from Ziad they wouldn't come back to see why. If there was anything wrong with their portable radio, that was their tough luck.

Holland looked around at the surrounding peaks, jagged granite scars against the clear blue face of the sky. All hope that Kate—or any of the other passengers for that matter—

might have survived the crash faded as he surveyed the stark terrain.

"It's a harsh but beautiful land, my friend. It grieves us at the best of times that so much blood must be spilt over it."

"Then why bother?" muttered Mark angrily.

Sadallah turned to him. "Ah, Mark, how naive and bitter you can be. We hate extremes of any kind. Government should be 'by the people for the people.' Isn't that what your own Constitution says?"

"Something like that. But we don't believe everything we read. You should have stuck to medicine."

Ziad was silent for a moment. "I could have had a comfortable practice in one of the large towns or cities I suppose, at least until the revolution. But the need was in the country. It still is. One day I was on an overnight trip to a remote part of the region and when I returned to my village I found that government soldiers had paid it a visit the previous day.

"They had been looking for weapons, food, money. And women. They raped many women and they shot anyone who tried to stop them. My children tried to prevent one soldier from raping my wife and he killed them both. After he had violated my wife he killed her too.

"I buried my family and then traveled into the mountains, knowing that the freedom fighters were here. I joined them. It's that simple, really."

Mustapha walked across to them and Mark felt intensely grateful to the Arab for breaking up the conversation. "The men are ready to drop down the ropes to the crash sites. Any instructions, General?"

"Mark?"

"Tell them to search for the flight recorder. It's a bright red box. And to look for any burnt metal—but if they find any, they must leave it alone and call me. One other thing," he finished quietly. "Anybody finds the body of a woman, they should call me without touching her."

Mustapha nodded and turned to relay Holland's instructions. "Why burnt metal, Mark?"

"Something brought that plane down. A heat-seeking missile, anti-aircraft shell or machine-gun fire will all leave a trace of burning on metal and that will tell me at least how it crashed."

Sadallah nodded. "But not *who* brought it down."

"No, not right away, but it's a start. Besides, it could have come down through pilot error or just plain old-fashioned mechanical failure. Let's get down there."

The two men slid rapidly down ropes to the crash site. As they did, the knot in Holland's stomach told him that, however much he hoped it was so, this crash was no accident.

He had suspected as much from the air, but standing on the site he knew for sure that the plane had been sabotaged. His Air Force experience told him that when a plane crashes it leaves an impression where it hits the ground. In the case of this granite wall it would have broken off chunks, leaving telltale scars. He also knew that the wreckage would have been concentrated into a much smaller area had it simply hit the mountain.

For four hours, Mustapha and his men scoured the area looking for bodies, the flight recorder, and any clues to the disaster. Shortly before one o'clock one of the men hurried over to Sadallah and whispered anxiously. Sadallah nodded and in an instant was standing beside the American, who was busily examining a section of wing.

"My friend," he started softly, "one of my men has discovered the body of a woman."

Holland dropped the piece of metal he had been examining and wiped his hand over his forehead. He had dreaded this moment. "Show me," he said as he straightened to his feet.

The body was almost naked and lay in the fetal position behind a small clump of rocks. Holland stood for a moment looking at the unmistakable female body, his stomach churning at the sight of the massive injuries that she had sustained.

Holland reached a hand outward toward the long dark hair which covered the dead girl's face and with trembling fingers carefully brushed it away to expose her gentle features. He expelled his breath and shook his head. "It's not Kate."

All around him he heard the outward rush of air from lungs

which had been straining with the force of holding in expectant breath. A soft gaggle of voices broke through the stillness and two of Ziad's men stepped forward to retrieve the body.

Holland returned to the area he had been combing with a feeling of relief that the crushed body had not been Kate's, although he knew that it could only be a matter of time before the awful moment finally presented itself.

An hour later he turned at the sound of careful footsteps, and the look of Ziad's face told him all he needed to know. Another female body had been located. He stood up and absently brushed away particles of sand which clung to the fabric of his trousers. "Where is she, Ziad?"

"Over by that outcrop. I must warn you that . . . well, you understand."

Ziad again led the way to where the discovery had been made. Mark felt a wave of hopelessness flood through him as he looked down at the body. It was Kate.

Sadallah stepped back and indicated that the others should do likewise.

At length, Mark knelt and gathered the broken body in his arms, tears forcing their way from narrowed eyes and down his sun-bronzed cheeks. The small group of men parted to make way for him as he carried Kate away.

They worked without pause through the long, hot day. Shortly after the discovery of Kate's body, they found the flight recorder. A burial mound was constructed of stones and the bodies of the passengers and crew were placed into it. Mark buried Kate himself on a shelf that looked over the wide valley far below.

It was Mustapha who finally shouted that Mark should hurry to the edge of the cliff where the plane had finally come to rest. "I sent some of the men over the side of this outcrop," he explained, "to see if any pieces had fallen over. One of my men is down there now and he says that there are several fragments and he can see many more that we cannot get to further down the mountain." Mustapha paused slightly before continuing. "He says that one of the pieces is a door. It is burnt, Mark. It looks like somebody cooked a sheep on it."

"Tell him to tie the end of the rope to the door and then pull it up here. I want to take a look."

He finished his examination within minutes.

"What have you found?"

Holland looked at the man and said quietly, "It was deliberate. A bomb!"

"Are you sure?"

"I'm sure. This is a cargo hatch. This jagged metal protruding outwards is away from the blast. The burn marks are on the inside. It was a bomb. No doubt about it."

"Well that takes care of 'how.' Now what?"

"I don't know. I suppose that we might as well return to your base; there's nothing more we can do here."

A sudden shout from the ledge below startled them. The Arab who had found the door to the cargo area was calling hysterically to his companions.

"He has found another body," explained Mustapha, "but he says this one looks as though he's the Devil himself."

In moments, Ziad, Mustapha and Mark slid expertly down the ropes and were studying the corpse that had been discovered.

"Holy Christ, no wonder it scared the guy," whispered Mark as he stared in fascinated horror at the sight before them.

A corpse was wedged obscenely among the rocks, the right leg bent back unnaturally. It was a man, that much was apparent. It wore a light-weight tropical suit of the sort that could be bought at most department stores for a hundred dollars.

The man's left eye socket, almost empty except for a small portion of pupil, winked gruesomely as the sun flashed off the suppurating tissue. The lips were gone, baring teeth in a feral grin.

The right side of the face was almost completely torn away and the bones on that side of the head could be seen clearly. Blood stained the material of both the suit and shirt. He had bled profusely.

Mark tore his eyes from the apparition. "What do you make of that?"

Sadallah also had difficulty in removing his gaze. He said

at length, "Poor devil. I should say from the position of the body that he did not die right away, but survived the impact and then crawled into this niche. I suppose he hoped that rescuers would find the site in time to save him. He had a broken leg; the pain must have been excruciating. Obviously, he was too badly injured and died from his wounds. I am afraid that I could not be exact as to the time of death, but I would not think he lasted long."

Sadallah returned to the unfortunate passenger and sadly shook his head.

"But what about his face? That wasn't caused by the plane coming down."

"No, you are right. And it is not decay. There are the ants and flies though, and birds of prey. But it is incredible that so much damage has been done in so short a time."

"Jackals? Could they have caused injuries as extensive as this?"

"Yes, my friend," agreed Ziad, "if this were the desert or even further down the mountain, but look around you," he added, sweeping his arm around the terrain. "The whole area is barren of vegetation. Nothing comes here to graze and so the jackal stays where he knows there is food, or at least the prospect of obtaining food. It would be most unusual for carnivores to climb to this height in search of food."

Holland leaned forward to examine the man's face. "His skin is shredded. What could have caused that?"

Sadallah leaned over Holland's shoulder. "I don't know, Mark. The lacerations resemble injuries similar to those sustained by metal fragments smashing into the body, but normally the skin would be forced inward, not like this."

The men stood transfixed and tried to imagine the animal or circumstances which had caused the man's death. Finally, Sadallah broke the silence. "It must have been vultures."

"If I were a Christian," muttered Mustapha pointedly, "I would make the sign of the cross to prevent the sight of this from coming to me in the night. By Allah, I have never witnessed such a thing!"

Mark shook his head. "If it is as you say, Ziad," he said,

looking into the clear blue sky and shielding his eyes against the painful brightness of the sun, "why are there no carrion birds circling? In fact, we didn't see any sign of vultures or crows when we came in this morning, yet by all the laws of nature, with as much food as there is around here, you would think the place would have attracted swarms of them."

"I don't know. You are right, of course, it hadn't occurred to me. Another mystery, or is it just providence we got here first?"

"You know as well as I do they would have been here within the hour of impact. But maybe it's as you say—providence."

Mark turned abruptly to the ropes that dangled from the ledge above. He quickly pulled himself up and was closely followed by Sadallah and Mustapha. Orders were barked to the assembled men and three luckless individuals were sent scurrying down to retrieve the body and prepare it for burial.

"That was the last one as far as we can determine. There is still time to recall the helicopters and return to our base if you have finished here."

Holland looked across the area of devastation. At the burial mound, at the twisted lumps of metal that stretched like a child's paperchase trail, at the ledge where under a pile of rocks he had buried Kate, along with his new found hope for life.

"Send up the signal, Ziad. We've done all we can here."

Mark walked away from the group of men toward her grave and sat quietly with her until he heard the even beat of the returning helicopters' blades.


"Well, my friend, there it is. The full list of the belongings that we removed from the bodies."

Holland ran his eyes down the pages of typewritten notes that Sadallah had prepared for him to take back to Addis Ababa. They had concentrated only on the belongings which had been found on each of the corpses, having decided there was little point in searching for the baggage that had been stowed in the cargo hold.

There had been twelve passengers on the aircraft and they

had found and identified all of them. They had also found the four-man crew. Sixteen names in all; their only memorial was the four pages he held in his hand.

The American sighed as he reached the name of Kate Carson and scanned the list of belongings itemized beside it. British passport, gold watch—Holland had bought her that as a birthday present just six months ago. A charm bracelet, one earring, one wallet containing credit cards and a few American dollars.

His eyes passed over her name and scanned the remainder of the list. At length he nodded, folded the sheets in half, and put them in his jacket pocket. "I'll make sure this list and their belongings get to the proper authorities, Ziad."

He studied the man for a moment and then added, "As far as I'm concerned, you and your guys are in the clear. I guess it's up to the Ethiopians to figure out the rest of the puzzle from here on in."

"I am delighted you have come to that conclusion, Mark. But I wonder if that's the end of the matter."

"I'll make sure the press gets the correct version of what happened here."

"I know you will, and thank you. But that's not really what I meant. There is something bothering me about the list of passengers. I typed it myself to make sure it was done accurately. Take another look at it, but this time read the list of belongings with more care."

Holland pulled the papers from his pocket and re-read them.

They had returned from the mountain exhausted, but had spent most of the night in compiling this catalogue of death. Now, Holland was sitting in the rebel leader's comfortable lounge, waiting for dawn and the helicopter which would take him on the first leg of his journey back to Ethiopia.

"The three scientists have U.S. security clearance identification cards . . ."

"Exactly. But they were also carrying identification as employees of Trans-Global Oil Company. Both cards are still current, but the intriguing thing to me is that the U.S. cards refer to a Station 17 in Livingston."

"Where the hell is that?"

"I looked it up on an old map which I have from our college days. It's in Montana, in the mountains. But how could these three be working in the Gulf *and* in the States at one and the same time?"

Holland studied the list again as though he expected the answer to the question to be implanted there.

"And there is one other, or rather two other questions which must be looked at. First, if the plane had left at the time it was supposed to, it would now be lying at the bottom of the Red Sea. It would never have been found. The second is more puzzling. Why was the plane in this area at all?"

"The first is easy enough. As a company plane it could leave whenever all the scheduled passengers were on board, or whenever the departure time arrived, whichever came first. I've done it myself, left a field earlier than expected. I don't get your drift on the second question, though."

Sadallah thumped his forehead with the heel of his hand. "Stupid of me. Of course, you wouldn't. You don't know exactly where we are at this time. But suffice to say that had the plane come down on top of us it would have been off its expected flight path. The fact that it came down even further inland is really strange. It was some two or three hundred miles off its route to Sana."

Holland felt his pulse quicken, but then he sank back into his seat once more. After the discovery of Kate's body he had become almost an automaton, doing what had to be done because of the need to keep busy, the need to avoid thinking. Now he was being forced to face further mysteries. Clear one up and two more take its place.

"I don't have the answers, Ziad, and frankly I'm too tired even to try to figure it out."

"Of course. There is time for a few hours' sleep before you have to leave. Get some rest now. I'll wake you when it's dawn."

Holland nodded and drained the last glass of whiskey before leaving. He was mentally and physically exhausted, more questions than answers running through his mind. He skirted around a stack of crates covered with a tarpaulin and started up the slight incline that led to his hut.

Ziad clasped Holland's hand warmly and then embraced the tall American. "Good-bye, and may you have a safe journey. Let us hope it will not be so long until we see one another again."

"I hope so, too, Ziad. You've given me quite a lot to think about. I couldn't get to sleep after I left your bungalow, thinking about those IDs for Station 17. I have a hunch that I can learn a lot from that place. I don't suppose you'd like to come with me, would you?"

Sadallah laughed. "For old times sake you mean? I think that I wouldn't last too long, Mark, there are too many people who would like to see me put up against the wall. Thanks for the invitation, though."

Holland grinned and slapped the man on the back in a farewell gesture before ducking under the blades and climbing into the cabin.

He looked back toward the rebel encampment as they swung to the south and saw the solitary figure of Sadallah standing near the helicopter pad.

A brief wave of the hand and he turned away toward the camp.

His stomach grumbled and he felt nauseous as the helicopter wove its way through the valleys back toward ferret-face and the Greek fisherman.

# CHAPTER SIX

"Do you mean to tell us, Captain," repeated the man, "that you were afforded the opportunity of visiting the crash site by the rebels? Don't you think this is all a little improbable?"

Holland looked past the questioner and allowed his mind to mingle with the sounds of the Addis traffic far below. Apart from the obvious skepticism at his journey, Holland knew there would be questions regarding his involvement with the freedom fighters and how he was able to arrange the trip in the first place.

He had been "interviewed" endlessly by government officials. Finally, the investigators appeared satisfied with the answers they had been given. Then came this press conference and he wished that Sandy Howard were sitting in the front row in place of this snide little bastard.

Holland leaned forward slightly and the man flinched instinctively. Holland pulled on his cigarette, aware that everybody in the room at the top of the Excelsior was waiting for an answer.

"I don't mean to tell you a goddam thing, mister," he snarled finally. "Like I've said before, my fiancée was on that plane and I got tired of waiting for the Yemen government to find it—or to get the courage to go up into those mountains.

"It's a matter of record that Sadallah and I shared an apartment when we were in college. We hadn't seen each other for a number of years and I guess he was curious."

"Jamieson, *Sunday Telegraph,* London," intoned another voice at the back of the room. "Captain, we understand you have in fact recovered the flight recorder from the crash site and it is now in the appropriate hands. I also understand you brought back with you pieces of the superstructure of the plane. What were your initial on-site findings?"

Holland looked around him. This was the million-dollar question, the one he'd been told by the Ethiopians to avoid until their aviation inspectors had the opportunity of examining all the evidence in more detail. But Holland felt he also had an obligation to Sadallah to help establish clearly that the rebels hadn't the inclination to bring down a civil aircraft. He could play it safe and avoid the question with a suitable "no comment," and who would blame him? Why ask for trouble.

"My initial findings indicated not only that the so-called freedom fighters were not involved, but that the aircraft was sabotaged. I discovered strong evidence that a bomb had been placed in the cargo hold."

Silence reigned for a moment and then the little man at the front called out another question. "What are your credentials for determining that, Mr. Holland?"

"I didn't catch your name, mister."

"Simon Graves, *Oil Standard International,*" he retorted self-importantly.

"Well, sonny, I'm afraid I don't quite understand your question. My 'credentials,' as you call them, include a near lifetime in the air. A session in the Korean War, where I saw a hell of a lot of planes shot down and had the chance to get into metal stress factors in combat situations. A degree in aeronautical engineering. That good enough for you?"

The man made hurried scribbles in his notebook and then looked back up. "Actually, no, Mr. Holland, it's not. The Korean War was a long time ago. I assume you were working on memory only with this particular crash. As to your much vaunted engineering degree, isn't it true you have not used that part of your, er, talents, since graduating? In fact, I understand you have spent the time since your college days flying a variety of obsolete aircraft for a variety of employers."

Mark smiled thinly. "I don't get your drift, mister. Make your point."

"Simply this. Perhaps you saw this little adventure of yours as a good way to obtain some personal glory, to elevate yourself above your present circumstances. I mean, a war hero who is reduced to flying for a construction firm in the Gulf must be a pretty bitter man—wouldn't you think?"

Holland appeared to the other reporters in this room as if he would willingly have cut the offensive journalist to pieces.

"Son of a bitch, that Graves," muttered one reporter.

"Bastard's going to get a knife in him for sure, one of these days," another agreed.

"Buddy, you can think and believe what you like," started Holland ominously. "But if your pea-sized brain put that bunch of crap together without help I'd be very surprised. Who's got any *relevant* questions to ask?"

"Captain Holland, why was the plane so far off course?"

The question had come from the center of the room. The questioner had not needed to raise his voice to be heard. Holland could see that he was an elderly man. Probably one of the senior journalists in Addis. "Good question. I wish I had a good answer for you, friend. Maybe the civil authorities can tell you."

"One theory has been advanced that it was directed off course deliberately in order that it could be blown up in rebel-held territory, to show those gentlemen up in a bad light. Do you subscribe to that theory, Captain?"

"No."

"Why not?"

"I should have thought that was obvious. The plane left earlier than scheduled. If it had left on time, as we must presume the person who planted the bomb thought it would, then it would have blown up over the Red Sea. Not in the mountains."

Several reporters ran from the room in order to get their news onto the wire. The next day's European and American papers would carry the story of a plane that, but for the sake of its pilot taking off earlier than scheduled, would have disappeared into the log book of aviation mysteries.

Mark stood. "I guess that's all for now." His tone left no doubt in anyone's mind that the session was at an end.

He moved through the throng to the bank of elevators just outside the door. Within minutes he had been escorted by a police officer to the door of his suite. Once inside he made for the small bar in the corner of the lounge.

He splashed Scotch onto the cubes of mineral-water ice, and as he lifted the glass to his lips he realized he was not alone.

"Who the hell are you?"

"Normally people say, 'How'd you get in?'"

"I don't give a damn how you got in, mister, but you'd better have a mighty good reason for being here."

The man lifted himself from the armchair and walked towards the bar. "My name is Volk. David Volk. I'm the press attaché at the United States embassy here and I thought I'd come along and see if there was anything I could do for you. I'd also like to hear your story, if you are disposed to repeat it all. My people in Washington would like me to file as complete a report as possible."

Holland accepted the offered hand and shook it perfunctorily, almost warily. He studied the man standing in front of him, noting with an increasing sense of unease that the man appeared far too muscular to fit the stereotype of a civil servant who enjoyed a foreign posting and the easy life which went with it.

Volk sensed the scrutiny and a sardonic smile creased the corners of his tight lips. The smooth Boston accent finally interrupted Holland's thoughts. "Perhaps if we have finished sizing each other up you could offer me a drink and then we can talk."

Holland splashed the Scotch onto the ice in a second glass and handed it to Volk. He had decided he didn't like this overly-smooth, overly-confident man, but he was curious about him and even more so about the purpose of his visit.

"If you wanted a debriefing you should have been at the one I gave the Ethiopians."

Volk absently brushed a nonexistent speck of dust from his coat. "I would have been, but I was out of the city. Only just got back," he replied blandly with the same sardonic, annoying, tight little smile.

"Too bad. Ask the Ethiopians for a copy of my report."

The smile vanished and a sharp glint appeared in the man's eyes. Holland could almost feel the coldness in the air as Volk's voice adopted a menacing tone. "That's a great shame. We much prefer our nationals to be cooperative."

Holland tensed at the change in Volk's voice and his own attitude hardened perceptibly. "Who is 'we'? Who do you really work for?"

"I've already told you."

Mark tossed the remnants of the ice into the small metal bowl and dropped three fresh cubes into the glass before covering them with a liberal amount of Johnnie Walker. He again stared at Volk as though trying to make up his mind about the stranger. There was no doubt that Volk was American and that he worked at the embassy, but the job title of this man just did not fit. He was too smooth, almost smarmy, and far too confident. He was, Holland decided, a man who was used to the higher power game, a man used to giving orders and having them carried out. No, he definitely was not a press hack.

"I tend not to trust or believe you, Mr. Volk, so unless you have anything really concrete to say to me I suggest you get the hell out of here."

Volk stood and walked silently to the door. He opened it and started through before, almost as an afterthought, he stopped, turning back to face Holland who had watched his exit with mild interest. "There is one other thing, Holland," he began in the same icy tone which indicated Volk was not used to being dismissed so summarily. "Keep your nose out of this business. We are on top of it and we don't want any more problems."

Volk nodded his head in farewell and started to close the door behind him.

"I don't like being threatened, Volk, or told what to do."

As the door closed Holland heard Volk laugh softly and his parting words just reached him as he drained the last of the Scotch. "Not threatened, Mr. Holland, warned."

Mark Holland spent several long moments analyzing the conversation and his feelings toward the man. There was no doubt he was being warned off, told to keep his nose out of the plane crash incident. He was stepping on toes by just being around and asking questions somebody didn't want asked. He reached for the telephone and after waiting impatiently for the operator to connect him, talked quickly to the desk operator at the Pan American office. When he replaced the receiver in its cradle he was booked on the night flight to New York.

After packing his Air Force flight bag, Holland left the room and went to the bar off the lobby.

He sat at the bar. It wasn't until he was on his second drink that he noticed an older man seated at the end of the bar. The man was studying Holland with more attention than the casual observer of bar life is expected to. Holland shifted his frame slightly so that he could ignore the man.

The man at the end of the bar moved his position and once again Holland could see him out of the corner of his eye. The move had been deliberate, calculated to impress on Holland that he was interested in starting a conversation. Holland sighed, expelling the air through tight, pursed lips and hoping the sound would register his annoyance.

The stranger left his own seat and walked toward him, carrying his glass. Holland prepared to give the man a curt "No" to the expected "May I join you?"

"Captain Holland, my name is Starling. I was at your press conference."

Holland looked again at the man and recognized him. Starling had been the journalist who had asked the question about the plane being off course. "I remember, but I've got nothing to add to what I said in there."

"I quite understand, Captain. No, I'm not trying to pump

you for additional information. Quite to the contrary. You told me all I needed to know. Confirmed my own suspicions, as it were. I simply thought you would permit me to buy you a drink."

Holland nodded in the direction of his glass. "Sure, if you want to, but there's no need."

"On the contrary, my dear fellow—two more Scotches please—there is every need. What you did was a very brave thing. I admire bravery, though I sometimes think it is closely related to stupidity. Like hate and love, I suppose. But there are those of us who would wish to be brave and there are those who simply react because that is the thing which must be done at that particular time. You are one of those who react. *Ergo*, one who would simply wish to act wishes to buy you a drink. That requires no attempt at bravery."

Holland laughed, "For a journalist you're pretty deep. I think you just called me an idiot who got lucky but is now called a hero for having pulled it off. I am not sure though, so I guess I can't take offense."

The two laughed together and Holland found himself liking the man who talked like a college professor. They knocked back their glasses and Holland indicated to the bartender they were ready for a refill. The door behind them opened and the soft rushing of air made him turn to see who had entered.

The girl glanced around the room, then looked directly toward the bar and smiled. She walked gracefully over and Holland wondered where it was he knew her from.

"Hello, Dr. Starling. I'm ready for that gin and tonic now."

Starling turned and beamed. "Ah, Stephanie. I was just having a drink with Captain Holland here and boring him with my theory of bravery."

"And confusing him terribly, no doubt."

"Oh, yes, of course. Wouldn't be any fun if I didn't confound my audience. Captain, may I present my colleague, Dr. Stephanie Caine."

Holland slipped off the stool and shook the offered hand. Dr. Caine smiled at him warmly. "I'm pleased to meet you, Dr. Caine," he said before indicating a stool for her. She settled herself on the stool and flashed the warm smile at him again.

"Are you a medical doctor?" asked Holland after ordering her a gin and tonic.

She shook her head. "No, my science is entomology. I'm an ex-student of Dr. Starling's. I received my Ph.D. from Oxford University shortly after Dr. Starling was asked to head the Center for Pest Research in London. It seemed an ideal opportunity for me to put my theoretical studies into field and laboratory practice, so I joined him."

Starling snorted good-naturedly. "My dear, you underestimate yourself." Turning to Holland he continued, "It truly is a case of the student teaching the teacher, Captain."

Holland smiled. "I thought you said you were a journalist."

"On the contrary, Captain, I said no such thing. *You* however made the assumption that because I was at a press conference and asked a question I must be. As to what the idea was or is—it's simply that we have rather an interest in this matter. In fact—"

"Wait a minute, I've seen you two before!" The girl had been looking up at Starling and the pose had nagged at Holland's memory. Suddenly he had it. "You were at Abha when the news came in that the plane had gone down! I remember seeing you in the doorway of the office while that guy was telling me about it!"

"That is correct, Captain, we were there."

"Why?"

"Why were you there?"

"To meet somebody."

"So, therefore, either we were there to catch a flight or we were there to meet somebody too."

"OK, which was it?"

"To meet somebody."

Holland looked from one to the other. "The Trans-Global flight?"

"Correct."

"Who were you waiting for?" Holland's voice softened with the understanding that they had also lost somebody on board.

"My uncle, Captain," answered the girl quietly.

"I'm sorry."

"I didn't really know him too well. In fact I only saw him about five times in my life. We lived in New Zealand for a long while and he lived and worked in the States.

"His name was Steiner. Dr. Albert Steiner. He and two other scientists were to have met us at Abha."

The image of the half-eaten face, the shattered leg, sprang to his mind. That had been Steiner.

"I wanted to thank you in person for having found his body," she was saying, "and giving it a decent burial. I would have hated to think that he, and the rest of the passengers of course, would never have been found. It will mean a lot to my mother."

"Your mother is—was—his sister?"

"Yes. As I said, we weren't very close, but she would want to know he was given a Christian burial. After the war, my mother married a British officer and they emigrated to New Zealand. My uncle went to the States."

"Captain, I wonder if you would tell me something. Did you see anything strange at the crash site?"

Holland looked at Starling carefully. "Yes, it was blown up and there were sixteen bodies. That's strange enough isn't it?"

"Forgive me," replied the man hastily, "I don't mean to be insensitive. I am aware of your personal bereavement, but I assure you it is most important for you to tell us if anything struck you as—unusual."

"Nothing."

"Are you *quite* sure?"

"I said there was nothing strange about the crash other than the bomb."

Starling sighed and turned to Stephanie. She looked disappointed.

"Well, I suppose that's one dead end."

"Look, you two, perhaps you wouldn't mind filling me in on what's going on. I get the feeling your interest goes beyond caring about the death of your Dr. Steiner."

Stephanie looked to Starling, who nodded acceptance. "Quite simply, Captain," began the girl, "as I said, we work at a scientific research center in London. Last Friday afternoon I got a telephone call from my uncle urging Dr. Starling and me to meet him in Abha.

"Captain, he was terrified of something. He wouldn't tell me what the matter was, or what trouble he was in. Only that we should meet him in Abha and he and the two others would show us something vital which the world should be told about. It was a very brief telephone call and once I assured him we would come, he broke the connection. But the tone of his voice is something I shall never forget—it was panic, pure terror."

"And that's all he said?"

"He didn't elaborate, Captain. We have tried to find out, but have gotten absolutely nowhere in the past week."

"He worked for Trans-Global. Have you tried them?"

Starling nodded. "I myself have spent hours trying to get someone there to allow me to look at Steiner's notes. To no avail, I'm afraid. I have even been warned off by a rather nasty American gentleman who said I should stop rocking the boat."

"That'd be Volk. I've had pretty much the same conversation with him."

"Well, as you may be aware, we scientific types are inclined to talk amongst ourselves and I tried that route. I spent several hours in the local bars getting to know some of the chaps who work at Trans-Global here in Addis Ababa.

"All very nice chaps and we got along really well. Until, that is, the subject of Steiner and what he was working on came up. Then . . ."

"They all clammed up," finished Holland.

"Precisely. They clammed up. Indeed, they became most agitated and excused themselves."

Holland thought of the security passes Steiner and the two other members of his team were carrying. "Does Station 17 mean anything to either of you?"

Starling and Caine looked at each other and shook their heads.

"How about Livingston?"

"The doctor?" asked Stephanie.

"No, the place. It's in Montana, in the States."

"And what is the relevance of these two names, Captain?"

"I haven't the faintest idea, Dr. Starling, but I found a security pass for each of the three scientists made out for a place called Station 17, Livingston. It struck me, or rather it struck Ziad Sadallah, as being strange that they would have security passes for an installation in the States while working out here."

"Yes, it is strange," agreed Starling. "Normally when one leaves a security establishment one is required to hand in one's pass. It's standard procedure. I should say the fact that they retained their passes would indicate they were still working there."

"That's how I read it. I'm going to Livingston to see what I can dig up. It may be a wasted journey, but I have the feeling a big part of the answer is there."

Starling and Stephanie glanced at each other quickly. "I'm going with you," said the girl.

Holland shook his head, then took in the determined set of the beautiful jaw. She knew where the place was, he had seen to that by telling them, and she seemed to be the type who would not be put off. He smiled, suddenly glad of the company. "I don't see why you want to, but the flight leaves at nine this evening. Pan Am to New York, then Eastern to Butte."

"Captain," interjected Starling, "are you *quite* sure there was nothing on that mountain which might perhaps give us a clue? Something that seemed normal, perhaps, but extreme?"

"I've already told you—nothing."

They lapsed into silence for a while and Holland called the bartender over for a refill. As the man was obliging, Holland turned to Stephanie. "How about you, are you sure your uncle didn't say anything else?"

"There was one other thing, but it was so crazy."

"The whole thing is crazy. What was it?"

"He said if he didn't get help, it would be the end of the world."

# CHAPTER SEVEN

"THE CURSE OF ALLAH AND HIS HOLY PROPHET MUHAMMAD will fall upon you all," the blind man screeched in the square near the fountain.

The milling crowd scarcely paid attention to the old beggar who could be found every day at the same place, uttering more or less the same promises of divine retribution upon the heads of the godless.

His message had been slightly different the last time Abdullah al Haique had been in Omdurman. Then it had been something along the lines that when the Prophet returned he would take the vengeance of Allah upon those who had sinned. Now, the old man was saying that the Prophet's agents were already among us.

Abdullah grinned to himself at the thought of yesterday's entertainment in the market place and then returned his attention to the task at hand. The blind man was a fool.

The camel train meandered slowly across the sands as the midday sun climbed to its zenith. The Nubian Desert was a ruthless equalizer for those who treated it with contempt or indifference, but to the nomad travelers it was a friend who trusted and understood them and was in turn treated with the utmost respect.

Abdullah had been born in this desert and had spent all of his years crossing it with one train or another. As a guide and leader he was undoubtedly the best, and thus in great demand from merchants to see their goods safely to their destination.

He had grown rich from it and enjoyed the repsect of his peers, who measured a man by his achievements. And indeed, there had been many. Was it not Abdullah al Haique who had taken a train across the Sudan during the great thirst? Was it not he who had found the route leading from the great salt flats when even those with their mechanical trucks had perished attempting to cross the wasteland?

He looked forward to completing this long trek from Omdurman to Haiya Junction. Waiting for him would be his wives who would gather around after he had bathed and eaten, and listen in dutiful awe to the tales of his latest journey—suitably embellished perhaps, to add the correct amount of spice and adventure.

Abdullah shifted in the saddle to ease the slight numbness he was experiencing more often these days. No matter how good a man had been, old age surely came to everyone. The day would come for him, perhaps not too far away, when he would have to abandon his role as guide for the trains and spend his time swapping lies in the coffee stalls with the other old men.

He spat into the sand in disgust.

A movement across the horizon caught his eye and he looked for a while in consternation. Recognition dawned as he watched the shadows lengthen over the dunes. Not dangerous, but it would mean they would have to stop and tether the animals to ensure they didn't run off in fright.

Abdullah's terse orders were conveyed from one man to another and quickly the camels were brought to the ground, their legs shackled with hide ropes to prevent them from rising.

The darkness that came as this task was completed was the darkness of night. Abdullah, crouching by his mount, knew he was again witnessing the capricious spirit of the land wherein he traveled. Never, though, had he known it to be as bad as this. Truly something to speak of when they got home.

One of the camels shrieked and pulled loose from a badly-tied halter and Abdullah shouted to the men who were in charge of that section to re-tie the animal before it had the chance to stand completely upright and race away. The imbeciles should know their creatures were skittish and took fright at the smallest of noises. All they had to do was to secure them firmly until the strangeness was past.

A sharp pain in his calf made him wince and he looked down at the exposed limb to see a thin trickle of blood coursing its way through the dark hairs. He felt another sting, this time on his cheek. He brushed at it absentmindedly, then suddenly became aware his hand was now smeared with blood.

He stood and stared about him with a growing sense of fear and of bewilderment, as his men raced in blind panic to avoid the terror. But Abdullah understood they would not succeed, there could be no escape. He prepared to accept the judgment of the desert, as he had done all his life.

The camels screamed and brayed as they thrashed around on the sand, unable to stand and run because of the bonds.

Abdullah shook his head slowly as the red mist flooded his eyes. It wouldn't have mattered after all if they had been loose. There was only one ending to the final journey. The old man in the marketplace had given the warning and he had failed to heed it. Failed to make amends for all his wrongs. Before Allah he was as nothing.

He felt again the searing pain as more flesh was torn from him and he prayed silently to his God for mercy.

The sign at the beginning of the town said:

## WELCOME TO LIVINGSTON

Population 948, the last time we counted.
Drive carefully and you can stay!
Sign erected by Hank's Motel, Main Street.

"So this is beautiful downtown Livingston," said Stephanie dryly, as Holland drove the rented Chevy station wagon onto the town's one and only street.

The trip from Addis to Butte, with the long delay in New York while they waited for their airline connection, had seemed to take forever and their arrival in this small, midwestern town was just part of the anticlimax. As they pulled the car into the Sunoco gas station, Stephanie began to doubt that any piece to the puzzle could possibly be found.

They climbed out of the car and stretched taut muscles. The gas station stood on a strategic corner as you entered the town, at the head of the long main street which ran in a straight line through the heart before it again became the U.S. highway stretching away toward the mountains.

Stephanie looked around her, noting the small schoolhouse set back off the road surrounded by a pleasant garden on the opposite side of the street. Nearby was a freshly-painted clapboard church, which indicated the residents of Livingston cared enough to ensure that Sunday worship was conducted in a decent atmosphere.

A block away from the gas station, which stood apart, almost as though it were abandoned by the rest of the town, the business section began with a Seven-Eleven store which seemed altogether too large for the small population. Next to this was a drugstore and past that a small jewelry shop with a faded sign proclaiming it also served as a dry cleaner.

From somewhere further down the street drifted the sounds of a juke box loudly proclaiming the latest Olivia Newton-John tune. That would either be a bar or the ubiquitous diner which always managed to earn the proprietor a living no matter what the current state of the tourist industry in middle America.

Stephanie looked fondly, even with some relish, around the small town, at the odd piece of paper which scurried across the street and the slight layer of dust covering the hot tarmac.

"You look miles away, Stephanie."

She smiled without turning toward his voice. "I was thinking how much this town looks like my own home. I love places like this. They make you remember what life is supposed to be for."

An old man wandered casually out of the office, wiping nonexistent grease off his hands onto a oily rag in the universal gesture of the working mechanic.

"Howdy, strangers, nice to see ya. What can I do for ya?"

"Christ, he talks like a bad John Wayne movie!"

"Ssh. Hi there. Fill it up."

"Come over the mountains?"

"Yeah, from Butte."

"Better check under the hood then—oil and water get pretty low after a drive like that."

"Hank's the best place to stay around here?" asked Mark, as the old man prodded under the hood looking for the oil stick. With a grunt of satisfaction he found it and withdrew it from the engine block.

"Only place to stay, less you want to stay at Ma Allan's, but she'll talk your damn ears off. Hang right at the bottom of the street for Hank's. Can't miss it."

He grunted in satisfaction at the result of the investigation of the oil level and water. He nodded, happy that all was well with the car, and banged the hood down as the gas pump gave a loud "ding" in panic as it sensed the gasoline backing up the pipe. He removed the nozzle from the tank, replaced the cap and slammed the license plate cover back into position.

"How much?"

"Twelve fifty. You here for business or health reasons?"

"Neither." Mark peeled off two five-dollar bills from his roll. "Keep the change, and thanks."

The old man looked at the ten dollars. "Anytime. Don't forget, hang a right at the end of the street."

Hank's revealed itself to be another item off the Hollywood set. It was a large wooden building which seemed to take light in without ever letting any out. Stephanie grimaced at the sight of the lopsided sign. "Alfred Hitchcock lived here," she muttered as they walked up the stairs to the porch.

Hank himself greeted them, agreeing that he just might be

able to squeeze them in somewhere. "Come to think on it though," he said good-naturedly, "you could take your pick of the rooms. Don't get many up here nowdays. Everybody's in too much of a hurry racing around giving themselves ulcers to want to come to a quiet little neighborhood like Livingston. Get some hunters in the season, but mostly it's kinda quiet."

Mark decided Hank might be the type of midwesterner who liked to drink and talk. And if you took care of the former, the latter would almost certainly follow. After settling into their rooms, Mark retrieved one of the duty-free bottles of Black Label from his flight bag and returned to the porch. Hank followed him out, carrying three glasses in anticipation.

"Like the rooms, mister?"

"Real good, Hank, nice, clean and a soft bed. Just how I like it."

"That's good. Where's the young lady?"

"Long trip, she needs time to freshen up."

Hank filled two of the glasses without waiting to be asked and flopped into one of the chairs. He pushed back and kicked his feet up onto the porch rail, crossing one cowboy boot over the other. He drank deeply from his glass and then allowed himself time to examine the feeling as the Scotch probed its way down into his stomach.

"Now that," he said at length, "is one damn fine whiskey."

"Scotch," corrected Holland.

"Damn fine whiskey," repeated the hotel owner. "Reminds me of the taste of the good stuff I used to drink when I was in Europe in World War Two. You ever been to Europe, son?"

"I've—"

"Damn fine place, everyone should go once," continued Hank, not giving Mark a chance to reply. "Cause once the Russians get to take over, there won't be no chance for a fella like you."

"You liked it, eh?"

"Sure did. But once the war was over I couldn't wait to get back here. Had a bellyful of fornicatin' and fightin'. Some peace and quiet is what I wanted. Know what I mean?"

Holland nodded in serious understanding of Hank's point of view and offered the bottle. Hank refilled his now empty glass.

"So what brings ya all the way over the mountains to Livingston? Ain't much to do around here 'cept fish, and the young lady don't look like no fisherman I ever saw!"

He laughed loudly and slapped Holland on the leg in a stinging whack that belied the man's apparent frailness and age.

"Oh you know how it is, Hank, man gets tired of the rat race and wants to rediscover his roots, unwind a bit away from the hustle."

"You come from around here?"

"No, but a town pretty much like it. Thought we'd base here and take a look at the park and stuff like that. No schedules to worry about and no other tourists getting in our way."

"Sure picked the right place for that. Get to the other end of the Yellowstone and it's like Coney Island. Always wondered why a few water spouts and Yogi Bear could be so attractive to people. Hell, we got some of the best damn scenery in the whole world at this end, but because we ain't got none of them geyser things, people don't want to know. I guess they like to be photographed beside them spouts just to prove they been to Yellowstone National. Kinda sad I s'pose, but that's city folk. Never know how to be an individual."

"I guess you're right there, Hank. Another drink?"

"Don't mind if I do."

"One of the reasons I wanted to visit here," began Mark cautiously, "was that I was told by a buddy I could get to see a bit of real America. He said he could have spent the rest of his life here with no problem at all."

Hank looked interested and drank the Scotch, then burped with relish. "He from around here?"

Holland shook his head. "No, he just worked here for a while. He's a scientist or something. I never really did catch on to what it was all about."

Hank reached for the bottle and poured. "Shit, you mean that goddam Bug Hutch place!"

Holland's heart quickened. "Bug Hutch," he said, fighting to keep the interest out of his voice, "what's that?"

"Damned if I know, and that's the truth, son. Fact is even old Ma Allan couldn't find out, and she knows everybody's business if you give her enough time to dig. About three years ago the army came in and built a road; it starts about three miles out of town. Well they built this road right into the park toward the glacier and at the end of it they built a compound and that was that.

"We figured sooner or later we would get to meet the guys working out there, but no sir. They never once came into town, not even on Saturday night, for Chrissake! Three goddam years and not once did anybody come into town. Got a lot of traffic passing through, but none of it ever stopped.

"We reckoned they must have been bringing their own supplies in and taking their own garbage out. Sure kept to themselves. We called the place the Bug Hutch."

"Didn't anybody from town go in there?"

"Tried to. Got turned around and sent back at the road leading in. They even had guards out in the park to stop anyone from getting too curious and trying to get near from that direction. Matter of fact, couple of the boys got themselves arrested for being too persistent."

"Arrested? Who by?"

"Government agents. Turned out it was the Secret Service who was guarding the place. Just as though the president himself was living there."

Mark looked thoughtfully at the crossed cowboy boots.

"It's still there though, isn't it, Hank?"

"It's still there, sure. But nobody in the place. Don't know when it happened, but one day one of the Indian boys came into town and told us it was deserted. Just like that, they was all gone, as quiet and as quick as they come!"

"When was that?"

"About three months ago, I reckon. Why?"

"Just curious about things I don't understand."

Hank roared and slapped his leg painfully again. "Then you'd have driven yourself crazy, son, if you had been here when they first moved in. That's for damn sure, cause I sure as hell near went over the hill trying to figure it out!"

He roared with laughter until the tears ran down his face and then he wiped them away with a stained shirt sleeve. "Guess we may as well finish the bottle, son," he said unashamedly, "be a damn pity to let it go flat now we broke the seal off it." He roared with laughter again, and Holland joined in.

"Good morning. How do you feel?"

"Great. Did I really sleep as long as I think I did, or have I been dreaming?"

Holland smiled. "You slept. When supper was ready I came up to see if you were ready to eat and you were flat out. At ten o'clock, Hank's wife went up and put you into bed. Breakfast is on the table if you're hungry."

She shook her head. "Thanks, I just had coffee and toast. Where are we going? It's so early."

Mark finished checking the tools he had borrowed from Hank's shed and tossed them into the back of the Chevy. "Six thirty in these parts ain't early, doggone it!" he said, mimicking Hank's speech. "Get in, unless you want to miss the action."

He drove to the opposite end of town, toward the park, ignoring her pleas to tell her where they were going and why. Finally, he spotted what he was looking for. "There it is, that's the road Hank said the army built."

"Army? What army? What is going on, Mark?"

Briefly he told her about the conversation he had had the previous evening. She listened intently until he had finished.

"Funny name," she observed after a moment.

"Bug Hutch? Yeah, I guess it is. Hank said he didn't know who had named it, or why."

"It's the name the English give to an insane asylum, but I'm surprised the term would be used out here." She stared again at the road. "It looks very narrow, Mark. Are you sure this is the right one?"

Holland studied the entrance through the overhanging trees, the rough pitted surface and deep holes which would put off any driver who didn't have a four-wheel drive. "Hank said if we found a track that looked as if a mule couldn't walk down it then we'd found the right place. This fits, so hold on, we're going in!"

The car bounced and shook for half a mile before the road suddenly widened, becoming smoother. "Clever. Build an obstacle course for half a mile to discourage explorers. Hank said a lot of trucks came this way, so we should have a smooth ride the rest of the trip."

They drove for an hour. As they rounded a bend, with the mountain looming almost on top of them, they saw the area Hank had known as the Bug Hutch.

A locked steel gate blocked the road and what had once been a guard post leaned lopsidedly against a tree. Behind the wire fence sat seven single-story wooden huts. Off to the right was a concrete structure which in turn was surrounded by its own high fence.

Stephanie joined him at the gate and jiggled the heavy padlock and chain. "Now what?"

Mark turned without answering and walked briskly to the rear of the car. Opening the trunk he fished inside the pile of borrowed tools before hauling out a hefty pair of bolt cutters.

"When I open the gates you drive the car through. I'll close them again in case anyone else should happen to come along. Take the car around the back of that first hut."

Stephanie came toward him as he walked down the slight incline from the gates with the cutters. "Car's hidden. I looked in that hut," she said, nodding toward the one behind which the car was parked, "but it was empty."

"I thought they would be, but it's all we have to go on. Let's check them first."

It took no longer than five minutes to ascertain that the seven wooden huts were, indeed, completely empty. Mark returned to the station wagon and pulled the tool bag out, then retrieved the bolt cutters which he had placed against a large, white painted rock in what would have served as the main thoroughfare for the complex.

"What next?"

"That concrete bunker is all that's left," he answered over his shoulder as he hurried toward the second gate.

She stared at it for a moment and then ran after him. "Mark, I don't know if you should break in there. We don't know what was going on here and the structure might be dangerous."

Mark snapped the padlock off and pushed. The gate swung open with a slight squeak of rusting hinges.

"What makes you think it could be dangerous?"

"The building! It's the sort scientists put up when they want to keep something in."

"Or keep people out. I figure if there was anything dangerous in there this place wouldn't be left unguarded."

Holland examined the door. It was solid enough, but had obviously been built for short-term occupancy in a well-guarded compound. He selected a fourteen-pound sledgehammer before moving Stephanie out of his way and smashing it into the hinges. It took five swings before a loud crack indicated he had broken through.

He pulled flashlights from the bag and stepped inside. The two beams of light danced around the one-room building, re-vealing rows of laboratory benches that stood, ghost-like, in the gloom.

They searched the room carefully. Other than the wooden benches, it was empty.

Stephanie kicked idly at a small stone as they sat on the grass, unable to stem the disappointment they both felt.

"I really thought we'd find something around this damn place that would at least give a clue about what has been going on here."

Holland stretched out in the grass. "I suppose it was really too much to hope for. Christ, I don't know why I'm here in the first place. As far as I was concerned, it was all over for me after returning from Yemen. But that clown Volk trying to warn me off made me decide to come over and check things out. That has to be the lulu of all idiot moves!"

"I know how you must be feeling," she said, "but I think we both felt we had to check out every possibility which pre-

sented itself, to check any lead, no matter how slender. I felt
then and I still feel that it really was important. I only wish
my uncle had given me a clue. Some clue!"

Her voice broke slightly and as Mark turned to her he caught
sight of the grass at the far end of the compound. He stopped
and lowered his head and the grass looked normal. He raised
it again. Then he jumped to his feet, pulling her with him.
"We're not finished yet. Come on!"

Stephanie staggered after him, trying desperately to maintain
her footing as he pulled her along.

"What . . . what is it?" she gasped breathlessly when at
last he stopped.

"From back there . . . as I started to get up . . . I could
see this piece of grass was flatter than the rest. Look, it has
grown less than the grass in the surrounding area."

"So? You're going wild just because someone did some
extra mowing?" Stephanie stopped suddenly, scanning the area
around her before breaking into a smile. "It's grown differently
because it's been constantly flattened. It was a path, leading
away from the main complex towards those trees!"

They trudged along it for ten minutes before entering a
clearing which had once been a lush forest. Stacks of trees lay
to each side, while the tree stumps showed that whoever had
cut them had been no professional. Mark guessed it had been
the Army Corps of Engineers.

Ahead of them, at the far end of the clearing, lay the first,
rock-strewn slopes of the mountain. Further up the valley, the
sun's dying rays made the glacier glisten darkly.

Stephanie stared up toward the high, jagged peaks and let
out a deep sigh. "God, it's magnificent, isn't it?"

"But what was happening? Why have they cleared *this* site?"

She turned back to him reluctantly and also tried to find an
answer. "Landing field?" she offered hopefully, knowing the
tree stumps made that an impossibility.

"Sure," he said. "Package tours to the doorstep of Yellowstone Park."

"What?" she shouted. "What did you say? Yellowstone
Park?"

Holland looked at her as she grabbed his arm. "Yeah, Yellowstone. It's a National Park and . . ."

She turned quickly and looked back at the glacier. "My God, that's it. I should have realized it."

She pointed to the glacier. "That's Grasshopper Glacier. There's a network of dark, horizontal layers beneath the ice. Thousands upon thousands of grasshoppers are buried in it. I'll tell you about that later if you like, but the important thing is that it was the glacier they were working on, not this clearing. I want to have a closer look."

Stephanie started to scramble up the slope hastily. He followed until they were perched on a ledge some forty feet up the mountain face. Her dark eyes were alive as he pulled himself up beside her.

"Look, they have dug right into the ice down there taking samples. I'll bet if we were to cover this entire side of the glacier we would find they have done the same thing at varying levels."

"Terrific."

"But don't you see? That was my uncle's science, entomology. Oh, he moved to biochemistry in later years, but this is what he was really about."

"OK, so that puts him here, at this site. But it still leaves the problem of why he was in the Middle East with an oil company and why he called you."

She sat down on the rock. "I guess we're no closer, are we?"

"Not a lot," he replied softly. "Come on, let's get back down. Once night starts to fall up here it comes down with a rush. We still have to get back along the road."

She allowed herself to be led down again, pausing only once on that path to glance back. Holland stopped outside the concrete building and bent to retrieve the bag of borrowed tools.

"A flashlight," she said suddenly, "give me a flashlight!"

Holland dropped the bag back to the ground and handed her one of the heavy-duty flashlights. She ran to the building and stepped inside. Curious, he followed her, snapping on his beam as he entered the building.

She was on her knees under one of the work benches. "I knew it, I just *knew* it!" she exclaimed with satisfaction. "Mark, come and look!"

He walked across the room, dropped to his knees and wriggled under the table as she explained. "I've worked for large organizations—the sort who can afford to bankroll this type of operation. They all have one thing in common. They brand their property. Every Bunsen burner, bed sheet and fork has the company logo on it."

He looked where her light held steady under the table. A metal disk was attached to the underside of the bench. It bore the embossed design of the world with the letters "T.G." set in gold paint beneath the globe.

"Trans-Global Oil," he muttered half to himself. "It's starting to look as though all roads do lead to Rome."

"Or at least right to Trans-Global's doorstep," she replied dryly.

Holland pulled out his package of cigarettes, thoughtfully drawing in the harsh smoke as he sat on the cold cement floor and looked across at Stephanie, her face eerily distorted by the yellow glow from the flashlight. "So, what do you make of it, Stephanie?"

"I must confess, I really don't know. There are several things which I find puzzling. What about you?"

He shrugged. "I suppose I agree with you. Why was the Secret Service involved in protecting a civilian establishment? Why was this place built to begin with? What's the tie-in between the crash and this place? There seem to be more questions than answers."

"Yes, but it does explain why that Volk man was so determined to keep you from investigating Kate's death any further."

"How do you figure that?"

"Well, first, if his attitude was belligerent, that's not exactly the press and public relations image you'd expect from a press attaché. Second, you discover from Hank that the Secret Service protected this facility. Well, surely Volk was afraid you'd be able to tie the owners of the crashed plane to this site. The coincidence would be too much to ignore. He would realize that and want to warn you off in the same way he did Doctor Starling."

"Which means he must be more than a press attaché?"

"Not necessarily. After all he could just have been passing on a message, but I'd bet that he is in government security somewhere."

He suddenly jumped to his feet, pulling her up as he did so. "Come on, let's get out of here and back to the motel. I need a bath, a drink and some good food before I can even begin to figure this lot out."

As he walked to the car Stephanie closed the door to the workshop and after a moment's hesitation she followed, a slight smile touching the corners of her mouth.


"Well there, folks, have a good day?" Hank called to them from the veranda as they pulled up in front of the seedy motel. Sitting beside him was an even older man, whom they could see had spent most, if not all, his life in the outdoors.

"Not too bad, all things considered," Mark replied to the hotel owner's question. The thought crossed his mind that he must remember to return Hank's tool bag to the shed without him noticing. He had decided against asking for permission. It had been safer to simply borrow them without his knowing.

"Like you to meet Jeremiah Two Horse," began Hank, jerking his thumb toward the man who shared the porch. "Best guide in the district if you want to get some fishin' in while you're here. He knows these woods inside out and can move faster and quieter than a snake when he has to."

Holland shook the Indian's hand. "No time this trip, Jeremiah, but I'll keep it in mind for the next."

Jeremiah grunted and Hank chuckled. "Don't say a whole lot, ol' Jeremiah." He nodded in the direction of an earthenware jug. "Take yerself a swallow of that stuff, boy. Jeremiah brought it down with him from the mountains!"

Mark accepted the jug and stuck the first two fingers of his right hand through the handle before popping it into the crook of his arm and tipping it back to drink straight from the neck. He took a long draft of the moonshine before depositing it back at Hank's feet, trying his best to smile.

It burned like the fires of hell all the way down his throat and seemed to attack the very lining of his stomach.

Hank looked at Holland with admiration and Jeremiah allowed himself another grunt. "Not bad at all . . . for a city boy. You took a swallow like you knew what you was doin'. Reckon he ain't no stranger to a little moonshine, eh, Jeremiah?"

The Indian grunted and Holland burped loudly in final surrender to the fiery liquid. "Used to take the odd taste back home when I was a kid. But I can tell you," he added, rubbing his stomach, "that was the roughest stuff I've tasted. It's got a kick like a mule crawled inside the still and died!"

Jeremiah made a sound similar to a chuckle and Hank roared in appreciation. "You'll do, son. You'll do." Suddenly he was serious. "I told Jeremiah to hang on till you got back cause he used to guide fer some of them fellas we were talkin' about last night."

Mark's eyes narrowed slightly. "You said nobody from town ever got to meet anybody from the complex," he said accusingly.

"And that's right enough. Nobody did. But Jeremiah here isn't from the town. He lives in the mountains you was just takin' a look at. Besides, he doesn't talk a helluva lot so I guess they reckoned that was all right."

Hank studied Holland's face for a long moment and Mark felt as though he were being taunted in some way, but he didn't know how or why.

Hank spat over the rail. "If there's anything you want to know about these people, then here's your chance, son. Jeremiah never got to go inside the place, he always waited down at the lake for any that wanted to go fishin' or up at his camp when they wanted to hunt."

He spat again and Mark turned to Jeremiah. "Did you ever hear them discussing what went on in the complex?"

"No. Talk about fish or deer all time. Drink much, tell stories about selves. Never about camp."

"Was it always the same people who went, or different?"

"Depend. Most time same three men."

Stephanie started and went into the hotel. Mark could hear her footsteps receding as she ran up the stairs to the first floor.

"How often did you take them out?"

"All time. One man say they like to relax in woods. Good for them to join with nature. Lotta crap like that."

Mark smiled and looked up as Stephanie burst through the double front doors. She thrust a worn photograph at the Indian. "Was this one of the men?" she demanded breathlessly.

Jeremiah looked at the photograph without taking it. In the distance a car horn blared noisily, causing four large black crows to stop their scavenging in the garbage bins at the end of the drive and take to the air.

"That the one who say crap about joining with nature," agreed the guide.

Mark looked at the photograph. It was Steiner.

"Jeremiah, I gather you talked with this man more than any of the others, is that right?"

A grunt confirmed this.

"Then are you sure he never said anything to you about his work, or about the complex at the glacier?"

The Indian looked off into space for what seemed an eternity. In the distance the car horn sounded again as the driver vented his impatience. The sound seemed to cause Jeremiah to remember he had been asked a question.

"Last time we go fishing in lake, just day before they leave. He watch snapping turtle chase little fish. He say bad things in the world. Things that cause much misery and suffering. He say was going to stop such bad misery in a place a long way off. I told him he should stop misery in this place first, before he worry about other places. He say thing he going to stop would do good things for all."

"Did he say what he meant?"

"No."

The interview was over.

Jeremiah reached for the jug and took a long drink before handing it to Hank. Mark thought about what the man had said, shaking his head when the jug was offered to him. At length he nodded.

"Stephanie, go and pack your stuff. We're leaving. Hank, make up the bill, will you?"

"Shoot, that's easy enough. Five bucks each for the beds and three bucks for your supper last night. Breakfast included. That's thirteen in all."

Mark started peeling off the bills as Hank added, "No charge for the tools you borrowed this morning!"

Mark paused only slightly at the jibe and carried on counting to twenty.

"I appreciate that, Hank. Use the rest to get a bottle for you and Jeremiah."

The money vanished into a shirt pocket and Hank spat again. "Kind of you, son."

Jeremiah grunted in agreement and Mark turned toward the hotel entrance. Walking up the stairs he could hear the two men laughing softly.

# CHAPTER EIGHT

A HUNDRED MILES OFF THE COAST OF OMAN, IN THE ARABIAN Sea, the Portuguese navy cutter *Independence* hailed the ocean-going yacht.

They had first noticed her an hour before when the radar officer reported a craft that appeared to be drifting. The radio operator had been unable to raise the vessel and her captain had ordered a course change to investigate.

Captain Luis de Gardo el Jimminez had been at sea for over forty years and had experienced more things in one lifetime than most other men would in ten. A drifting, abandoned vessel was not an unfamiliar object to Captain Jimminez. During the course of his career, the captain had boarded ships where the entire crew had jumped overboard with madness at the solitude of the sea and ships where murder had suddenly exploded amid the incredible silence and solitude of the ocean.

As his first officer shook his head to indicate a lack of response, Captain Jimminez felt annoyance at this unscheduled stop in their homeward journey. Courtesy calls to foreign countries were all well and good, but the constant pressure of being on show was tiring and they all, officers and men alike, looked forward to completing the long trip home.

"Board her, Lieutenant. See what's going on over there," he ordered.

"*Si*, Captain."

"But do not take any chances. Take your sidearm, Lieutenant. It is far better to err on the side of caution than to come back a dead man. Good luck."

The young officer saluted briefly and then dropped over the ship's rail into a small launch below.

Five minutes later, the captain observed the young officer haul himself aboard the yacht and give rapid instructions to the men who made up the boarding party. Captain Jimminez trained his binoculars on the wheel house and then ran along the entire length of the vessel. "Ah, to own such a ship as that and sail the world at your leisure," he muttered enviously to himself.

A sudden flurry of activity indicated radio contact had been established between the cutter and the yacht. "Captain, Lieutenant Rodriguez requests you join him with all haste aboard the yacht," reported the master-at-arms.

"Why? Ask him what is wrong."

"Aye, aye, sir."

The Captain looked back at the yacht. He could see the young officer in the wheel house of the craft, talking into the microphone of the yacht's radio. Within moments, the master-at-arms stuck his head back through the bridge door.

"Sir, he says he prefers not to broadcast on an open wave band until you have had a chance to examine the ship for yourself. He says once you have visited the yacht you will agree he acted in the correct way. He's sending the launch back for you now, sir."

The Captain smiled. "Then I assume he gives me no choice, eh, Phillipe? Very well, but this had better be worth leaving my ship for, or else I think that we shall be looking for a new first lieutenant."

Ten minutes later, after the captain had looked into the five cabins and the yacht's sumptuous day room and seen this thing for himself, he knew that the first officer had had no choice.

\* \* \*

On the Pan Am jet to London, Mark was silent for a long while. Stephanie slumped slowly into his shoulder to sleep the rest of the way to London. As her hair fell across his arm, she reminded him, disturbingly, of Kate. Soon, he too allowed his tired body to take over, and he slept restlessly, images of Korea flitting in and out of his mind, mingling with a vision of Crazy Horse chasing General Custer. Custer got a flat tire and Crazy Horse killed him.

They arrived at Heathrow at eleven o'clock London time, to an England that sweltered in a rare heat wave. Stephanie entered the line designated "U.K. and Commonwealth Passport Holders Only," while Holland joined the longer line under the sign "Others."

The immigration officer flipped the passport open and studied Holland before turning his head slightly to his right. The man who had been standing at his shoulder stepped forward and took the green booklet. He too looked at the page that bore Holland's photograph and personal details before turning his attention to Mark, who began to get impatient.

"Mr. Holland, would you come with me please!" It was delivered as an order rather than a request, but Holland hesitated before moving around the desk. They walked through a door marked "Private" which led into a short corridor with offices on each side. The officer led the way, without once looking back to ensure that Holland followed, to one of the doors on the right. It was marked "Interview Room" and he opened the door for Holland to enter and wait.

Mark looked around the room. Except for a table and three uncomfortable-looking chairs it was empty. The place was as clinical as an operating room.

The door opened and Stephanie was ushered in. "I saw you being taken out of the line," she said angrily, "and then they pulled me! I've never been so embarrassed. What's going on?"

"No idea. The guy who brought me here didn't say a word."

The office door opened again and Holland started.

The man walked in, closing the door behind him. "Good morning, Mr. Holland, Dr. Caine," he said. "I hope you both had a pleasant trip?"

Stephanie looked to Holland for an explanation. "This is Mr. Volk, Stephanie. He says he's a press attaché at the U.S. embassy in Addis, but he has a good routine in warning people to stay away from things which don't concern them. Your Dr. Starling has met him."

Volk smiled. "Ah yes, how is Dr. Starling? Well, I hope?"

"He flew back to London, but I imagine you already know that."

"Indeed I do, Mr. Holland, but I thought it might be appreciated if I showed my concern by asking after him. Because, make no mistake about it, I am concerned."

"That's nice," replied Holland sarcastically. "Just to prove it, perhaps you wouldn't mind telling us what's going on here. Are we under arrest?"

Volk indicated they should sit. "Not at all. The British Special Branch arranged for me to have a little chat with you before you were cleared into the country."

"And if we don't want to make with the small talk, they throw us out. That the idea?"

"That would be up to the British authorities. Mr. Holland," snapped Volk menacingly. "I have little influence here. Besides, Dr. Caine has a work visa."

"Which could be revoked. OK, what do you want, Volk?"

Volk suddenly stopped smiling and Stephanie shivered slightly.

"I should like to know," he said, "why you trespassed on a U.S. government installation and why you caused it damage."

Stephanie glanced quickly at Holland, but he continued to look at Volk.

"Who are you *really*, Volk? And what's it got to do with you?"

"I ask *you* the questions, I don't answer them."

Mark reached into a shirt pocket and withdrew a cigarette from the pack. He flipped the lighter into action and drew deeply. Volk had just confirmed what he had suspected in his Addis hotel room.

"We got lost, and figured maybe there was a telephone there we could use," he said. "And there wasn't anything to indicate it was a government place. In fact there was a lot to show the reverse—that it was an oil company installation. Trans-Global Oil, to be exact. You CIA boys really dropped the ball in clearing out that place."

"Very perceptive of you. But what conclusions did you draw from your visit?"

"None. Other than the fact that Trans-Global was running scientific operations which had the blessing of the Central Intelligence Agency, before the place closed down three months ago."

"Seems like a long way to go for nothing," observed Volk tightly.

"Dr. Caine and I are very persistent people."

Volk continued his questioning, often asking the same one twice to gauge if the second reply matched the first. At length, he reached inside his jacket and extracted their passports. He tapped them thoughtfully on the table for a moment before sliding them across.

"The British have already stamped them. You can go."

Holland opened the door for Stephanie and she stepped through. Mark started after her, waiting for Volk to add something. He wasn't disappointed.

"One other thing, Mr. Holland." Mark paused and turned to face the CIA man. "You didn't listen to me in Addis when I suggested it would be better for you to stay out of this. I suggest you listen now. It could be dangerous for you and that pretty lady friend of yours. So I hope you'll take it as friendly advice."

"You know, Volk, a bucket of shit would make a better friend."

They walked to the taxi stand to the left of the terminal building.

"What now?" Stephanie asked.

"A hot shower for me, I guess. What about you?"

"I could certainly use one as well, but I can't just yet. Look, I have a two bedroom flat in Eaton Square. Why don't you stay there? It'll be more comfortable than a hotel. I must go over to the office, so you can do what you like."

Holland didn't argue. Forty-five minutes later the cab had dropped him off at the apartment and taken her on to her office.

Holland let himself in, dropped his flight bag in the hall, and looked around the place.

It was, by any standards, an apartment that matched the prestigious Eaton Square address. Off to the left of the hallway were the two bedrooms, separated by a large bathroom. To the right was an exceptionally large kitchen.

Beside the kitchen was a paneled room that looked as though it had been intended to be a study, but now served as a lab and utility room.

At the end of the hall stood a set of double doors which Holland opened to reveal the living-dining room. It stood at the corner of the building and so had windows along the length of two walls. Running around the outside of the windows was a wide balcony providing breathing space for a veritable jungle of potted plants.

He opened the balcony door and the sounds of the London traffic below flooded into the room, breaking the silence. He stood for a moment looking at the living room furnishings. It was almost a *House and Garden* picture with all the trappings. A home that had not been set up with a temporary residence in mind. He suddenly felt he was on the outside looking in.

A small bar stood in the corner and he thought briefly about a drink before remembering that while it was after twelve in London, his body clock said it was only shortly after seven A.M.

Holland walked back to the hall and recovered his flight bag, which he dropped on the bed of the smaller room. Stripping off his clothes, he padded across the plush carpet to the bathroom and within minutes was enjoying the feeling of the steaming hot water on his aching body.

He was just making his second cup of coffee when the telephone rang. He hesitated for a moment before reaching for the wall-mounted instrument beneath the kitchen cupboards.

"I hope you're finding everything!"

"No problem. I'm beginning to feel a little more human. Where are you?"

"In Dr. Starling's office. I've filled him in on everything that's happened and I think it might be a good idea if you came over. Starling has a theory that—"

"What's the address?"

She told him and explained it wasn't far from the apartment. He forgot about the coffee and quickly dressed in his one spare pair of slacks and blue denim shirt. If nothing else, while he was in London he'd have to buy some more clothes.

He had noticed a dry cleaner in the street to the left of the main entrance to the apartment building. Before hailing a cab to take him to Wright's Lane he deposited his now heavily-soiled suit with the shopkeeper, asking for the two-hour treatment.


"Ah, Captain, how very nice to see you again. Stephanie has told me all about your trip. Very interesting. Very interesting indeed."

She had been waiting for him in the reception area of the Center for Pest Research, and had quickly steered him through the various offices to Dr. Starling's room.

Starling was bent over a table cluttered with maps and was hastily scribbling on a yellow pad. The atmosphere seemed charged with subdued excitement, heightened when the scientist at last realized that Holland was standing beside him. He beamed warmly and gripped Holland's hand with both of his in a genuine expression of pleasure.

"Captain, you look very tired. Perhaps you really ought to consider easing off."

Holland laughed. "Dr. Starling, that's the second time today I've been warned to take it easy. I'll start thinking I'm getting old if this keeps up."

"Well, I'm afraid I tend to err on the side of caution, so I advise abandonment of the inquiry."

Holland shook his head. "No chance, Doctor. I don't know

what's going on, but by Christ I intend to have a good try at finding out."

"Yes, of course. But how would you expect to carry the search on from here? As I understand it you don't have anything tangible to work on."

Holland was suddenly irritated by the man's negative posture. His face hardened to reflect that displeasure. The change in Holland's appearance didn't go unnoticed.

"Look, Doctor, let me make myself real plain. I'm not going to give up just because Volk and you warn me off. I guess the answer has to lie back in the Gulf somewhere and I'll find it if I have to turn over every grain of sand in the process. Stephanie can stay here if she wants. I'd prefer it if she wasn't crucified on some Arab hilltop. But I have to go."

Starling patted Holland's arm reassuringly. "Good for you, Captain. Sorry about the backtracking, but I did want to know if you were still as determined as you were in the bar in Addis Ababa.

"For my part, I must confess I am a little fuddled as to what has been going on and more than a little unsure of the next step. Following your visit to Livingston we do have further solid clues to go on. They all point in the direction of Trans-Global. Let us approach this problem in as scientific a way as possible.

"I have looked at the passenger list and, with all respect to your Miss Carson, there appears to be only one person or group of persons who would be important enough to warrant blowing up a plane. It is an extreme act. We must assume that whoever wanted those people dead had to make sure there could be no mistake, no chance of missing the target.

"We know the plane left early because all of the expected passengers had arrived on board. In itself this is not suspicious because it is quite acceptable for privately-controlled aircraft to depart when they are ready rather than waiting for their expected time of departure, providing, of course, that the local air traffic control can accommodate such an early departure. Now then, had the aircraft left at its scheduled time it would have exploded over the Red Sea and all traces of it would have been lost. Obviously, some careful thought went into the planting and timing of the device—planning which was circumvented by that most unpredictable of all objects, the human decision-making factor.

"So, the plan of the murderers was that the aircraft would come down in open water and even if there were any survivors the chance of them lasting for very long would be remote indeed.

"I feel one hundred percent sure it was Steiner and his colleagues who were the targets. None of the other passengers qualified for action as severe as this. Or rather I cannot conceive of secretaries, nurses, oil workers or construction workers incurring such wrath from someone they had dealt with during their normal working day so as to lead to this sort of retribution. Scientists, on the other hand, often incur the annoyance of fanatical organizations, governments, businesses and politicians. They often learn or discover or create situations which one or all of those three categories wish to suppress or punish them for. I remember, as an example, the case of a chap whose wife gave birth to a horribly malformed baby and he set out on a campaign against those scientists who had invented the drug she had taken during pregnancy. He got three out of a team of forty research workers before the police finally stopped him.

"Add to this the very strange telephone call Stephanie received from her uncle, and I believe we are safe in postulating he and his two colleagues were the targets. The fact that thirteen others went to their deaths is incidental."

Holland's mouth was dry as he listened to the man behind the desk clinically analyzing the situation. As though he had read the American's mind, Starling smiled softly.

"She's dead, Mark. Words can't hurt her anymore."

Holland nodded.

"Now, we turn to the problem of the installation you both visited in Livingston. We should assume the area was established by Trans-Global, for whom our Dr. Steiner worked, and it was protected by the CIA. Strange but not in itself unusual. There are many installations and factories both in your country and in England which, because of the sensitive nature of their work, are protected by the government. The situation is simply indicative of the importance which was attached to whatever was going on.

"Stephanie, I shall shut up at this point and let you explain to the good captain what we know about this particular area."

She sat forward on the couch and turned slightly to face Mark. "What do you know about grasshoppers?"

"Little, bordering on nothing," admitted Holland. "They can be pretty devastating if they happen to get at your crops. That's about it."

Stephanie smiled. "Well I shall now tell you more than you ever wanted to know. To start with, the word is a euphemism used to describe what is really the locust.

"During the development of the American midwest, a strain called the Rocky Mountain locust ravaged the entire area, causing untold amounts of damage and misery to the settlers and farmers.

"It seemed the plagues, for there were several over the course of some twenty years, were sent deliberately to test the new settlers. Churchmen postulated that the insects were sent by God because the farmers had turned away from the church, and the president even called for a national week of prayer toward the end in an attempt to ask for divine intervention in what had become a real national emergency.

"Newspapers of the time show us that the populace was really terrified of the creatures and many false reports circulated about the abilities of the locusts. I remember one editor of a newspaper in Buffalo seriously printing a report which claimed a swarm of locusts had eaten one farmer's crops and then proceeded to eat the wooden barn, house, and outhouse. It closed with a statement that as the house vanished in front of the eyes of the farmer and his family the still-hungry insects began on the iron railings and iron plough.

"Patently ridiculous of course, but the story does indicate the seriousness of the American plague and the seriousness with which it was viewed by the population.

"Anyway, to cut a long story short, in 1878, shortly after

the president called for his prayer week, the locusts disappeared, much to the delight of the churchmen who welcomed the return to full churches. It wasn't the normal recessionary period all locust swarms go through, but a literal vanishing act. Overnight the swarms disappeared. Not even solitary locusts could be found, and everyone was quite naturally delighted and happy to attribute it to the Lord.

"Then at the turn of this century, a party of prospectors was attracted to a mountain area and to a particular glacier which had caught their eye because of an unusual darkness under the ice.

"On closer examination they found the dark areas were, in fact, dead insects. Locusts. The entire glacier was a locust graveyard. It was only when you said we were in Yellowstone the penny dropped.

"Anyway, reports from that period state that around the glacier's terminal moraine were piles of rotted locusts and through the ice more of the insects could clearly be seen. A scientific expedition was hastily put together by the Department of the Interior and they discovered at Grasshopper Glacier the Rocky Mountain locusts which had disappeared so suddenly years before.

"But, in finding that out, they uncovered one of the greatest mysteries in entomology. How could an entire swarm of insects be suddenly wiped out? What caused them all to settle there?"

"What do you think?"

She shrugged. "It really is a tremendous mystery, Mark. There is no other occurrence in the insect world to compare with this mass gathering, and quite honestly we haven't the faintest idea what instinct brought them all together. Equally, we can not explain to ourselves what caused them all to die at Grasshopper Glacier. They might have been on a migratory path, or blown off a migratory course, settling on the mountain during the early evening. Once there they could have been caught in a cold snap and any moisture on their wings would have frozen, which would have prevented them from escaping in the morning. Successive exposure to thin atmosphere, moisture, and freezing would eventually entomb them.

"Or, the other theory is that after arriving at the mountain through instinct or accident, they then succumbed to a bacteriological infection which wiped them out en masse. Or it could be a combination of both theories or any one of a dozen more theories."

"That doesn't answer me, Stephanie. What do *you* think?"

"Bacteria probably. Then a cold winter added the touch of mystery by obligingly depositing a mantle of ice over them."

Holland studied the floor for a moment and now it was their turn to allow him a few moments reflection. "So you think your uncle was involved in some sort of investigation into those Rocky Mountain locusts. But how does that all tie in with the rest of it?"

Dr. Starling took up the story.

"The key is the word 'bacteria,' Captain. Stephanie has told you entomologists think this is what wiped out the Rocky Mountain swarm. Please accept it would have been an exceptionally virulent type of bacterium to have done so.

"Presumably you are already aware that Steiner, like us, was basically an entomologist. What you may not know is in later years, since the Second World War in fact, his principle science has been biochemistry. Specifically, he was working for the United States government on a program deeply involved in germ warfare.

"You must understand that Steiner was a man who was basically a survivor. He was of value to the Nazis developing the anti-personnel nerve gas tagun and after the war he became of value to the Allies, again through his work in bacteriological warfare gleaned through a need, a desperate need, perhaps, to be powerful. Power to Albert was quite simply a drug, a security blanket in an uncertain world where you obtained riches through achievement. It mattered little to Albert that his work was in a field which many of us consider to be the most heinous of scientific research.

"When the Johnson administration was forced to close a number of these so-called research establishments, as a result of public pressure, many of them were simply moved to top security military bases or to other sites under the auspices of the CIA.

"Many of them were closed down altogether, it's true—usually amid a great fanfare of publicity. But this was invariably because those centers had served their purpose and the program was already drawing to a close, or because they had originally been set up as dummies, established against that day. What better way of showing the world you mean only good towards all men than by closing down the most evil and horrendous of armament facilities—especially if you know they were harmless to begin with?

"Albert Steiner worked at one of the places that wasn't harmless, but nonetheless his operation fell to the governmental ax. The CIA, however, did not want to relinquish their best bio-warfare man, and they arranged for him to have another center put at his disposal. That center was funded, in part, by Trans-Global Oil. His task was simply to discover the bacterium that wiped out an entire strain of insect."

"How have you managed to learn all this, Doctor?"

Starling shrugged and waved his hands in the air. "Your government and mine spend a small fortune keeping quiet about their own business and trying to learn what the other chap is up to. If they revealed more to the scientists in their employ they might save themselves a lot of money. We are a competitive lot, so we like to know what one another is up to. A few telephone calls this morning gave me the information. Incomplete though it is, I think it does allow us to make a guess at our outstanding question.

"Why was the plane blown up? Perhaps to punish Steiner and the others for having become involved in germ warfare. If that's the case then we are looking at an extremist group. But it is more likely that it happened to shut him and the others up."

"And what took him from Livingston to the Middle East?"

Holland's question was unanswered. Then Stephanie broke the silence. "He must have been on a field trip to test the results of his work at the glacier."

Starling looked like a contented schoolmaster. The affection he felt for his younger colleague was obvious.

"Excellent, my dear. Yes, I should say it would be the logical thing to do, following three years' work into the demise of the Rocky Mountain locust."

The scientist stood and walked to the window overlooking the quiet London street.

At length he turned. "I should hazard a guess he had conducted his experiment involving human guinea pigs and that was why he called us. He must have been appalled at the results, and wished to ensure nothing like it could ever happen again. It seems that he has not been able to."

# CHAPTER NINE

*It was whole. At last, the mass sensed that it had gained the necessary strength. It felt the correct balance between the outer edges and the heart, and it knew the time was near.*

*Once more it rippled and felt the excitement build as it accepted the knowledge that it would again be powerful.*

*Knowledge! Not knowledge, so much as an instinctive knowing of its oneness with the elements that surrounded it. Elements from which it had continued to draw succour. Elements that had remained unchanged for millennia. The mass knew these and understood them. Soon, they would help it feed without limit, without mercy.*

*It sang to the elements and they replied by helping it to move, to stretch, to explore.*

*The mass stretched and felt the heat. Was aware of the flies and the lizards scurrying across the rocks four miles away, equally of the earth-burrowing creature at the very center of the valley where, for the moment, it rested. The consciousness was a unifying thing, from end to end, extremity to extremity.*

*Looking to the sky, it took in the first change of rhythm that indicated something was different. It became aware of the noise.*

*There was something that didn't belong, was alien to itself. A threat.*

*The center of the mass reacted without thought, and a part of it rose into the air and moved toward the source of the vibrations that had pained the outer edge.*

*The first helicopter was smothered as it swept low, spraying chemicals onto the ground below, the stinging chemicals that had caused the mass to react. The intake valves clogged and sputtered, trying to supply much-needed air to the engine. The blackness dragged the helicopter to the valley floor.*

*Rapidly and with frightening speed the other two helicopters and their crews were dashed to a rock-strewn grave, their only epitaph a thick column of black smoke to mark the place where they had died. Their only witness, the mass itself.*

*It settled back and again surveyed the situation. It had not been hurt beyond repair. It would recover. But now it felt a greater need. The vibrations had stirred their longing, pushed forward the decision about when it would leave this place for the other.*

*It would not wait much longer.*

# CHAPTER TEN

THE TAXI DRIVER DROPPED MARK OFF AT MAIDEN LANE, AND as the cab pulled away Mark regretted not having had the man drive him directly to the hotel. It wasn't the thought of the darkened side streets down which he would now have to walk which bothered him, but the hard, spitting rain that heralded the approach of a violent storm. He would probably be soaked by the time he walked the six or so blocks that stood between him and the Waldorf.

Mark had received a telephone call from Volk while they were still in Starling's office. Volk had sounded agitated, and insisted they meet.

The route he selected would take him past the popular theater-goers restaurant, Luigi's. It had been one of Kate's favorites and they had eaten there the year before when she had brought him to London to show him off to her family and friends. He was to meet Volk nearby in fifteen minutes. The irony of the situation did not escape him.

He had left the cab early so he could retrace the route Kate and he had taken on their last night in London. She had loved this part of the city, a shrine for millions of pilgrim tourists

and opera lovers—Covent Garden. They had walked around
the bustling streets into the early hours, joking with one good-
humored flower seller or sampling the produce from another
merchant. He could hear her laughter now, echoing around the
corrugated stalls. He could see the laughter in her eyes.

Stephanie had wanted to go with him, but decided against
it when Starling asked her for help with an analysis of current
locust activity in Saudi Arabia. In some ways, Mark was grateful.

Starling had explained that now was the season for the
insects to start swarming and, as always, there was neither
enough time nor willing hands to handle the flow of information
that was both received into and distributed from the Center for
Pest Research.

At this relatively early hour in the evening, the streets were
virtually deserted. The theater-goers were safely in their seats
for the evening performances and the club crowd would not
arrive at the discos for several hours yet. As for the tradesmen,
they were gone. Gone to the new wholesale market on the
south side of the Thames. And with them, thought Mark, as
he maneuvered his way around a stack of garbage cans, went
most of the character of the place.

The rain splashed heavily onto the pavement, creating instant rivulets across his path, and began to soak through the
sleeves and shoulders of his jacket. He cursed himself for not
having had the sense to carry a raincoat. He had forgotten just
how quickly the English weather could change.

As he hurried along, looking down to avoid the glistening
puddles, a figure slipped out of a side street and hurried forward
purposefully.

Mark reached the half-way point of his journey through a
small, deserted street, when a tall figure stepped in front of
him, blocking his path.

"Captain Holland?"

Mark stopped and glanced into the unsmiling face. "Yeah,
who the h—"

He sensed rather than felt what was happening behind him
and twisted sideways to try to avoid the blow. The sharp pain

that bit into his left shoulder told him it would have been better if he'd kept his eyes open along this road rather than dwelling on the past.

He grunted with pain and brought his right foot up toward the man who had spoken. He kicked hard and caught him between the legs. The face registered amazement and then burning agony as a second later he sank to his knees clutching his crotch.

The man behind had plenty of time to ensure that the second swing of his blackjack did not miss the target. Mark fell against the lamp post and slid slowly to the ground. He placed his hand in front of him and felt strangely comforted by the feel of the wet pavement. A foot was raised and he was aware of its target, but he had neither the will nor the strength to remove it from harm's way.

He didn't feel the pain. There was no room left in his brain to handle it after the blow his head had taken. He saw the man raise his foot again and the breath left his body in an effortless gasp, refusing to return to the bruised lungs. He rolled into the gutter, retching and fighting for air.

Then he felt himself being grabbed by the collar and hauled like a broken puppet halfway to his feet. The man's breath assaulted him with as much venom as his voice. "You should have stayed out of the Steiner affair, Holland, now I'm going to wrap the lamp post around your fucking neck."

Mark didn't bother trying to reply. He felt like he was watching a silent movie in a deep freeze. The man raised his hand with the edge of the palm angled for a chop and was about to bring it smashing down into Mark's face when they heard a shout. The attacker looked quickly down the road, in the direction of where Mark had left his taxi. Mark felt the hand smash down onto the bridge of his nose. Before he slipped gratefully into unconsciousness he saw a huge shape lumbering toward them and his two assailants running toward a open car.

"How do you feel?"

His eyes rolled toward the top of his skull and he felt himself drift away again.

"Mark, how do you feel?" The voice was more insistent this time and he fought the blackness that threatened to swamp him. Gradually he had control of his senses and his eyes unglued from their lids.

Stephanie was standing over him. He tried to smile.

A second voice reached him and he recognized it as Starling's.

"He's going to be all right, my dear, don't worry. Nothing broken, just badly bruised."

He felt the glass at his lips and drank instinctively. The cold water cleared his head only marginally, but it did make him feel slightly better.

"Jesus," he muttered, "talk about walking right into it."

Full consciousness came rapidly now and he looked around with a start. He was back in her apartment.

"I'm not saying it's not a wonderful surprise, but how did I get here?"

Stephanie smiled. "The man who chased them off . . . and that Volk creep . . . both brought you here. They called me at the center and said you'd been hurt."

Mark remembered the image he'd had shortly before losing consciousness—the man running toward him. There had been something familiar about the lumbering shape.

"Who was it . . . that found me?"

"He's in the living room, talking to Volk. Tough looking character if ever I saw one."

"Thank God for that then, Doctor. Help me up, will you? I want to have a talk with those guys."

"For Christ's sake—"

"Stephanie, leave me alone. Please!" He had been more abrupt than he had meant and felt instant regret as she flinched at the sharpness of his words.

Dr. Starling walked to the bedroom door as Stephanie helped Mark to sit upright in the bed. "Gentlemen, Captain Holland would like you to come in now."

The first person through the double doors to the living room was Mustapha.

"Hello, Captain. Good to see you are not hurt too much,"

grinned the Arab. "I always was told by the general you were a man who could take care of himself. It seems the bad men have got tougher over the years, eh?" The Arab laughed loudly and walked forward to the side of the bed.

"I thought I recognized you, you big ox. What the hell are you doing here?"

Mustapha waved his arms airily. "Sightseeing. All rich Arabs come to London during the summer, so I think—why not a poor one as well?"

Stephanie handed Mark a brandy. After they were settled Mark looked from Mustapha to Volk.

"I don't mean to sound ungrateful, but what the hell were you doing there? We were supposed to meet in the hotel, a good four blocks away."

"I was walking with Mustapha," Volk said simply. "It was just as well, wasn't it?"

"I suppose it was. I gather you two know each other?"

"Oh yes, we know each other." The reply was matter of fact. Mark sighed and eased himself back into the pillows. Suddenly his chest hurt, and he didn't care.

"Would somebody please tell us what is going on?"

Volk gave Stephanie his plastic smile. "But, of course, you and Dr. Starling wouldn't know about Mustapha, would you? He is Ziad Sadallah's right-hand man."

"But that doesn't explain what he is doing in London, or how it is he was with you."

"That," acknowledged Mark, "is the million-dollar question." There was a pause as Volk chose his words.

"The fact of the matter is my department has, shall we say, cooperated once in a while with Sadallah and his men. We met to exchange information."

"When you telephoned you seemed pretty agitated. What did you want to see me about in such a hurry?"

Volk placed his empty glass on the bedside table before reaching for the raincoat which lay draped over the arm of a chair. He pulled it on without appearing to have noticed the question. Holland was too exhausted to repeat it.

"I received the report from Addis today on the flight recorder you retrieved from the crash. I thought you might like to know what was on it."

"How did you guess?" replied Holland sarcastically. He struggled painfully forward and Stephanie reached out a supporting hand. He was glad of it.

"Apart from the normal in-flight conversation between the crew and brief conversations between the ground stations and the aircraft, the only thing which went against routine was a request from Dr. Steiner to detour to a place called Niah Valley. The stewardess apparently told the captain that Steiner desperately wanted to check something out."

Stephanie glanced sharply at Holland. "Surely an aircraft captain wouldn't change course just because a passenger requested it?"

Holland shook his head. "No, of course he wouldn't in normal civilian traffic. But this was a company plane. I've changed course myself for senior executives, or to pick up previously unscheduled passengers or equipment. The whole idea of a company owning its own aircraft is the flexibility it provides for both the company and its personnel. But still, you wouldn't see a pilot change course at the whim of just any employee. Steiner must have carried a lot of clout. The sort of influence only senior staff would have with the aircrew."

Holland shifted position slightly and rubbed the bruised hand his assailant had stamped on. Starling had said nothing was broken, but his hand at this particular moment wasn't too sure. He turned to Volk. "How far is this valley from where the plane crashed?"

"About ten miles further up the range. They never got to see whatever it was Steiner showed interest in."

"And that was what you wanted to tell me?"

"Yes, that was it. I thought you might like to have heard it from me rather than just read it somewhere."

"Very thoughtful of you. I appreciate it," said Holland dryly.

"My pleasure. Now if you will excuse me, I really must be going. Dr. Starling, Dr. Caine, goodnight." Volk walked with Mustapha toward the living room door and suddenly turned.

"By the way, I did warn you to stay out of it. Tonight you were lucky. Next time you might not be. Goodnight."

"I definitely do not like that man," Stephanie said as she returned from seeing Volk out. "He's supercilious and unpleasant and—"

"A liar."

"Liar?"

"Yes. I can't imagine any senior CIA officer turning into my fairy godmother overnight."

"You know your problem?" Stephanie said. "You're always just too ready to think the best of someone." She smiled and then turned on her heel, heading for the kitchen. Holland watched her go, admiring the way she moved in the loose silk shirt and blue jeans.

"Lovely girl, Captain," Starling said. "Like a daughter to me."

"How long have you known her?"

"Oh years. I was at her christening in Christchurch. Her father married the woman with whom I was in love."

Starling noticed the expression on Holland's face and chuckled.

"Right after the last war, Stephanie's father and I were stationed in Frankfurt. One of the German interpreters was a girl called Frieda. She was, and still is, very lovely. I fell for her, hook, line and sinker. The trouble was, so did William." Starling refilled his pipe and sat back in the armchair. "We chased her like mad and did the most awful things to try and prevent the other chap from seeing her. We were both second lieutenants, so neither had the advantage of rank. One day I was ordered to replace a sick officer, who had the duty of supervising a ration convoy to Berlin. This was before the Berlin blockade, of course, so it was quite an easy duty. It was only after we were halfway there that I found out from the sergeant that the sick officer was William. Needless to say, he was no more sick than I.

"Well, once we got to Berlin we were re-routed to some other place and once there on to another and all in all we were away from Frankfurt for two weeks. When we finally got back William admitted he had persuaded the medical officer to sign him off and then arranged for a cousin at headquarters to have the convoy shifted about for a few days. He also told me he and Frieda were married."

Starling re-lit the pipe and swirled the brandy around the balloon glass. "Of course, the situation couldn't have gone on indefinitely. One of us had to be the loser. The only thing I have ever regretted is I didn't think of dealing with William in a similar way. Rather a superb checkmate, I have always thought."

"Yet you all remained friends?"

"But, of course, Captain. As I said, I was at Stephanie's christening. I'm also her godfather. William has done well by Frieda and she is happy. And that, after all, is the main thing, isn't it?

"But more than the personal relationship with Stephanie, I do have a strong academic one. You may recall she told you she was a student of mine and a very fine one too I may say. Rarely does a teacher come across a student who has such a grasp and feel for the subject he is trying to get across.

"Stephanie was my rare student. She excelled at university and subsequently she has built an exceptional reputation in a very tough and demanding field. Professionally I also have the highest regard for her work. A natural ability, you might say, combined with a strong dose of humanitarianism. Really rather special."

Starling struck another match with which to coax the reluctant tobacco into flame.

"And you? You never married?"

"Didn't really see much point in it," mused the scientist. "Frieda was the one I wanted."

Stephanie returned, bearing a large tray with omelettes, toast, and coffee. Throughout the meal they talked more about the past, a past Holland tried to remember without bitterness. As he said goodnight to Starling, he felt more refreshed and alert than he had for a while, despite the insistent ache of his bruises. Holland watched Stephanie clear the remains of the coffee cups and turn out the hanging lamp over the small table. The silk rustled and her dark eyes shone. Kate would have smiled like that. The thought took him back momentarily to the bare mountain side and he experienced again that feeling of hopelessness he had first known after Fong Lee, after Bob Strake had killed himself.

"Do you want to talk about it?" she asked softly.

He looked up at her.

"About what?"

"From the look on your face, I'd say you were remembering Kate again."

Her scent reached him. She smelt fresh and musky and as she reached a hand up to brush a shock of hair from her forehead the silk moved against her breasts.

He studied her face for a moment and then allowed his gaze to wander over her body. His eyes lingered on nipples swelling against the light material of her blouse, then travelled down past curved hips and tapering thighs. He knew she was watching him as he examined her and he felt that first flush of excitement as she moved her legs slightly, causing the denim to tighten across the inside of her thighs.

Holland looked back into the brown eyes and then reached for her. She came readily, hungrily into his arms and moaned with expectant pleasure as he caressed her hair and crushed her mouth and her body against his.

# CHAPTER ELEVEN

GORDON BANWELL WAS BLOODY MISERABLE. HOW ON GOD'S earth could such a thing happen to him, mechanic extraordinary and hustler beyond compare?

Banwell had been working a rig in Iran before the revolution started making things uncomfortable for nationals and foreigners alike. He had grown moderately well-off from his job as a maintenance mechanic and very rich indeed from his role as a supplier of pornography to the other on-site workers. Unfortunately, most of his co-workers had been Iranian and the new regime had decided he was most definitely a corrupter of public morals.

His first taste of work in the Middle East had come as a shock. The money was great, sure, but by God they expected you to slave like a bloody Arab for it. Once he had taken a leave, however, he felt a little differently about things. The girls loved the deep tan he had acquired and his mates envied the thick wad of money he carried. The girls liked that too.

A few of the boys had asked him to bring back some magazines from London and he happily obliged. He knew the risks he ran. If the Saudis found them in his luggage he would really be in the shithouse. But they hadn't and his mates had eagerly grabbed for *Playboy, Penthouse, Oui* and the rest.

Banwell had also taken back harder material for his own amusement and he was surprised to find that these were even more in demand, even by the blokes he had always thought of as following the straight and narrow.

Then he knew he could capitalize on their deprivation. They would pay plenty for a little aid toward releasing their frustrations.

At that point, Gordon Banwell, mechanic, became G. D. Banwell, merchant of Arabia.

First of all he recalled the magazines he had brought with him and spread the word that he was operating a lending library. He charged high. Ten dollars for half an hour. There was no shortage of customers, few complaints at the charges.

His foreman allowed him all the time he needed, during working hours, to develop and control the business. "He recognizes the importance of keeping the lads sane," Gordon had thought when the man relaxed the rules for him. "He's a prick," thought Gordon, when in due course (after all the hard work had been done) the money was rolling in and the foreman informed him it was time to take a partner.

But it was a fact of life and whenever a new foreman was put in charge, or when he moved to a new site, Banwell had had to make sure the boss received a slice of the action. It paid dividends. There wasn't any competition, and Gordon consequently made a lot more money.

Then he had been moved to Iran and the mammoth oil fields. It was Heaven, the Lost Dutchman Mine, an Inca treasure trove and the U.S. mint all rolled into one.

The Iranians were more relaxed in their approach to Western "art" than the stiff, inflexible Saudis, and there were more men. Banwell kept supplies artificially short to increase the demand. From there, it was an easy step to buying a house and installing a few girls—twenty or so—a good bar and a couple of heavies. All the while he maintained his job in the oil fields—an essential measure in order to avoid deportation.

It was a good life. Until, that is, the Shah and his cronies had been ousted by a bunch of religious fanatics who preached what they didn't practice.

Word had reached him that they were coming, that there was every likelihood that after a quick trial he would end up against the wall. There was a chance they would just bounce him out of the country, of course, but Banwell wasn't in the mood to take chances with his neck.

A quick bribe in the right place and he was sailing across the Persian Gulf to Dhahran.

Now, he was sitting on the rocky slope that led from the sea, wondering where to go next. He knew he was in Saudi but he hadn't the faintest idea which way Dhahran lay. The fisherman hadn't said a word all the way over and he had only realized they were coming ashore when the boat had grounded into shale.

He looked to the left and then the right. No lights on the horizon, and the stars were no bloody help. They just glinted mockingly. Was he north of the town or south of it? If he guessed wrong and started walking, the mistake could kill him.

He figured that on this side of the coast he'd not see another settlement to the north until he reached Kuwait—if he could walk that far, which was unlikely once the sun came up.

He had all but decided he would go to the left when he heard a soft, slithering noise on the sand, coming from the direction in which he had decided to aim.

Banwell's skin crawled. The moon slipped behind a large cloud, cutting him off from his only source of light. He cursed his stupidity at not bringing a flashlight. It was tough enough to have lost all his money in Iran, without having the shit scared out of him by whatever it was crawling closer.

He tried to remember if they had tigers in Saudi Arabia and then, when he couldn't, he started to whistle through dry lips. The rustle stopped for a moment, as though the source of it were trying to understand the significance of the sound. Then it started again—but now, it seemed to the terrified man, with a greater sense of urgency.

"Fuck it then," muttered Banwell, as much to hear the sound of a human voice as to reassure himself he could still talk. "To the right it is." He stood and walked rapidly away in the new direction, knowing that whatever was crawling around on the sand was now following him. It was after him. It *must* be a tiger.

He broke into a run and heard the sound increase its own tempo to keep up. A sob broke from his parched throat. He rounded an outcrop of rocks and in the near distance lights beckoned from the blackness. He sobbed again, this time in relief.

He raced along toward the town and all the while he could hear the slithering noise behind him. Gradually, it faded from his hearing and he was safe.

Slowly, the noise filtered through his sleep-encrusted mind and he stretched languidly, feeling the fresh sheets on his tired body.

He winced at a slight pain, which reminded him of the beating he had taken the evening before. But the sharpness was no longer there and that reminded him of what had happened afterwards.

Her musky perfume, the memory of the smoothness of her skin still lingered. He had needed her, and the thought both comforted and appalled.

Stephanie kicked open the door of the bedroom and walked in carrying a tray laden with cups and plates of food. She was dressed in a loosely-buttoned white cotton shirt and as she passed around the foot of the bed, the light of the early morning sun streaming in through the windows highlighted the curves of her body.

She placed her tray on a side table and he felt a stirring in his loins as he looked at her. He had explored every inch, every portion of her with his eyes, his hands and mouth the night before, and she his. He wanted her again now.

"How do you feel?"

"I guess I'll survive."

There was a moment's awkward silence and then they both spoke at once.

"Mark . . ."

"Stephanie . . ."

They laughed together, each understanding the other's discomfort, and the laughter made it easier.

She shook her head slightly as he looked into her eyes, but then he kissed her gently and she came into his arms. He could feel her desire rising as he ran his hand over her breasts, brushing the nipples with his fingers.

She pulled away suddenly. "Time for breakfast, Mr. Holland. Then a shower and then Starling would like to meet us at the center."

He reached for the tray and pulled it onto the bed between them.

"Did he say what it was about?"

"No. Just that he'd like to see you."

She grabbed a piece of toast and headed for the door, calling over her shoulder as she went, "I'm for the shower. Eat your breakfast."

He watched her go and suddenly he was very glad she had come into his life.


They were greeted by Starling as they walked into the large Situation Room from which the Center for Pest Research kept a constant watch on areas throughout the world that were likely to develop into trouble spots.

"Feel better, Captain?"

"Much, thanks."

Starling nodded and glanced at Stephanie. She blushed and Starling's smile grew brighter. He knew at least what *that* smile meant.

He waved around the room where men and women were busy at telephones and telex machines and others shifted markers around on massive charts which depicted the world in segments.

"Ever see anything like this, Captain?"

Holland nodded. "It reminds me of a war room."

Starling slapped Holland on the back and then quickly apologized as Mark winced. "Sorry, Captain. I'm afraid I forgot your injuries. Yes, it is a war room. From it we wage war on nature's toughest fighters and man's most resilient enemies.

"Mark, you have worked in the Middle and Far East for many years and I assume that you have seen the carnage that pests can cause. Indeed, you may well have flown through a swarm of locusts and experienced just how dangerous that can be to an aircraft.

"Well, from this room we control our worldwide activity against many forms of insects. Termites, the East African army worm, locusts, the cotton leaf worm, the list is endless. But the Center for Pest Research doesn't just concentrate on chasing bugs off farmers' crops. We are involved in research of insect viruses at Porton Down, and are equally committed to the maintenance of the ecostructure.

"For example, we have a field program being carried out in several countries selected for varying soil and climatic conditions. The objective is to study the effects of pesticides on soil structure and function in the tropics, because preliminary studies have suggested that toxic residues may affect soil fauna and flora, soil fertility, nutrient cycling and other properties of fundamental importance to the balance of nature.

"We have always recognized the importance of working with nature rather than against her. Our success in controlling pests has been due in large measure to understanding the need for ecological balance. If you cut down a forest in Thailand you deprive the insect of natural food and it must seek alternative sources. Usually it has to look no further than the nearest farm, then the farmer is confronted with a problem he has never experienced before. So we have to educate him on how to combat this new threat and educate the forestry people by showing them they shouldn't alter the environment without careful thought and analysis of the consequences."

Starling looked with pride around the busy room. "In this room we can show you graphs of, for instance, locust activity in Kenya in 1943. For any *month* in 1943! For years we have been plotting wind and weather reports each month and matching them with reported insect movement. In this way we have a unique source of reference. If weather conditions match with activity, say in Tanzania this month, we can track back to find a comparable situation. Once we have a match, we can issue a projection as to the likely route of a swarm.

"Of course, these days we back it all up with a little help from our friends at NASA and their satellite tracking stations. But, in essense, often it all comes down to knowing the enemy."

A white-coated assistant hurried forward and handed a message to Stephanie. Scanning it quickly, she handed it to Starling.

"Speak of the Devil. Captain, I'm afraid you'll have to excuse me for a while. Stephanie will show you around the rest of the establishment."

Holland watched the doctor walking hurriedly away from them, towards the bank of telex machines. He felt strangely disturbed.

As he turned to Stephanie he spotted a familiar figure hurrying through a door at the end of the large operations room.

Mark darted forward, leaving Stephanie startled at his sudden movement. He ducked through the door and was faced by a short corridor. Two doors led off it, to the right and left. One, smaller than the other, looked to be a broom closet. The corridor terminated in a dead end. There was only one place he could be.

He stood in front of the door for a moment, listening to catch any murmer of conversation. There was nothing. He took a deep breath and swung it open.

Volk sat behind a desk with his feet up, languidly cleaning his nails. He lifted his head slowly and smiled. Mark stepped into the room.

"You creep around here as if you belong, Volk."

"Is that a statement or a question?" replied Volk as he swung his feet from the desktop. Without waiting for an answer from Holland he indicated Mark should close the door and sit down.

Mark sat in front of the desk, accepting the offered cigarette. He sensed that Volk's attitude toward him had changed, and it made him, if anything, more wary of this man who had originally claimed to be a press attaché, but who hadn't denied

Holland's assertion at the airport that he was with the CIA. Holland drew on the cigarette and returned Volk's bland smile.

"It bothers me when you're nice, Volk. What are you doing here?"

Volk elegantly tapped the ash of his cigarette into the ashtray. He looked at Holland as though trying to make his mind up about something and then suddenly the smile was gone and a seriousness came over Volk's face. "I need your help, Holland, and in order to get it I'm prepared to level with you.

"You were obviously surprised yesterday to see Mustapha in London. He came with a message for you from your friend Sadallah."

"Why didn't he give it to me?"

"Because he's one of my men, Holland, and I told him not to until we had the chance to evaluate the options. Sadallah wants you to fly out to the Gulf to meet him. He says he has something to show you. We don't know what it is—even Mustapha doesn't know—but he does know that whatever it is has got Sadallah pretty excited."

Holland stubbed the remainder of his cigarette out. "I thought Mustapha's loyalty was with Ziad and the cause."

"It is, one hundred percent. But he recognizes that sometimes friendship between two individuals can often cloud judgement. Mustapha wants to win that war and he knows they can't do it without outside help. CIA help. He plays ball."

"So you want me to go out there to look at something."

Holland spotted a slight flicker of uneasiness.

"All I know is that Sadallah says it's important and he's asked for you. I reckon that's good enough and Washington agrees. Sadallah isn't prone to overstating a situation. Incidentally, he says it could have something to do with the plane crash. Will you go?"

It was an ace delivered at the right moment. "I'll go," he said softly. "When do I leave?"

"A plane is waiting now, at Northolt Royal Air Force Base."

"I need clothes."

"I took the liberty of getting you some. Your car is waiting, and the driver will fill you in on the rendezvous point and return pick-up arrangements. He'll also give you money and your passport. Good luck, Holland. I'll explain to Dcotors Starling and Caine for you."

Holland stood and walked toward the door. Just as he was about to open it he stopped and turned around. "Seeing as you want to be open with me, Volk, did you or your people have anything to do with killing Howard on the beach?"

"No. We are pretty sure it was agents of Trans-Global Oil, but I can assure you we had nothing to do with it."

"And Livingston?"

"Yes, that came under our protection and sphere of influence. As a matter of fact it still does."

Holland smiled. "I figured Hank was more than a hotel keeper."

"Harvey is his real name. He was one of the agency's best operatives before Castro's boys worked him over six years ago, after he got careless in Havana. When we got him back he was fit only for internal security work. Once we knew we were going to be involved in Livingston, Harvey was sent in to buy the hotel. It's a good spot to watch for strangers."

Holland nodded to Volk and without another word stepped through the door and walked quickly down the hall.

Volk looked through the window of the office as the driver opened the rear door of the embassy car and Holland climbed inside. He glanced upward at Volk for a moment before walking quickly to the driver's seat.

The car pulled away from the curb. As the door to the office opened, Volk watched it weave through the busy London traffic.

"Will he be all right, David?"

Volk turned and faced the woman.

"You've done a good job, so far. For Pete's sake don't let go on me now. OK?"

She nodded. "I've grown quite fond of him."

"I know you have, Stephanie, I know."

# Book Two

# EXODUS

*Thou canst not make the dead to hear, nor canst
thou make the deaf to hear the call, when they
turn their backs on it; nor canst thou guide
the blind out of their error. Thou canst make
only those to hear who believe in Our Signs, for
they submit. When the sentence is
pronounced against them, We shall bring forth
for them an insect out of the earth, which shall
bite them because people did not believe Our Signs.*

The Book of Al-Namil
in the Holy Koran

# CHAPTER ONE

THE U.S. AIR FORCE JET HAD BEEN WAITING AT THE AIRFIELD and within moments of Holland climbing into the copilot's seat, the pilot had fired the engines and was moving along the tarmac.

The cockpit cover slid forward and down. Holland again felt the uneasy thrill of being enclosed in a finely-honed instrument of war. He snapped on the oxygen-radio mask and listened to the familiar chatter between pilot and Air Traffic Control.

"Er, Tango Gypsy Delta, you are cleared for take-off, runway two, over."

"Roger, control. Tango Gypsy Delta, runway two. What change in the weather, over."

"Tango Gypsy Delta, storm possible over the Swiss Alps, but there's little to trouble *you*. Hot and sunny all the rest of the way . . . you lucky bugger, over."

"Tango Gypsy Delta, I'll send you guys a postcard. So long, out."

And then they were away. Holland had been surprised at the speed with which they had pulled into a steep, banking climb, the American pilot apparently disregarding the "stack" that circled the area daily, waiting for landing clearance to nearby Heathrow Airport. The pilot must have understood Holland's puzzlement.

"You must be a really important guy, Captain," squawked the voice in Holland's ear. "I was given a flight path that cut right through the stack. They must have ordered West Drayton to detour every ship in the vicinity for you. I thought they only did that for the royal family!"

Holland laughed but was impressed. The CIA really was putting a Top Priority stamp on this mission—A USAF jet fighter to whisk him across Europe and special clearance normally reserved for the top VIPs.

As they flew across the English Channel at 60,000 feet, Holland went over the instructions the driver had given him in the car. The plane would take him to Abha, to the same airport where he had waited for Kate a mere week ago. From there, a helicopter would take him to the border region where, if all went well, one of Ziad's helicopters would be waiting.

It was, he thought, a far cry from their first meeting.

The powerful engines forced him back into his seat as the pilot increased thrust and then he was leading his wing to attack Fong Lee, flying in, dropping his bombs and feeling the familiar judder in the aircraft as the weight was released. Flipping the safety catch from the machine-gun trigger and strafing the village.

Screaming in low to take another look after Bob Strake's voice came eerily over the radio and then the image of the Korean woman being consumed by napalm, but still trying to save her child.

The flashback continued in faster sequence, almost as though his mind were trying to relive the whole nightmare just once more before expunging it forever. Finding Strake's body in the bathtub of the Officers' Quarters with his skull blown away and, covering the wall, his brains, skin tissue and bright blood.

Colonel Gaines's face just before Holland saw again how his fist had smashed into the pudgy features.

The court-martial for criminal negligence, Gaines sitting in the witness chair with the nerve to lie while staring straight at him.

Sweat was pouring from Holland's face and he wiped at his forehead with a gloved hand.

The voyage home, then the nightmares. Always the burning woman with the child. The misery of it continued to haunt him.

His father's anger at his court-martial, at his imagined disgrace. His father. He had not listened when Mark had tried to tell him that he was framed. The Air Force doesn't do that sort of thing. His father at his mother's funeral. Get out and don't ever come back. He hadn't. Not even for the old man's, scarcely two years later.

He had planned to go, though. With Kate. But that was over now as well. The crumpled wreckage on the mountain had seen to that.

"We're coming down, Captain, be there in ten minutes."

Holland snapped his mind back to the present. The entire flight had been a blur. He wiped his forehead again and checked his watch. Two hours. He had lost two hours with his self-pity.

"There it is, Captain, that Saudi chopper. I'll taxi over, save you the walk."

"Appreciate it. Thanks for the ride."

"My pleasure. I'll be here when you get back."

"That's comforting."

The pilot grinned and waved as Holland unbuckled and climbed out into the stifling heat. A Saudi Royal Air Force officer stood near the doorway of the Chinook and he offered his hand as Mark approached.

"Good day, Captain Holland. My name is Hourani. I'm to escort you to your destination."

The helicopter lifted rapidly into the air and sped toward the southeast and the People's Democratic Republic of Yemen. As the helicopter flew over the familiar ground, Mark gazed silently out of the small window. Half an hour later the jet helicopter slowed perceptibly.

They circled and landed amid the dust cloud beaten into a frenzy by the Chinook's rotors. Two hundred yards away was Sadallah's helicopter. Holland jumped down and the Saudi officer called after him as he ducked instinctively to avoid the blades far above his head.

"My orders are to wait no longer than four hours, Captain. Don't be any longer."

Holland waved over his shoulder in acknowledgement and pulled himself into the second helicopter. The pilot grinned.

"Hello, Mark, my friend."

"Ziad! I didn't know you could fly one of these things."

"Needs must, my friend. One never knows when such a talent will come in handy. Hurry. We cannot be too long."

Holland hastily pulled himself into the seat and grabbed for the door as Ziad took off. He slammed the door shut before shouting above the roar of the engines.

"What's the rush?"

Sadallah pointed to the sun dipping low in the horizon. "It's nearly dusk."

"Scared of vampires?" shouted Holland.

Ziad looked sharply at him. "Something like that."

An hour later, Sadallah banked to the left and settled the helicopter down into a flat, even area of ground in the jagged mountains. He allowed the blades to stop before turning to Holland.

"In the locker under your seat you will find a couple of handguns. Dig them out, will you, Mark?"

He did as he was asked and wordlessly followed Ziad as he scrambled up the rock face toward the crest of the small mountain upon which they had landed. After twenty minutes of hard climbing and walking, Sadallah motioned to Mark that they should crawl quietly over the next outcrop.

Holland looked over the ridge into the wide valley that seemed to stretch endlessly away on either side of them. Directly across from their position, Mark could make out the shadow of the opposite range.

He looked below their position at the rich, black earth covering the valley floor. He thought he could discern a movement in its midst, but when he looked again it had stopped. He could make out a skeletal structure lying embedded in the floor, but although it looked familiar he couldn't identify it.

Other than that, the valley was quiet. It was the first time he had used a five-million-dollar plane for sightseeing. He looked quizzically at Sadallah.

"This is Niah Valley, Mark," explained the freedom fighter. "You may remember I told you of it once. It's also called Locust Valley. It has been a favorite breeding ground for them for many centuries."

Holland looked at the still, skeletal shape across the valley and then turned back toward Sadallah. As he did so, a soft, slithering sound wafted toward him on the soft mountain breeze. There was also the smell. Holland snapped his head around.

The whole earth seemed to be swaying, moving into rhythmic, pulsating life. The black earth undulated and swayed. Mark stared with fascinated horror. The earth itself was alive.

"What you can see," explained Sadallah quietly, "is a fifth instar of locusts moving, marching. They are in the final stage before swarming."

"I thought it was the soil, the shadows," he said, unable to keep the sense of awe from his voice. "There must be millions of them down there!"

"Yes, many millions perhaps. Certainly it is the biggest gathering I have ever seen . . . and the most dangerous. Mark, this valley is roughly fifteen miles long and four miles wide. That 'black soil' you see stretches from end to end, from side to side. On its own, that would be cause enough for the greatest alarm to the agriculture of the Middle East and probably North Africa as well."

"On its own? There's more?"

"I believe there is, Mark." Sadallah edged forward slightly and pointed toward the skeletal structure. "That was a helicopter not so long ago, with a crew of four—there are two more just a little way down the valley."

"The shape of it was familiar. Looks like it crashed."

"It did, in a way. Mark, you and I have known each other for many years. I want you to listen to what I have to say with the greatest care," Sadallah said as he withdrew from the edge of the ridge and settled himself carefully against a large rock.

"A couple of days ago, one of my men was scouting this

area. We do it often to make sure the government forces are not trying to approach from this side in order to launch an attack.

"Anyway, this man was suddenly surprised to see three helicopters fly over the ridge near where we landed and head this way. He thought they were government gun ships and he hid. But they were not.

"He watched them sweep in low over the valley and start to spray the locusts down on the floor. At that time they would probably have been in the fourth instar and as yet unable to fly.

"He swears to me those locusts rose into the air and deliberately, *deliberately* swamped the helicopters.

"My soldier described it as a wave reaching up from the valley floor and washing over each helicopter in turn, bringing them to the ground.

"Obviously the locusts got caught up in the air intake, and the engines, starved of air, flamed out."

Sadallah wiped his mouth with his hand and tugged the ends of his moustache as he struggled with himself over how to proceed.

"Mark, those helicopters were not flying very high. You probably remember how low you used to go when you were a crop duster. When they came down I am told that the crews survived. My man said he saw all four men run from this near one and when he looked at the other two wrecks he could make out the figures of their crews."

"Lucky escape."

Saddallah shook his head sadly. "No, Mark. It was not a lucky escape at all. They would have been better off if they had died in their craft."

"Why?"

"My friend, the locusts devoured them."

After one final look at the swirling floor Ziad led him away, back to the helicopter. By the time they settled into the cabin, they had a little less than two hours until the rendezvous with the Saudi helicopter.

"We have seen this before, haven't we?"

Ziad nodded. "I know it sounds too incredible, my friend, but they apparently tore those men to pieces. It was as though they were angry at the insecticide, and they retaliated.

"That's why I wanted *you* out here—to see how big that swarm is, too see the crashed helicopters and to listen to what I have to say. The story isn't finished yet.

"Over the last three or four days I have been receiving reports of more incidents. A village wiped out, lone travelers found mutilated. Not many cases, I grant you, but in all there was evidence. I myself saw a village—six huts, half the bodies were stripped of every vestige of meat and the others were hacked and cut as though millions of tiny knives had been at work on them.

"Mark, I think there are more than those in Niah Valley. But the one in the valley is getting ready to swarm, it can't be long now, and when it does—if they really are the same as those I believe killed Steiner and decimated that village—then we are in trouble."

An hour later, with the sun now dipped behind the horizon and darkness covering the desert, Sadallah landed his helicopter near the Saudi Chinook which had turned on all its lights and seemed like a welcoming beacon as they swept over the Empty Quarter.

Sadallah gripped his arm wordlessly in a final salute, then Holland got out of the craft, closed the door and stepped away. As the guerrilla leader swept back toward the mountain, Holland allowed himself to wonder briefly if he would ever see the man again. Then he turned and joined the Saudi officer.

The return to London was as uneventful as a Sunday afternoon stroll in Hyde Park, and they chased the sun, landing at Northolt in the early evening. An agent and the embassy car were waiting for him and he was carried swiftly across London to Stephanie's apartment in Eaton Square.

"Mr. Volk thought you might appreciate the chance to clean up before you give your report, sir," explained the burly agent. "I'll be back to collect you in an hour, if that's all right with you?"

Holland grunted and climbed from the car.

She wasn't in and he felt a pang of regret. He had wanted to tell her what he had seen—to draw agreement and support for the theory he had formulated before meeting with Volk again.

All too soon, it seemed, the buzzer announced the return of the car and he grabbed a light jacket before closing the door to the apartment.

Outside it was now dark and the gloom of the staircase made him remember the darkness of Maiden Lane. He hadn't given a thought to his bruises since this morning. It seemed like a month ago.

He reached the foot of the stairs and walked across the short hallway toward the glass-fronted main doorway. The car accelerated away to Grosvenor Square and drew up in an alleyway behind a row of offices to the left of the American embassy. The driver left the car and went to a door where he spoke rapidly into an intercom. Within moments, two brutal-looking individuals escorted them into the building.

In the large office that overlooked the square, Stephanie and Starling were waiting with Volk for Holland's report.

He gave Stephanie an encouraging smile and accepted the glass of whiskey from Volk.

Stephanie exploded with impatience. "Well? What *did* you find out there? Mark, will you please tell me what is happening?"

Holland told them what he had learned—about the villagers, the reports of travelers found in the desert, the three Trans-Global helicopters, and finally of the guerrilla leader's belief that there were more swarms apart from the one in the Niah Valley.

There was silence when he finished and Holland allowed his news to sink in before continuing.

"Dr. Starling, when Stephanie and I came back from Livingston, you postulated on the final use for a bacterial agent. Remember?"

Starling nodded gently, sucking hard on the uncooperative pipe. "I remember the conversation, Mark. It seems logical.

A man who has switched to the destructive side of research, bacteriological warfare, and who puts three years of research into a potential bacterium, as yet unknown, must be doing so with a view to the development of an anti-human agent."

"I agree, Doctor, it is logical, but perhaps you were also influenced in arriving at that conclusion because you didn't like Steiner?"

Starling colored slightly and clamped his teeth over the pipe stem. "Possibly," he said at last, "although I'd like to think not. My calculations were based on the facts as I saw them. Steiner wasn't a likable man, that's very true. He was, as I have said, power hungry, but not mad for power. He changed scientific disciplines because he recognized the values in doing so. Not for humanity, but for himself within the scientific and government structures. No, I didn't like him, but I sincerely trust that if, as I suspect, you have evidence to contradict my scenario of Steiner and the aim of his research, you will not accuse me of falsification."

Mark held up an appeasing hand. "Of course not, Dr. Starling, I don't mean to imply anything of the sort. Where you went wrong, where we all went wrong, was in assuming that the character of the man would come through right to the point of extracting a highly contagious, and potent, bacterium. It wasn't helped by the fact that the CIA protected Livingston or by the fact that Steiner worked with the CIA program to develop germ warfare agents in the past.

"It was logical, therefore, to assume that if Steiner was working to see whether the Rocky Mountain locusts were destroyed by a virulent bacterium then he would only be doing so with a view to isolating that germ for the purpose of incorporating it into the existing germ warfare program the American government is supporting.

"Volk will confirm this perhaps, but it's my guess he did, in fact, discover a germ at Grasshopper Glacier, but at no time was it anybody's intention that it should be used against humans. I think the bacterium was to be used to eradicate the desert locust in the same way it wiped out the Rocky Mountain plagues. Somehow, something went wrong and he realized he was breeding a new form of mutant locust. Perhaps he felt the only way of ensuring that his mutants and his new bacterial strain would be destroyed was by going to the public through his niece. He knew the CIA would never allow him to publish the results of his experimentation and that was why he called you, Stephanie, in such a panic."

A heavy silence descended on the room and all eyes turned toward Volk, expecting confirmation.

"Yes," he said at last, "you are quite correct, Holland. Steiner was a genius but he had an incredible ego. He wanted, expected, to be hailed by his fellow academics as a great scientist, while in truth he only rated as a very good technician. His haste in wanting to ensure his own personal niche in history made him skip normal safety precautions which all scientific research undergo prior to field testing.

"You are also correct that the CIA was running the Livingston facility in conjunction with Trans-Global Oil, and are equally correct in stating that the bacterium was never intended to be used as a human toxicant."

Volk brushed absentmindedly at his coat as he sought to place in chronological order those facts which the group could be told. "Although Steiner had worked with us in the past, he was basically expendable. If it had not been for his involvement in entomology, he probably would have been expended and this conversation would not be taking place now. He wrote a paper for a small-circulation magazine a few years ago, one of those scientific journals which are read by a very small number of similarly interested groups. Anyway, as he was associated with the agency, this article was circulated, and eventually arrived at Covert Action.

"The possibilities this paper presented to us were immediately apparent. It dealt with the scientific phenomenon of the locusts at Grasshopper Glacier and postulated the theory that it must have been a bacterial infection which wiped out the swarms so suddenly and dramatically. Steiner was able to prove, reasonably conclusively anyway, that the weather at the time was mild and couldn't contribute to their demise. It was, I suppose, the sort of paper which would normally rouse only mild interest from us, except at the time the paper was published the agency had foreseen massive political turmoil and an anti-American move in the Middle East.

"Part of this turmoil would be, of necessity, our own making. In 1979 we discovered the Shah of Iran had cancer. We knew that when he died his son would never be able to hold together the various factions in Iran; he just wasn't the same type of man as his father. We projected that once it became known the Shah was dying his rivals would move in with a concerted program to take over the country and our oil supply would be irrevocably cut off. At worst this would have led to a major conflict and the Russians wouldn't have been able to stay out.

"We decided the best thing was for the Shah to be deposed by a fanatic—a religious fanatic—who would drive the country so far down that its people would pray for a return of the Shah and his relatively liberal ways. We accepted the inevitability of the venomous hatred which has been emanating from Iran for the past four years because we are aware a great deal more hostility is being directed inward toward the Iranians themselves.

Volk smiled grimly. "Indeed, it is essential to our scenario that this be the case. Soon, quite soon in fact, there will be a military takeover of the country and the mad priests will go, which the population will welcome. Needless to say, normal relations between Iran and the U.S. will be resumed soon after the coup, probably stronger than ever."

Volk carefully lit another cigarette before continuing. "You are probably wondering how all this relates to Steiner. Quite simply we recognized the need to immerse ourselves in the psyche of the Arabs—much the same way the English and Americans think of themselves as being so closely intertwined. Steiner's article started us thinking that if we could help eradicate the greatest scourge the Arab farmers face, then they would be grateful to the extent of repaying us as a nation with a continuing source of oil."

"So the agency's plan was to deliberately cut off one source of oil for a period to ensure later continuity and to supplement the future supply by creating a situation of greatful bondage from those countries whom the government would help agriculturally by way of pest control?"

Volk smiled at Stephanie. "Yes. But more than oil was involved, of course. Iran poses a particular plum for us insofar as we can keep a very close watch on the Soviets.

"It was Steiner who came up with the ace. He isolated the germ which had wiped out the Rocky Mountain locust. All we had to do was breed that bacterium into the desert locust and within a few generations, meaning several months, the desert locust would become as dead as the dodo.

"That was the theory and we decided it was the best route to go. Trans-Global fronted the research and stood to get more oil concessions than they would know what to do with, if everything fell into place.

"Representations were made to a few carefully selected oil producing countries who suffered locust infestation, and they all fought to be the first to be cleared of locusts and sign oil contracts with Trans-Global in payment.

"The two scenarios together indicated we wouldn't have to worry about the Russians for many, many years. Then Steiner went on his damn field trip and it all started going wrong. You, Captain, have just confirmed what we suspected. Far from wiping the goddam things out, Steiner has quickened the life cycle and made them hardier. Inside two generations his crossbreeds have turned carnivorous. Steiner has produced a mutant more terrifying than the thing we wanted to destroy!

"He wanted to warn the world about his creatures—that's when he called you, Dr. Caine. Trans-Global tried to stop him from blowing the whistle but he wouldn't listen. He was scared stiff. Terrified at what he had done. We now know he was bringing you samples of his work when he was killed.

"We know from the flight recorder the plane went off course, at Steiner's request, to check on the breeding ground at Niah, and therefore came down—was brought down—over the mountains. The samples must have escaped the crash, free to merge with other locusts in the area."

Holland sat forward. "Steiner's face looked as though it had been torn away down one side; Ziad said he saw the same thing in the village."

Volk nodded. "He would have been the first. They would have been the youngest of the new mutants and not in need of much nourishment, otherwise you would have seen all the bodies mutilated in the same way."

Mark's eyes blazed at Volk, his jaw set hard. "Who blew up the aircraft, Volk?"

"The same people who have been after you. Trans-Global. They took unauthorized action. We would not have considered such a step, it would have been recognized as causing more problems than it would be worth. They decided there was too much at stake to risk word getting out that they had been involved in something like this—however good the intentions. Had the plane taken off when it was supposed to, those creatures would be at the bottom of the Red Sea right now.

"However, there are now reports reaching me from all over the region of attacks on humans, cattle, sheep, horses, camels—you name it. There was even a yacht the Portuguese navy found. The passengers and crew reduced to skeletons.

"Sadallah was right in thinking there are two groups. But he was wrong about the group you saw at Niah Valley. Part of them, a large part, has already swarmed."

"Then why don't you destroy the valley now, before the rest of them have a chance to get airborne?" Stephanie demanded.

Volk turned to her patiently. "Trans-Global tried, losing three choppers. But worse, the insecticide had no effect whatever, other than causing them to swarm. It seemed to act as a catalyst."

"Shit!" exclaimed Holland with disgust. "It would have been better if you and your agency had spent the time and money developing something else to drive your fucking Cadillacs."

"Perhaps so," replied Volk testily, "but the fact of the matter is the United States government recognized our oil needs and oil by-product requirements were escalating, practically doubling every ten years. We estimated that by the year 2000 we would be in bad trouble. Our own reserves were running low and new discoveries, although they were coming along every year, didn't meet the estimated requirements. We started stockpiling in great quantities as far back as 1968. But even the stockpiling would only be a solution for a limited period of time.

"We looked at ways of getting oil into the United States. Any method had to be examined and we even built a pipeline from Alaska, across Canada into our refineries. Expensive, but necessary to keep the oil requirements topped up. Then the Arabs finally put the heat on as we had expected and we had the big shortage. If an industrial country hasn't got oil, Holland, you can wipe it off the map. It's as simple as that—survival.

"Steiner and his bacteriological experimentation was, we thought, the answer. The idea was that inside a single season, the desert locusts would become infected with the disease and die out. Steiner estimated they would, in fact, lay sterile eggs. He was wrong."

"So you and Trans-Global are doing everything you can to prevent the news getting out—including murder. But where do we go from here?"

Starling coughed and studied his pipe for a long moment before taking it up for Volk.

"Locusts have plagued man ever since he first began to sow seeds in order to grow crops. Early records dating back to 2520 B.C. refer to desert locust swarms and the eighth great plague of Egypt is recorded in the book of Exodus. That dates around 1300 B.C. There are also records pertaining to the Oriental migratory locust in Chinese literature as long ago as 707 B.C. Much of Europe, as well as large parts of Asia, have been visited by the little devils at some point in time. The American continent, as you are now aware, had its own problems with the rocky mountain locust.

"It is true to say every continent and acre of land in this world, with the possible exception of Antartica, is liable to receive a visit from a swarm at any time, providing conditions are right.

"You may remember the summer of 1979 in America. There was a tremendous locust swarm across the northern U.S. They clogged air conditioners and got into vehicle radiators; roads were covered with them. For a while there was a general sense of fear and certainly there was general chaos caused by the swarm.

"Put it into perspective, Mark, by simply realizing the desert locust, which we consider here at this center to be one of the world's most serious agricultural pests, is only one of many strains. A single swarm, in a single season, can infest an incredible eleven million square miles. That's twenty percent of the land surface of this planet.

"Now individually, the locust is an incredibly well-constructed bug, with quite a lot going for it. Put it with others of its kind and it turns into the Mr. Hyde of the insect world. A little while ago we tracked a single swarm of desert locusts in Somalia that covered four hundred square miles. That's about a quarter of a million acres and as we know that there are about forty to eighty million locusts in a single square kilometer of swarm, that swarm could easily have comprised around forty-thousand million munching their way across the Somali Republic.

"A locust weighs two grams and it can eat its own weight in a day. That computes to this particular swarm eating eighty thousand tons of food per day. You can easily see how serious the situation is by relating that quantity to human needs. Eighty thousand tons of corn would be enough to feed four-hundred thousand people for a year."

There was complete silence in the room as Starling continued.

"I cannot stress enough that all your H-bombs and man-made weaponry can't possibly equal the destructive power of the insect world. In fact, despite trying very hard, we have never, ever, been able to eradicate *any* species of insect. Animals, yes. But the insect world seems to be a law unto itself."

"But surely all you have to do is wait for the little buggers to pop out of the eggs and spray them," Mark said.

Dr. Starling laughed. "Stephanie, you answer this one. Let me rest my tongue."

"It's not that easy, Mark. While you can have a mass the

size Dr. Starling has described quite visible once it is swarming, the actual breeding point, or outbreak area as it's called, can be very small and will not be seen until the outbreak occurs. Even with the benefit of satellites, you have to know where to look.

"For instance, imagine the outbreak area in this room. Within twenty-four hours the swarm flies and within a week New York is infested. That's the size of the problem."

Starling came in again. "We have a very intense program of counterattack. But let me give you an example of what we face. In 1960 we estimated the northern region of the Somali Republic was invaded by four main waves of swarms covering some seven-hundred-fifty square miles. What weapon could be devised to combat that? In the old days, one method of counterattack was the ploughing of fields after locusts had laid their eggs. Another was to dig huge trenches and try to direct as many locusts as possible into them in order that they could be burned.

"These methods took a great deal of manpower, of course, and they were only moderately successful. The campaign against the locust became much more effective in their breeding grounds with the introduction of chemicals. The earliest poison used against them, quite extensively, was sodium arsenate. This would be mixed in with something the locust would eat, such as chopped maize cobs, wheat bran, chaff of various kinds, even sawdust. The mixture was then spread on the ground in the path of the locust and bingo, large numbers were eradicated. Unfortunately, so were a number of cattle who ate whatever was left over."

"So this method was stopped?"

"Oh, no. Baiting continued for several decades, but then the introduction of insecticides for specific purposes came about, a tremendous boost for us. Sodium arsenate is a general poison, you see. The first of the newer poisons developed for use against the hoppers was the gamma inomer of benzene hexachloride.

"In one attack against them in eastern Africa in 1953, one thousand tons of baited poison wiped out more than one-hundred thousand hopper bands of all sizes. To put that operation into perspective, let me tell you we needed eighty-three trucks and over a thousand men to spread twenty thousand sacks of bait.

"And that is the operative word here, of course. A very high proportion of our campaign costs were incurred by having to buy foodstuff to act as an attractant and a very small proportion of poison was actually distributed. In that particular operation, of the one thousand tons of bait spread, only one and a half tons of actual poison was used.

"Clearly this couldn't go on. During the 1950s a simple system was designed, known as the Exhaust Nozzle Sprayer— it operated by pressure from the vehicle's engine. We used the poison Dieldrin with great success. It is so powerful that when sprayed with a twenty percent mixture of oil, to give it a tackiness to enable it to adhere to leaves, its effect would last several weeks.

"The method we used was to spray several parallel bands, knowing, as the hoppers usually proceed in the same direction, that even if they didn't eat enough poison to kill them in one band they would at the next.

"This method had great advantages because formerly we had to locate the hoppers before going into action. Now we simply plot their expected course and set to work—lay a trap as it were."

"What about aircraft?" Mark asked.

"They have been brought more and more into the fight since the Second World War, but even under normal circumstances there are drawbacks. In order to minimize wastage of insecticide sprayed by aircraft, it is essential that as many locusts as possible be between the aircraft and the ground. In view of this, and since locusts collect more insecticide when they are flying, the best chances for a good kill occur in the morning and evening, when they are close to the ground. A good example of the effectiveness of a modern insecticide, Diazinon, applied in this way, was the destruction of one-hundred-eighty million locusts with a single light aircraft load of sixty gallons. But that's only the equivalent of one square mile of land covered!"

In the air-conditioned office, Holland felt the sweat sting beneath his shirt. Stephanie watched the blue eyes harden.

"So you see, Captain, they are an international problem. In the Rome headquarters of the Food and Agriculture Organization of the United Nations there is a Locust Office—an indication of the importance that the U.N. place on combating the menace presented to the food suppliers of the world.

"I don't think it's blowing our own horn too much, nor overstating our importance, when I say that without the center there would be a lot more misery from famine in the world today.

"Here in London, and in the field, we are constantly testing new methods and ideas. With insecticides, yes, but also with pheromones, sex and food attractants, and, perhaps most promising, virus and bacteria control."

The pipe was refilled. Starling struck a match and applied it to the overflowing bowl. At last he was satisfied with the cloud of smoke he was drawing.

"Of course, there are other problems we have to face. In some parts of the world the locust is welcomed, if not in vast quantities. In Africa the natives rush out when a swarm appears. They eat them. Quite a good source of nutrition. There is even a tribe in Zaire which thinks of them as gods. Revere the little buggers as they chew their way through the harvest.

"They are also involved in folklore and religions closer to home. I've mentioned Moses bringing the plague down on the Egyptians. They also warrant a piece in the Koran. As I recall, it goes something like this: 'When the sentence is pronounced against them, We shall bring forth for them an insect out of the earth, which shall bite them because people did not believe Our Signs.' And, of course, we have the piece from Joel: 'The day of the Lord cometh . . . The land is as the Garden of Eden before them, and behind them a desolate wilderness; yea, and nothing shall escape them. . . .'

"Gentlemen, Stephanie, the premise we must work on is that these mutants are more powerful genetically than their forebears. Their breeding and life-style patterns appear to be much altered, as do their eating habits.

"Of particular concern must be Mr. Volk's assertion that the insects have mutated to a carnivorous state. Couple this with what can only be described as a heightened attack pattern as evidenced by their almost intelligent counterattack on the Trans-Global helicopters, and I think we can all agree we face, potentially, the most disastrous situation any of us has ever faced.

"If the reports Mark brought back with him are correct, and frankly we have no reason to doubt them, the insects' migratory abilities are equally heightened. And this is where our real danger lies. The longest recorded flight by a single swarm was from the Canaries to the British Isles—sixteen hundred miiles. The norm for a single flight is about fifty miles.

"Assuming the insects are genetically strong all round, I feel certain we shall see flights of sixteen hundred miles, or thereabouts, as the norm rather than the exception. The danger to Europe at this point must be extreme. I would advise the total and immediate destruction by whatever means available of the Niah Valley.

"Those insects must not be allowed to swarm."

Ishmail Khalkali walked onto the balcony of his sumptuous Paris apartment, staring idly out at the throngs of motor vehicles surging on the wide avenue far below him. The smell of Paris assailed his nostrils and we wrinkled his sun-tanned nose with distaste. God, how he hated it here.

His visitors had left only a short time ago and once again he had been left with the feeling of total abandonment. Every day the handful of his followers, who had gone into exile with him from Yemen, came to the apartment and talked. God how they talked! About the time when the holy war, the jihad, would be called and of how he would take the rightful place as the Mahdi to lead the Muslims against the infidel.

Ishmail was more aware than his fifteen followers that it could never be, certainly not in his lifetime. His country was divided and, even if it were not, Western ideas, money and political influence would ensure talk of the jihad was kept to the domain of mullahs and madmen. The people didn't care.

They hadn't raised so much as one voice in protest when he was exiled. To Ishmail Khalkali it was inconceivable that the holy war could ever take place and he knew that he was destined to spend the rest of his life reclining in splendid comfort like a deposed emperor.

He stood on the balcony, immobile, dreamily imagining a triumphant return at the head of the huge Muslim army he would control. The sound of the traffic giving way to the adulations of thousands standing beneath his balcony in a city far away, calling his name: "Mahdi, Mahdi, Mahdi." The chant rising and falling like waves on the sea shore. Then the crowds drifted away in a haze and he was left only with the honking horns and Klaxon sirens of a Paris police car rushing to another emergency.

He sighed and returned to the interior of the apartment. Dreams. Dreams of a man with no country and nowhere to go. But if he himself had started to doubt his destiny, what of the followers? If they too lost faith then surely all would be lost. He relied on them for all things. Money, spiritual support, communication with the homeland and the band of malcontents which still waited for his return.

Khalkali wandered into the kitchen and poured himself a glass of ice water. They had been forced to leave Yemen and sought sanctuary in Iraq. The Iraquis had been pleased to support Khalkali and his group and had offered them every assistance in fermenting unrest in their old homeland. But then things had changed, as Khalkali had known they must.

Iraq had patched up its differences with Yemen, and in the political arena Yemenis had suggested it wasn't very friendly for the Iraquis to give sanctuary to a rebellious mullah whose aim was to destroy existing ways of life and replace them with an authoritarian Muslim regime.

His former friends couldn't wait to help him on his way, and, with what Khalkali had deemed unseemly haste, he was the subject of an equally unseemly trade-off with the French. France agreed to give him sanctuary, thus relieving the Iraquis of the embarrassment of his presence, in return for something the French had wanted. What it was Khalkali hadn't the faintest idea, nor did it matter. He had been the pawn and now the pawn was moved even further from the board. What could he do this far away except lose hope?

He moved aimlessly into the living room and sat heavily on the silk brocade couch and began to glance idly through *Paris-Match*.

If nothing else, he thought to himself as he scanned the world news section, he would live out his life in luxury.

Suddenly he stopped and re-read a small item which normally would have been overlooked. A tingle ran down his spine and he shivered as he read again the nine-line item. It isn't possible, he said aloud to the empty room. But it was; he knew it was the sign he had waited for all these long years.

It was time for him now. Allah had sent the sign just as the Koran had prophesied. The insects of the desert were turning against the infidel and all those who had lost the way. He read again the small article about the unconfirmed report of a village being attacked by locusts, and hastily reached for the telephone.

After dialing wrong twice, he calmed himself and carefully redialed the six digits. At length, in an Arab restaurant on the Left Bank, the call was answered. Khalkali talked rapidly to the man who would put into motion the plan which carried their hopes and aspirations. At length and near to tears he concluded the telephone conversation. "Allah has sent the sign. I am the Mahdi. Let the jihad begin."

# CHAPTER TWO

"I HONESTLY DO NOT UNDERSTAND, YOUR EXCELLANCY, WHY you won't support this request."

The scientist had pleaded and cajoled with the Saudi Arabian ambassador for fifteen minutes. He was getting nowhere, but he was the only person in the room who didn't accept it.

Holland looked at his watch. It was nearly eleven o'clock in the evening. Time was slipping inexorably away. Taking into account the time difference between England and Saudi Arabia, they had a little over three hours before dawn crept across the desert. It wasn't known if the next day would see the swarming of the remaining locusts in Niah Valley, but it was known they didn't have many more days left.

They had presented the facts without embellishment. At length, Volk had advised that the Saudi Air Force be alerted immediately in preparation for a napalm run on the valley.

The Saudi ambassador had refused.

"Mr. Ambassador, I quite understand the reluctance of your government . . . of your king . . . to order a strike against your own country. But it is an uninhabited area. The only casualties will be the mutants."

The Saudi ambassador held up his hand to stem Starling's tirade.

"Dr. Starling," he began in a cultured voice that spoke of a Western education, "I have listened to all the facts with great interest. I was also advised by my king some hours ago of Captain Holland's report on his return from Niah Valley. I assure you our decision has not been made lightly, but has been arrived at following consultation with our cabinet and with other advisers."

"But sir, with the greatest respect, if these things are allowed to swarm they will not only devastate your country, but all the Middle East, Europe, perhaps eventually more. You must support—"

Again, the regal hand was raised, this time to cut Stephanie's earnest appeal.

"Dr. Caine, I repeat: This decision has not been made lightly, nor, I might add, easily. I have already explained to the American ambassador the reasons why we have made it. Now, if you will excuse me, I have things to attend to."

The Saudi rose and brushed cigar ash from his Savile Row suit, then shook hands with his American counterpart before walking to the door without further comment.

As it closed softly behind him, a sigh escaped from the throats of those left in the office.

"Goddam it," muttered Volk. "Mr. Ambassador, that guy must be made to see reason."

"Mr. Volk," began the U.S. ambassador darkly, "that guy, as you put it, is one of the best, most concerned men on the whole planet. He also represents the kingdom of Saudi Arabia and, as such, speaks with the full sanction of his country. But, I suppose people like you have a more casual attitude to authority."

Volk colored as Ambassador Howe continued.

"The fact is, that the Saudis refuse to order a strike because the king's religious advisers are putting the heat on. They say this is the sign the faithful have awaited and it heralds the return of Allah and his Prophet. There is even a report of a Mahdi calling for a holy war!"

"Oh Christ," groaned Mark. "Bloody religion."

"You of all people should know the Saudis are basically a simple people with simple beliefs."

"Sir, can't we order a strike and worry about the consequences later?"

George Armstrong Howe smiled gently. "Mr. Volk, I have already said the Saudi ambassador is one of the best. He's already thought that through, and has come to the conclusion we must not attempt it.

"If we did destroy those locusts, the religious fanatics in Saudi Arabia would rise up against the king and against any non-Islamic party. There would be a holy war of such intensity, I doubt if a hundred years would be enough to heal the rift which would exist between Saudi Arabia and the rest of the world."

"So what happens, Mr. Ambassador? Are you saying we do nothing?"

The ambassador rose from the desk and walked to the French windows. He stood looking out into the quiet square.

"Officially yes. The president concurs with the decision not to attack Niah Valley on the basis that we can not afford to lose another oil-producing country. Iran was bad enough. However, a full emergency program has been initiated to try to develop bacteria that can be administered surreptitiously."

Starling stood and Holland could see he was shaken.

"My God, Mr. Ambassador, doesn't the president realize that could take months, years? Steiner worked for three years before isolating the germ that created these mutants."

Ambassador Howe turned from the window.

"He realizes, Dr. Starling. But the scenario that's been written for this emergency indicates it is the only route that can be followed in order to maintain the status quo—"

"Status quo?" exploded Starling angrily. "My God, man, there won't be anybody left to care about your precious status quo!"

"Doctor, there is nothing to be gained by outbursts like this. The president has authorized me to tell you this because we are going to need your help. I might add the Kremlin is aware of the crisis and also agrees. They are as anxious as we that the balance of power as it exists now should be maintained. Perhaps it does sound ridiculous to you to talk of this when we are faced with a situation of such horrendous proportions, but please remember those locusts in the valley are not the only problems we have to worry about. There are others. We can't handle a holy war as well. Do you understand?"

Starling glared at him, but not in anger now, so much as at the hopelessness of the situation they were in.

"I apologize, sir. I'm afraid I got excited. It's just—"

"I know," said the ambassador. "I have never in all my life felt so helpless, and personally so afraid."

Howe moved slowly to the cocktail cabinet and extracted a bottle of white wine and four glasses. He placed these on a silver tray and then took the whiskey bottle and poured a full five fingers of Scotch into a cut-glass tumbler. He returned to the desk, handing Holland the Scotch before pouring wine for the others.

"What I don't understand, Mr. Ambassador, is how you have managed to get moving so fast on this problem. The Saudi ambassador communicates with Riyadh, the king with his advisers, and you with the president, the president with the Russians, a scenerio gets written. How could it be done in a matter of—what, three hours?"

"Obviously, we knew within hours of the plane crash we might be in trouble. Our contingency plans started being prepared last week. Your visit to the valley simply confirmed our fears."

Silence descended on the room as each thought over the events of the last hours. Volk broke the silence.

"Is there nothing we can do, sir?"

"I don't honestly know. The Sixth Fleet is sailing from Singapore to Aden at this moment. SAC is on full alert and agreement has been obtained from several African countries to initiate bombing raids when, and if, locusts are spotted in their territory.

"The idea, initially at least, is to try to contain the outbreak areas to the Mideast. If that can be achieved, we have time to beat them."

The idea was incredible, thought Holland. Curtail the spread of the locusts within the Gulf area. In plain English it meant the Mideast would be a feeding ground for the insects and the people of Islam their willing sacrifices. All because of an obscure paragraph in the Koran.

A slight drizzle started to fall as they left the embassy. It was in many ways a fitting epitaph to the evening. Holland turned to his three companions. "Fascinating to see how the world can be turned over in such a short space of time. What now?"

Starling, Stephanie and Volk exchanged quick glances and then Stephanie spoke.

"I'm going out there, Mark," she said simply.

"Are you crazy? Haven't you been listening to what's going on?"

She shook her head dismissively.

"Mark, we have to have live samples of those creatures if we are to have any chance of beating them biologically. We have discussed it and I'm the obvious one to go. I know what to look for and I am the senior researcher at the center."

"You're also vulnerable as hell, woman!"

Volk stepped forward. "Captain, Dr. Caine is right. Apart from the scientific reasons we also have the security aspect to take into account. If we bring anybody else into the picture we run the risk of the story getting out before we are ready. It came down to either her or Dr. Starling."

"And I'm afraid I'm a bit too old to be gallivanting around in the sun, Captain Holland."

Mark slammed his fist on the hood of the waiting car in sheer exasperation. "Goddamit, Volk, you must have a dozen scientists capable of this sort of thing. Why not use one that's on your payroll?"

Stephanie reached for his arm and squeezed gently.

"I want to go, Mark. You must understand that. My uncle started this and I must help to reach a solution. I'll be all right.

I shall be able to get into the valley, take my samples and get out before there is any real danger."

"That's what the helicopter crews thought."

"Not the same thing, Mark. Those helicopters were attacking the insects—I won't be. There is no reason for them to retaliate."

"Unless they're hungry!"

"We are having protective suits flown in that will withstand even a concentrated attack for a short while," interjected Volk. "Dr. Caine will not be going very deep into the mass, nor staying long. With any luck she will be there before they start to swarm."

Mark looked at her and could see that her mind was made up.

"When do we leave?" he said.

# CHAPTER THREE

*THE SUN BROKE THROUGH THE NIGHT AND SWEPT ITS RAYS ACROSS the sand, and across the mountain range. Warming fingers stabbed forward, forcing the bitterly cold night air away from the mass.*

*The ripple of movement started at the very heart of the resting insects and spread with a murmur to the edges. As the sun rose higher, moment by moment, the fluttering wings increased their tempo and the noise reached a crescendo.*

*Each locust communicated with its neighbor and one isolated thought became the thought of them all. The wings touched and spread the feeling.*

*The instinct was felt by all. The knowledge there were others of their kind was understood by all. The desire was kindled in all.*

*At last, the time had come. The dew was dried from their wings and the ripple of movement culminated as they lifted joyously, soullessly into the air.*

*They circled and swam in the warm morning air, until the valley floor was empty and the darkness of the mass blotted out the light from the sun.*

\* \* \*

The heat seared the backs of the oilmen as they labored in the desert. Paul Maclusky swore with a hearty Newcastle accent as he slapped the holding chain around the pipe which would feed another ten feet of drilling rod into the ground beneath them.

Below the rig, the crew foreman shaded his eyes and looked up at Maclusky, before turning back to the man beside him. "That fuckin' limey sure can work, Ed. I'da never believed the English could work so friggin' hard without gripin'."

Ed Fellows, Shell Oil's field superintendent in this sector, smiled. Although he had been born in New Jersey, he had been raised with the smell of oil fields in his nostrils and had worked as a rigger before he had been able to read and write.

"Jimmy, you got an opinion of the British that stinks," he laughed. "Here, have a can of cool old American beer—smuggled it in myself."

The foreman wiped his hands on his T-shirt before gratefully accepting the lukewarm beer. One thing you could rely on in this hellhole, he thought to himself, was the boss bringing a few precious cans back to Saudi after one of his trips to a neighboring "wet" state.

"I first started working with British crews in the North Sea rigs," Ed continued after they had swallowed half their drinks. "Believe me, any guy that can put up with the bitching weather on those things can put up with heat like we got here. Maybe it's what they say about the English—give 'em a chance and they'll work their asses off. But it's gotta be worth their while. That Maclusky kid up there was with me on two rigs and I seen him do the work of three men. He's a worker all right."

The foreman nodded slowly. "That's as may be, Ed, but 'cept for him and a couple of the 'mericans we got here the rest of them are as green as grass 'bout workin' a rig. Shit, I had one asshole who was smokin' on the friggin' thing last week. Could'a blowed us all to hell and back. What I mean, Ed, is why the hell can't we get some experienced oilers out here?"

"Come on, Jimmy, you know the score. We work for a partly British company and they gotta be able to prove to their government that they're givin' jobs to Brits. Otherwise they're goin' to be in the shit with the Department of Labor, or whatever, in London. Besides," he finished resignedly, "this is a low priority test hole and the head office figures it'll be good training for them out here. Can't screw things up too badly."

Jimmy spat into the sand and growled, "Yeah, make me a fuckin' mother hen to these wetasses. Shit, Ed, you an' me been in this game long enough to know half these shitheads won't last the month out."

"I know that, Jimmy," replied Ed sharply, "but we need to check this site out and we need trained men at other places. Now that's the way it is and there's not gonna be no changing it for the next coupla months. At least, not as far as you're concerned. Understand?"

Jimmy understood well enough. Three months previously the Saudi religious police had caught him and a sixteen-year-old girl, both drunk. He had broken two of the kingdom's prime laws—no alcohol and no fooling around with the local women. Jimmy had compounded the felony by getting the girl bombed and that meant a hell of a lot more than a flogging offense. He had heard of guys who had been thrown in jail for fifteen years for supplying liquor to Saudi nationals.

The company had told him he would have to stand the penalty for his crimes, but had then done all they could to get him a light sentence. Somehow, he had been let off with a stern warning and sent back to work. No deportation, no flogging, and, mercifully, no more time in a Saudi jail. No doubt about it, he owed the company a debt and they, in turn, had started extracting payment by putting him in charge of a test well in the middle of nowhere with a bunch of trainees. Well, at least Maclusky knew what the hell to do.

"Come on, Jimmy boy, it's not as bad as all that. Another month or so and I'll be able to move you back to the fields at Abadan. Then you can start havin'—"

"Hey boss, look . . . over to the north."

Both men swung their heads toward the shout. Maclusky was pointing to the north, frantically gesticulating. Jimmy and his supervisor followed his gaze.

"What the hell . . . duststorm, Ed?"

"Moving wrong for that," mused the supervisor. "Let's go up the derrick, get a better look."

Both men clambered up the staggered ladder that led from the desert floor to the drilling platform. The five-man crew was looking anxiously toward the cloud and Jimmy snarled that the drilling bit shouldn't be left unattended. Nobody took any notice of him and it continued to bite deeper into the sandy floor as the six watched the swirling cloud move closer.

"What in the hell is it?" mumbled Jimmy to no one in particular.

"Sand storm?" asked one of the men nervously.

"No sand storm," repeated Ed, "moving all wrong for that. Jesus, look at the size of it though!"

The cloud appeared to be moving away from them toward the south and Ed was sure now it wouldn't do them any harm.

Maclusky chuckled. "You guys are scared shits. Have you never seen a rain cloud before?"

Relief ran around the crew. A rain cloud. Unusual out of season, but that's what it was. A large but straightforward rain cloud.

"Balls," shot Jimmy, "no rain cloud moves that fast, son. And I ain't never seen a rain cloud that big, nor movin' from north to south like it were a snake wrigglin' across the sky."

As they watched, fascinated, a large portion of the cloud seemed to detach itself from the main body and sweep across the sky toward them. Daylight turned to dusk as it obliterated the sun and a sense of foreboding swept across the derrick.

Suddenly, a hollow laugh rang out from the field supervisor. "Jesus Christ. Locusts. That's all it is, a bloody cloud of friggin' locusts lookin' for food. Take a good look, boys. You'll never see a swarm as big as that for the rest of your lives. That's really somethin'!"

Jimmy let out a sigh of relief. "Right, lads, get back to work. They can't hurt you, but I sure as hell can if you lose that bit. Now haul ass!"

Three of the workmen moved back toward the drill. Maclusky hung back, shaking his head at the sight before his eyes

—the cloud that now moved closer towards their position. "Man, I've never seen nothin' like this, I'll tell you. Are you sure they can't hurt you, Jimmy?"

Ed and Jimmy laughed and Jimmy slapped his back good humoredly. "Don't you worry, son, they are as harmless as pussycats. Now go on, make sure those greenhorns don't lose the bit down that hole."

"Let's get another beer, Jimmy, I'm as dry as a dust hole."

The two men reached the halfway point down the derrick when the locust swarm reached the rig. The tiny insects clattered against the tin roofs of the store buildings like cascading hailstones in a summer storm.

The ground quickly became covered by thousands of the insects as they hopped and scurried in search of food. The sound of the drilling rig became obscured, and high above them four figures could be seen vainly swatting away the flying creatures.

Suddenly, all that could be heard was the inexorable growl of the drilling equipment biting deeper into the ground.

Ed reached the bottom of the ladder first, and moments later Jimmy jumped the last few steps to land beside him. They looked nervously at each other as the insects poured over their boots like a rush of crude.

Jimmy looked skyward and noted with fascinated horror that every single strut and beam of the derrick was laden with locusts. On the platform, the crew had moved toward the edge and they were looking down at their supervisors. The panic on their faces made Ed Fellows' blood go cold.

Jimmy turned to him. "What the hell's goin' on?" he whispered.

Ed shook his head. "I've got no idea, never seen them act like this before. It's like they was waitin' for somethin'. . . ."

As though in answer, a shrill whistle swelled from the main body of the swarm near the crew's sleeping quarters. The sound was taken up by the locusts on the derrick and immediately the air was once again thick with flying bodies.

A human scream reverberated from the derrick and the two

men on the ground snapped their heads upward. "My God," screamed Jimmy, "they're being attacked!"

Even as he spoke, a body came crashing through the gantry, hurtling the hundred feet to the ground. It landed only yards away from them. They could clearly see the bloody gashes and tears in the young man's face and chest before the body was covered by locusts once more. It was Maclusky.

Screams reached their ears again and Ed suddenly felt a sharp stinging on his own face and neck. "Get'em the fuck off me!" he yelled to Jimmy. The older man swatted ineffectually at his supervisor before realizing he had his own problems. His shorts left revealing stretches of leg for the insects to devour and they were making the most of their opportunity.

A second figure came hurtling down to the ground from the derrick and Jimmy decided enough was enough. "The truck, Ed, make for the fuckin' truck," he yelled, running at breakneck speed toward the blue oil company vehicle which had brought Ed out from Abadan.

Jimmy hauled himself into the cab and hastily wound up the windows. He kept the driver's door open slightly to enable his friend to scramble in. Ed walked dizzily across the space from the oil rig toward him, then crumpled to his knees in the sand. He looked toward the vehicle with pleading, hopeless eyes before making a last gesture with his hands, and falling face down into the seething mass which had gathered around him.

Jimmy slammed the door shut, concentrating on killing the insects which he got into the cab. He was bleeding profusely from a multitude of bites and lacerations. The experience of the last few minutes, coupled with the loss of blood, made him feel weak and nauseous.

He started the engine of the vehicle and slammed it into gear. As he pulled away from the test site area, he allowed himself one last look back. The sight would haunt him for the rest of his life.

\* \* \*

Stephanie slept as the Air Force plane left the French coast
and flew on a route which would take them over Sardinia before
turning east toward Egypt. From there, they would again turn
south for the run down the Red Sea to Abha.

Yammani had assured the American ambassador Saudi helicopters would ferry them to the valley. He had also told him
it would be the one and only time they would be able to mount
an incursion against the locusts. The religious leaders would
see to that.

Holland shifted slightly in his seat, relieving the numbness.
Stephanie's head moved slightly before she readjusted it instinctively to find the original comfort of his shoulder.

He stroked her dark curls thoughtfully to calm her back into
sleep. But his eyes were glazed as he somehow looked beyond
the present threat. Someone at Trans-Global had ordered the
bomb to be placed on the aircraft and killed Kate. No matter
what else happened, thought Mark grimly, that someone would
live to regret the act. But he would not live for long. Once this
was over he would get back on the trail of the men who had
both ordered and committed the murder.

Sunlight flashed through the window as the aircraft changed
course. Even with the protection of the plane's insulating shell,
Mark could feel the heat of the sun. For several seconds he
studied the way it highlighted shades of red in Stephanie's hair,
before pulling the shade down.

She stirred. Mark brought his hand down to her cheek. He
looked at the woman asleep on his shoulder and wondered
about her.

He had fought against feeling about her the way he did after
so short a time. But now it didn't feel wrong. It didn't really
even feel as though it had only been a week since the crash.
Maybe he was just clutching at straws. He sighed and fished
in his shirt pocket for a cigarette.

His thoughts were interrupted by the approach of the copilot,
who was moving hastily down the short gangway.

"Call from London, Dr. Caine. Mission aborted!"

Holland didn't bother to correct him. "Why?"

"They said to tell you it's too late. We have orders to land

and refuel in Tunis. The captain is turning back now. Sorry, sir!"

Holland nodded his thanks. The crew wouldn't know what their mission had been, so there was no point in attempting to elicit further information.

"Mark? What's happened?"

She lifted her head from his shoulder, and rubbed at the crick in her neck.

"Mission aborted. We're landing at Tunis to refuel."

"They've swarmed," she said quietly.

The Tunisian sun beat down oppressively as they stepped from the aircraft, causing Stephanie to gasp involuntarily as she collided with the wall of heat.

Although it was still early morning, the airport was crowded with vacationers from all over Europe, arriving and departing. The smug looks and sun tans walked proudly to their home-ward-bound aircraft while their replacements slunk into the country as though ashamed at the whiteness of their bodies.

Volk had obviously been at work. As Stephanie and Mark stepped onto the scalding concrete, a large American car swept to a halt before them, closed windows indicating air-conditioned comfort was only moments away.

"Hi, folks, name is Paul Edwards," grinned the youthful face which appeared from the rear of the vehicle. "Mr. Volk's instructions were to pick you up and take you to our Tunisian Ready Room. You can connect with London from there."

Edwards held the rear door open for them, then dropped the seat which was recessed into the back of the driver's compartment before climbing into the limousine. He sat facing them, the grin still in place.

"How much do you know about this?"

The grin faded. "Mr. Volk has appraised me fully, Doctor. My orders are to maintain the North African watch. Maintain the line of communication between Eagle's Lair and governments in this sector."

"Eagle's Lair?"

"The command bunker under the London embassy, sir. There

are several of them around the world. They were designed for use in the event of nuclear war, but I guess this emergency qualifies."

Holland nodded, looking through the smoked-glass windows of the now speeding car. The road led directly into Tunis and while it was wide and well made, it could easily have been anywhere in North Africa.

Camels meandered along its dusty edges in blissful ignorance of the cars and buses speeding between the airport and vacation spots.

Mark had been surprised they had not been required to go through the formality of customs inspection or passport control. Even the normally stringent regulation concerning smallpox vaccination certificates had apparently been waived in their case. The small things always seemed to be a measure of the seriousness of a situation.

The incongruity of it all was the number of vacationers still arriving by the hour aboard the loaded charter planes. Arriving aircraft could be rerouted or turned back if necessary, but for the moment it was a question of wait and see, take precautions, don't spoil the economy.

The heat rolled across the road in waves, scorching and blistering. In the car, the air conditioning kept them comfortably cool.

"What's the picture right now?" asked Stephanie apprehensively.

"Well, Doctor, as far as we can determine, the group you were on your way to take a look at has swarmed. By all reports it's a big one. The Saudis have told us they intend to close their country to all travel as of noon today. That gives us a chance to get U.S. nationals out.

"This Mahdi and his mullahs are already whipping up a storm, telling the populace this visitation heralds the return of the Prophet, stuff like that. We've had a few reports from inside there, but very sketchy I'm afraid. Don't seem to have been a lot of deaths so far. Once they start, maybe the Bible freaks—Koran freaks—will change their tune and ask for help."

Stephanie pulled a map of the Middle East from her bag and opened it out across her knee.

"Have you got a flight direction yet?"

The grin reappeared. "Sure have, ma'am. We're using every satellite in the sky to follow them. Russian, American, French, you name it."

*"Their flight?"*

"Sorry, Doc," the agent leaned forward and stabbed at the map with his finger. "The Niah Valley, across the Empty Quarter to As Salamiyah in the north, that's south of their capital city. To the west as far as Al Qunfidhah. We don't seem to have a problem yet with the eastern side of Saudi."

"My God, that's an incredible distance," Stephanie muttered as she stared at the coordinates.

"It's an incredibly big swarm, Doctor," replied the agent seriously. "And if that were all we had to worry about, perhaps it wouldn't be so bad. There are several smaller ones around North Africa. Unfortunately we don't know which are the mutants and which are normal locusts at this stage. The only way we can tell the difference is by plotting reports of attacks."

The finger darted out once again. "Here, in the Arabian Sea, northern Ethiopia, the Nubian Desert, El Khargo in Egypt, Al Kufra Oasis in Libya, as well as Marzuq and Sabbah—all reported areas of locust attacks on humans or livestock."

"Nothing further to the south?"

"No, Captain. Just the areas I mentioned."

"How big is the one moving across North Africa?"

"Big, but nowhere near as big as the one in Saudi."

Stephanie was shaking her head in disbelief. "It just isn't possible in so short a time." The beginnings of despair crept into her voice.

"I don't know about that, Doctor. All I know is the satellite put them in those locations in Saudi Arabia just before I left to pick you up. There isn't any mistake!"

"No, I'm sure there isn't, Mr. Edwards, but just the same . . ."

The rest of her thoughts were left unspoken and Holland

turned his attention back to Edwards. "The group that's crossing your sector, where are they now?"

Edwards looked through the window of the car as they turned into the American compound. He looked into the sky as though he expected to see them at any moment.

"Northern Libya. They hit Tripoli about an hour ago. Our agents in the city say it's a bloodbath."

Holland looked in disbelief.

"Dear Christ, man, Tripoli is near the Tunisian border. They could be here within a matter of hours. What's being done?"

Edwards shrugged indifferently. "Not a great deal. The Tunisians are hoping the swarm will bypass this area. I think they half believe it *is* Allah's messengers come to revenge them against Libya and Algeria. Particularly as it is the feast of Ramadan right now. The mullahs that know about it reckon it must be a sign. From what I can ascertain they don't plan to do much more than the Saudis have. Libya has already refused to help, but then that's typical of Kaddafi. He's as much of a religious nut as any of them.

"Doctor, Captain, you'd both better get used to the idea that people in this part of the world seem to prefer to trust in their God than in the United States Air Force. If ever a group of people had a death wish, it's these fucking Arabs!"

Beryl Markham and her husband, David, had not had a vacation for many years. There always seemed to be something else that cropped up on which the money could be better spent. Dentistry for the children, a new roof on the house to make sure their equity was maintained, clothes. Then their old car had broken down. David had to have a new one to get around and visit his customers.

For ten years he had slaved at his small car dealership. Selling was hard work at the best of times, but when you were competing against the giants in the business, you had to work all the harder just to maintain your clients.

Beryl rolled over to allow the Tunisian sun to baste her back. She dug her fingers lazily into the already hot sand and wondered what the children would be doing now. Probably still in bed, the lazy little buggers. They had thought long and hard—Beryl remembered the arguments all too well—before deciding to take a vacation together, alone. They'd had to explain it wasn't because they didn't love the children, but because they simply wanted to go away without them in order to rediscover each other.

Finally, the kids had yielded and enviously seen their parents off to Tunisia from Birmingham airport. And so far it had been a glorious experience.

The complete freedom to go and do just what *they* wanted when they wanted, without having to worry. Beryl rolled onto her side and ran her fingers down David's stomach. He smiled his quiet smile at her through closed eyes and sighed gently. He was happy too, she thought. The last few nights alone in bed without the children in the next room had also been a terrific boost. The thought of his passion aroused her and she moved closer to him.

"Want to go back to the room, love?"

He chuckled. "Christ, Belle, lay off for a bit, eh, you'll wear me out. Why don't you put some more of that suntan oil on me."

Beryl flicked a small pebble at him and reached reluctantly for the bottle: Guaranteed To Keep Off The Harmful Rays Of The Sun While Turning You A Golden Brown—Naturally. She poured the liquid on his chest and leisurely rubbed it in.

When she had finished she nudged David and handed him the bottle. "Now me, please."

David struggled to his knees and began repeating the process. "Lovely place this, eh, Belle?"

"Oh, yes. I'm so glad—get off you little bugger." She slapped hard at her thigh.

"Something bite you?"

"Funny, ha, ha—"

"No, I've got it. It's still alive!"

The pair looked over to where the insect struggled, falling back into the sand in a fruitless attempt at gettting to its feet.

"Christ, Beryl, look at the size of the bloody thing!"

"Never mind that, look at the size of the bloody bite it gave me. Can you get rabies from insects?"

Her husband didn't answer, still engrossed at the sight of the insect maintaining its attempt to get airborne. "It's a locust, is that. I never knew they bit *people*. I thought they was, you know, vegetarians."

Beryl shrieked loudly. David snapped his head in her direction. She was on her feet now, staring open-mouthed along the beach. He followed her gaze and was shocked to see a large number of people running toward them, waving their arms wildly in obvious panic. Directly above the throng he could see a black cloud darting and wheeling over the scampering bodies.

"Oh God, David, let's get out of here," moaned Beryl. Without waiting for an answer she raced from the beach toward the hotel some quarter of a mile away. David, paralyzed, watched for another moment before he too ran after his wife.

Just as he caught up with her stumbling figure, he heard the sound of rushing wings. Suddenly a shadow passed over the hot sand in front of them. He glanced up and back and groaned. In the time it took David to see them, Beryl had fallen into the sand, causing him to trip over her prostrate body.

The shadow descended. Beryl scrambled frantically toward him, reaching with trembling hands for his.

The insects crawled hungrily over the huddled pair, and Beryl screamed, and screamed, and screamed.

# CHAPTER FOUR

*THE MASS SWEPT HIGHER AND HIGHER AND FARTHER AND FARTHER as its shadow spread across the hot desert below.*

*The locusts had tasted flesh and enjoyed the strength derived from the food. The smell of the warm, sticky blood excited them, driving them the harder to search for more in this sparse land.*

*They sensed this was the right direction to find that nourishment. They would need more, much more if they were to make the long, hard journey to the Other Place.*

*Others of their kind were even now moving to the north in steady procession. It was as though they knew this was the correct route, knew why they had to proceed thus, rather than south to the warmer climates.*

*The scouts flew low over the desert floor, attracted by the smell and the wailing that echoed across the sand.*

*They settled on the high walls of the old city and tasted the air with their antennae, collecting the rising aroma of incense and sweat from the mass of bodies below.*

*Then they lifted into the air and sped away from the faithful praying in the Holy City of Mecca. The need of the mutants was great. In this one area they had found a bounty.*

\* \* \*

The communications center at the American embassy in Tunis was busier than at any time since the Cuban missile crisis. A full squad of technicians, military and civilian, manned the consoles that lined every available inch of wall space as well as the transmitters in the middle of the room.

From this double bank of equipment came a constant stream of demands for updated information. Into it went an equally constant supply of news gathered from other centers dotted around the Middle East and Northern Africa.

The scene of ordered chaos would be, even now, repeated in every sizable embassy around the world. The need for information was of paramount importance and the search for material would be pursued by any means possible.

Off to one side, a situation board had been erected so that the radio operators could check immediately the latest position of the two swarms of mutants.

Red crosses were drawn to indicate areas of actual attack against humans—attacks on livestock had quickly become too numerous to handle efficiently.

Blue lines which cut across the map of the African and Gulf regions gave a ready image of the path the swarms had taken. One technician constantly monitored the direct link with Washington, which in turn monitored the feed from satellites sending pictures back to earth stations. If the locusts moved so much as a foot it was noted immediately.

By the time Edwards had ushered Mark and Stephanie into the top security room, the blue lines on the Saudi Arabian portion of the map formed a wide V, with the right fork reaching almost to the capital, Riyadh.

The left had crossed through the town of Al Qunfidhah on the west coast and then shot forward to the north, missing Jiddah completely, but seeming to stop only inches from the ancient city of Mecca.

The swarm's passage across North Africa was similarly indicated, although it was apparent this swarm had not split. The weaving pattern looked for all the world as though a child had scribbled aimlessly across the chart. From the isolated red cross in the middle of the Arabian Sea to northern Ethiopia and the town of Asmara; to the Nubian Desert and then sharp left to the Jebel Abyad Plateau before completing the dog leg to Egypt and El Kharga. Then into Libya and the Al Kufrah Oasis, Marzuq, Sabbah and Tripoli.

Holland quickly scanned the board. He didn't need to have it explained to him, he had seen many such prepared in Korea. If anything, it was the sight of the board and the related activity, rather than what it portrayed, that made him feel suddenly ill at ease.

Shrugging off the feeling, Holland concentrated on the North African swarm, moving up the coast toward Tunis. They were right in the front line.

The technician moved the blue line past the town of Gabes on the Mediterranean coast and another technician added a red cross.

"They are getting close," muttered Edwards, licking his lips. "I hope this place stands up to them. I wouldn't want the little bastards getting into the ventilation system!"

Stephanie turned on the man quickly and screamed, "Fuck you, you shit! What about those people out there? They won't have a chance." Her dark eyes glistened with rage.

Edwards flushed scarlet at the outburst. "Sorry. I didn't mean that the way it must have sounded. I only meant if this station went down, there would be no monitoring . . ."

Holland turned away from them. "That mark near Mecca—how serious?"

Glad for the change of subject, Edwards moved to a desk and flipped through the computer printouts.

"Three or four miles away, if they carried on moving at the same rate as the last time the satellite pinpointed them."

"And Mecca?"

"Crowded for the religious holiday. Everyone wants to see this madman who claims to be the Mahdi."

"Have you warned them?"

"Of course!" Edwards dropped the sheaf of papers on to the desk and walked to Holland's side. "They said thanks but the will of Allah will prevail. The king has taken his family there!"

Holland turned back to the man, struggling to comprehend

what he had said. "You have got to be putting me on! Doesn't he realize what could happen to them?"

Edwards nodded. "He knows. He's not stupid, by any means. He understands what could happen in his country after the locusts have passed them over—if they pass them over—if the king, the defender of the faith, refuses to accept the Koran's prediction.

"You can bet your life he doesn't like it one bit, but his advisors will have told him he has to go to Mecca as normal for Ramadan, even more so now that Allah seems to be on his way back. He is in something of a bind, our friend the King!"

A call from one of the technicians interrupted their conversation. "Mr. Volk calling from London, Mr. Edwards. Wants to talk with you, Dr. Caine."

In moments, they were put through and the familiar Boston accent was coming over the desk speaker.

"Dr. Caine, it would appear we are too late. I trust that you are both safe?"

Holland turned his head in disgust at the forced pleasantries. Stephanie quickly said, "Thank you, yes. What's the picture in London?"

A short laugh came from the speaker.

"Quiet hysteria, I should say. The media broke the news to the public about an hour ago. It seems that a CBS news team was in Riyadh when the first reports started to arrive in the capital. There will be questions in the House of Commons this afternoon and the BBC is interrupting radio programs to broadcast updates."

Holland leaned forward. "Well, at least the public is getting the message. That doesn't seem to be happening in Tunisia."

"Captain, panic could and will kill more people initially than the locusts. Our job is to try to minimize casualties while we search for the solution to the overall problem. Each government will and is making its own mind up about how to handle internal problems relating to crowd control."

"Very nice, Volk," snarled Holland sarcastically. "That gets you ten brownie points for humanitarianism. What are your bright boys doing about it all right now?"

Static scrambled the voice form London and Edwards reached across the console to adjust a dial.

". . . the computer is running a profile at this time on variables such as trade winds in your area, to establish to as fine a degree as possible the scope of the problem. Contingency plans are currently being prepared for countries that are affected or which the computer feels will be affected."

"What *are* the contingency plans, Volk?"

"I can't tell you at this time, but I can assure you we are confident those plans will further slow the mutants' progress."

Stephanie groaned. "They already think Europe is in immediate danger."

"In other words, Volk, you're scared shitless because you haven't got a clue what's going to happen and neither have your people in Washington, or any other fucking place. Am I right?"

Stephanie placed her hand on Holland's arm. The room had gone quiet as the technicians stopped what they were doing to listen. They were as interested in Mark's outburst as they were in the answer to his question.

Volk sighed, the sound carrying clearly across the room.

"Something like that, I suppose. At the moment, North Africa is suffering badly with the infestation, but this will get much worse once the mutants mate with the relatively harmless domestic version. It is the next generation and the ones after which are the real hazard."

Stephanie leaned forward.

"Mr. Volk, what are the preliminary predictions for the swarm in this sector?"

"As far as we can determine, or rather as far as Dr. Starling thinks, the mutants will not at the moment cross the Mediterranean but will either swing south or continue along the coast in search of more food."

"What is the time prediction for total infestation of the continent?"

"Two weeks."

"My God, that's not possible," Edwards muttered, trying to convince himself as much as anyone else.

Holland spoke. "Volk, we know about the ones in this sector—what about the swarm in Saudi Arabia?"

Again the sigh came from the desk speaker. Stephanie glanced anxiously toward it. Volk sounded as though the strain was starting to get to him.

"It doesn't take a cartographer," he said at last, "to see there is no water break to stop them from crossing over onto the main continental landmass. Jordan, Iraq, Syria and Turkey are right in their path and then they can take their pick—left to Europe or right to Russia.

"If they go left, there is no telling the amount of damage that would be done, but we estimate by the end of the year, if nothing is done to stop them, ten million people will die."

Volk's words hit every person in the room like a seldge-hammer blow. To hear what they had all suspected spoken in plain English simply confused the senses. It was as unreal as an old newsreel of a forgotten war.

"And that adds up to the fact that by the end of the week they could be in London," concluded Volk with a ring of resigned finality in his voice. "So I want you both back here as soon as you can get mobile. Edwards, is the plane ready to leave?"

Edwards glanced to a technician who nodded. "Yes, sir, already to go."

"Fine, see that Holland and Dr. Caine get going as soon as possible. That's all."

The connection was broken.

Edwards glanced toward the board. The blue lines were drawing ever closer to Tunis.

"I don't want to worry you folks, but if you are moving now is the time. Captain, do you have a gun?"

"No, why?"

"A hunch. They're getting closer, and regardless of what you saw when we drove into the city, a lot of people knew about the locusts. You can bet they will want to get out of here. We may have trouble getting through to the airport."

"Jesus Christ, that's all we need."

\* \* \*

Edwards was wrong. They had no trouble at all retracing their path from the center of Tunis to the airport. The trouble started when they got there.

Edwards had given Mark a Colt .45 with the caution he should only use the weapon as a last resort. Mark had not wanted the pistol, but now, as he saw the howling mob storming the terminal building, he was glad of the weight in his belt.

A cordon of police and armed soldiers were holding the crowd back and trying to re-establish some semblance of order. Holland knew from experience that very soon the frantic mob would lose patience and beat their way inside.

It would be a futile effort at best; it was doubtful if there were enough aircraft to lift even a quarter of them away from the danger area.

Mark tapped the driver on the shoulder. "We'll never make it through the crowd. Any ideas?"

The driver grinned. "Sure. There's a small track back the way we came. It leads to a security gate. Through the gate and straight over the field to the plane. No sweat, but the Tunisians won't like it much!"

"Screw 'em. Get going."

The driver slammed the vehicle into reverse and drove back down the highway until he found the track. The limousine bounced over the potted road, until finally the driver pointed ahead. "There it is."

Holland was out of the car before it stopped. He walked to the gate and checked the heavy padlock and chain. Looking through the fence he could see the Royal Air Force Boeing 737 which sat waiting to take them back to England.

"I don't suppose you'd have a pair of bolt cutters in the trunk?"

"'Fraid not, Captain."

Holland sighed and heaved the Colt out of his belt. He took two shots before the lock fell to the ground and Holland was able to swing the gates wide. The car rolled forward and he closed the gate behind it.

"Right, let's go."

The driver gunned the engine and raced around the perimeter

of the field toward the Boeing, half a mile away. As they neared the aircraft, Holland sat forward and narrowed his eyes.

"Slow down some," he ordered quietly to the driver. "Do you carry a gun?"

"Yes. What's wrong?"

"The crew is at the bottom of the steps."

"So? Maybe they're having a smoke."

"These are British Air Force, pal. They wouldn't dream of smoking near the plane, and they wouldn't just be standing around. They should be carrying out pre-flight checks right now."

They drew closer. Holland's eyes grew tighter as he recognized the figures of all four crewmen. He turned to Stephanie and pulled her to the floor.

"Trouble ahead. Stay down and don't get out of the car until I tell you. You should be safe enough."

"What makes you think that—"

"The crew is just standing looking up the gangway. Even the steward is on the ground. No way. He'd at least be preparing for the flight."

They pulled to a stop and the driver was out of his door and moving toward the gangway before anyone knew they had arrived. Holland leapt from the back and raced after the man even as the British crew turned in surprise and the copilot started to yell a warning.

"Look out, they've got—"

A shot rang out from the cabin doorway and the crew dived for cover. The captain banged into Holland as they crouched out of gun range beside the steps.

"What's going on?"

"Actually, sir, it all happened in such a hurry I really don't know. All of a sudden three nut cases with guns were ordering us off the plane. That was about half an hour ago. They've been up there ever since. Not doing anything, just standing in the doorway."

"Must be waiting for somebody. Were they in uniform?"

"Yes. Sort of dark green."

"State police. Tough characters. Is there any other way into this baby?"

The captain thought for a moment. "Might be able to get in through the cockpit window if there isn't anybody up there, but otherwise, no."

After the one shot had been fired there had been no others and Mark thought it might be worthwhile to try to talk to the hijackers. He ducked back underneath the belly and told the driver what he had in mind. Then he stepped into the open. From here he could clearly be seen by the people inside, but as he hadn't appeared at the foot of the stairway, Mark hoped it would save him from a bullet in the chest.

He walked forward slowly. Out of the corner of his eye he could see the embassy driver and the copilot moving toward the cockpit. He hoped all eyes would be on him, and the hijackers would momentarily relax their vigilance at the front of the plane.

"Stop right there. That is far enough!"

Holland continued walking forward. He needed to be closer and he wanted to make sure the three men on the plane concentrated their attention on this possible line of attack.

A bullet slammed into the concrete, accompanied by another shouted warning. The next one would hit. He walked two more paces and stopped.

"You have boarded a British aircraft," he called out. "Why?"

"Our need is greater than the British government's," came the reply. They had a point. Holland was close enough now to make out two shadows on either side of the doorway. Where was the third man?

"What need?"

"We know why this plane came to Tunisia and we know it is ready for departure. The only difference from your original plans is that I and my comrades will be departing, not you! Now take your men and that car from this area, or we will open fire."

Suddenly a shot rang out from inside the plane and the man

on the right of the doorway moved forward slightly. The Colt leapt into Mark's hand and he fired.

The body jackknifed and fell through the open door. Holland ran forward and up the stairs before the remaining two could recover.

A machine gun barked and Holland put his head down, swerving as he reached the top stair. The doorway was empty.

The driver's bullet-riddled body lay in the entrance to the flight deck; just in front of him lay the body of one of the hijackers. Two down.

Mark glanced to the right, into the main cabin of the aircraft. Many of the seats had been stripped from the interior to make room for additional cargo. Behind one of these remaining would be the man with the submachine gun.

"Listen to me," called Holland, "you open up with that thing and this whole plane could blow up. Then you won't be able to get out anyway."

"Better than staying to be eaten alive, English!"

Left side, about halfway down. Holland slipped around the curtain, starting to move cautiously toward the area from which he thought the voice had come.

He reached the first emergency exit sign when the man made his move. Holland saw the barrel of the gun appear between two seats and aim toward him.

The Colt bucked, the report sounding like a thunderclap in the confined space. The seat exploded as the bullet tore its way through the padding and the gunman slid into the aisle.

Holland moved in fast, but already the first trickle of blood had begun to seep from the blackened hole in the Tunisian's forehead.

"Come on, let's move it," he called through the cabin door. "Move that car out of the way and let's get the hell out of here."

The copilot and engineer raced up the stairs with Stephanie close behind. The captain paced quickly around the aircraft to make sure there was no critical damage.

They lifted the driver's body out of the plane and carefully laid him in the back of his car and then lowered the bodies of the hijackers to the tarmac. The young copilot looked uncomfortably at Holland for a moment and then, deciding he ought to say something, began, "I'm sorry about your colleague, sir. What was his name?"

"I don't intend to go back for his birth certificate, sonny. The important thing is to get this airplane up. Let's go," he retorted angrily—as much at himself as at the man's discomfort.

They climbed back into the Boeing and Mark shoved the staircase away as far as he could. The captain would just have to manage. Stephanie ran forward as he slammed the outside door closed.

"For God's sake, those people have got onto the field, they're running this way. We must take some of them with us, there is plenty of room."

Holland shouted to the flight deck they were ready and led her firmly back to a seat. They wouldn't be waiting for clearance—there probably wouldn't be anybody in the tower anyway—trusting instead to the abilities of the pilot to steer a course through any incoming aircraft.

The plane reached the end of the runway and Holland looked back through the window at the hordes streaming toward them on foot.

"Why, Mark? Why wouldn't you wait for them?" She was unable to keep the disgust from her voice.

He sighed and yanked the seat belt tighter as the jet raced forward across the uneven runway.

"Stephanie, this plane could, if we pushed it, carry a hundred and seventy people. There were at least ten times that many back there. How would you decide who came? That's even supposing they would let you. It would have turned into a fight like you've never seen. The plane would probably have been destroyed and nobody would have gotten away. They'd fight to get on and fight to stay on. Better this way. Forget it."

# CHAPTER FIVE

THE MULLAHS WALKED AROUND THE BALCONIES THAT ENCIR-
cled the seven minarets set at the corners of the great wall
protecting the Great Mosque and the Kaaba, which housed the
holiest of holy relics. The plaintive wall of the muezzin called
the faithful to prayer and the pilgrims responded by prostrating
themselves in the courtyard before symbols of Islam.

Twenty thousand of the faithful lifted their voices in dutiful
prayer and the sound carried beyond the high walls into the
town that had grown haphazardly around the ancient stones.

Twenty thousand heads rose and fell in unified supplication
to the east and so it was that the flight of the locusts from the
southern region of the city went unnoticed. Even had it been,
the chant would simply have turned to the Muslim prayer: "I
seek Thy protection from Satan and the Accursed." The word
had spread rapidly across the community that Allah's messengers were flying from kingdom to kingdom, spreading the word
that had long been awaited.

Allah would protect the faithful and punish the transgressors.
Allah would doubly protect those in His Holy City. Was this
not the place of the Kaaba? Was not the king, the defender of
the faith, here with the most truly loyal among Allah's servants?
Had not the Mahdi come as had been predicted?

The sun's light was snatched from the sky. The locusts, as one, changed direction and swept down into the town and into the huge square enclosing the mosque.

.

"Mr. President, we have to act and we have to act *now!* The whole balance of power in the Mideast is going to crumble and those damn Russian bastards are sure as hell not going to let the advantage slip away from them. Regardless of what the Saudis say, we have to hit those damn insects wherever we can."

It had been a long cabinet meeting, with opinions split evenly between those who supported the sovereignty of Islamic nations—so the oil taps would not be turned off—and those who advocated immediate steps to ensure that the Russians did not try to take advantage of the upheaval now rapidly spreading across the Middle East.

"General Carthy, I can only repeat. I have talked with the Russian premier, and I am convinced the Russian leaders see the first objective—getting rid of the locusts—as being of prime importance.

"I do not have cause to believe, at this time, the Russians plan to do anything other than cooperate with us in the fight. They have, after all, opened some of their top secret military satellites to us, in order that we can constantly monitor the progress of the creatures. But I agree it is the Russian habit of making capital from adversity and we shall have to watch very carefully that the Soviets don't try to make inroads while the emergency is on. Let's work together where possible—but don't trust them all the way."

General Tom Carthy was a hawk and nothing the Russians did would lessen his distrust of anything tainted by the hammer and sickle. The fact that the Russians had allowed the Americans access to their satellites was beside the point, totally irrelevant.

The general knew there were over two thousand satellites circling the earth at that particular moment, and even without

Russian assistance the American forces would still have been able to keep a constant watch on both swarms. No, it was simply a Russian trick to lull the president into a false sense of security—perhaps to gain access to U.S. military installations. The best course of action when dealing with the Russians was not to deal with them at all. Keep as far away as possible.

Carthy sighed. He had been a member of the joint chiefs of staff long enough to know when an argument was lost. He had attended enough cabinet meetings to sense when a political decision was going to outweigh need for a logical, military one.

"You're the boss, Mr. President, but I still want to say I think you are wrong and I'd like the record to show that."

The president smiled his famous smile. "I understand, General, and it is so recorded. But if *you* are right then maybe nobody will ever read that transcript and if *I* am, than I'd think you wouldn't want anybody to."

General Carthy smiled back at the president. "Touché, Mr. President."

"OK, that's settled then. Now, are the contingency plans ready?"

Carthy shifted and flipped through a folder marked with a heavy red "Top Secret" stamp. "Yes sir. If we are faced in the final analysis with a major catastrophe in the Gulf then our people will move in under the guise of medics and Red Cross workers to secure ports, airfields, and of course all oil installations. Our existing forces on the ground and American military advisers to friendly oil producers have already been advised to keep their powder dry in case they have to move fast to help our forces.

"We do expect, Mr. President, that the Russians will also be making much the same move down through Iran and Afghanistan. It's going to be a race, particularly to secure the Straits."

"I appreciate that, General, but it's essential we secure those areas before the Russians. Let's remember that the American eagle moves faster than a lumbering Russian bear. OK?"

The laughter in the room broke the tension. The president

allowed a few moments for the edginess to dissipate. He often thought of himself as a schoolmaster at these meetings. He knew what should and would be done, while they, the pupils, wanted to take the romantic, dramatic measures they thought would sit well with history and the media.

The president was into the middle of his second term and it was at times such as the present crisis he wished he hadn't allowed his wife to talk him into running again.

But Marilyn loved the cut-and-thrust of Washington politics, reveled in being the First Lady. Even his daughter was starting to act the prima donna at various functions the president had taken her to, against his better judgment.

The president tapped lightly on the huge oval table and gradually the clamorous excitement died.

"For the moment, gentlemen, we shall observe the rights of nations to manage their own internal affairs. However, should these insects threaten American territory or American lives then we shall act, and act with the full force of our capabilities. For the moment it would appear the outbreak areas are confined to Muslim and pro-Muslim countries, and, therefore, we cannot act without serious repercussions."

The president drank the glass of orange juice in front of him before continuing.

"If Iran should become infested then that would ease a troublesome situation. It is therefore advisable we hold back any counterattack until the fullest possible picture is before us. The secretary of state has prepared some figures for us regarding the Christians and other minority groups in the Mid East and at this time it might be worthwhile to hear those. Mr. Secretary?"

The secretary of state cleared his throat and shuffled the papers in front of him before finding the relevant material.

"Thank you, Mr. President. Gentlemen, at the president's request we at State worked on the premise that no Islamic country would call for aid. The thought among Muslims is that these locusts are the bearers of the word of Allah and Muhammad. In other words, that a prediction in the Koran is about to come true; the Prophet is ready to return to Earth.

"Accordingly, we concentrated on determining the number of Christians, Jews, and other minority religious groups in certain countries.

"The figures are as follows: Egypt, seven and a half percent, or three million people; Iran, one percent; Iraq, five percent; Jordan, four percent; Saudi Arabia, one percent; Syria, ten percent; and Turkey, two percent.

"Gentlemen, when put in percentages, those numbers may seem hopeful, but in fact the task we are left with is still quite unmanageable, even with more time. Christians and Jews alone in those countries I have mentioned number nearly five million. That means five million people who might want to get out of the combat areas. If we launch a rescue operation, and use aircraft seating two hundred people each, it would take twenty-five thousand planes to lift them out!

"I leave it to the mathematicians among us to calculate how long such a rescue operation would take to accomplish!"

General Carthy glanced from one of his colleagues to another. He didn't give a shit about those foreigners. Americans were his concern.

"Mr. Secretary, those numbers are mighty impressive and I agree we should protect everyone we can in our own backyard. But what about American civilians and military personnel in the area? What's being done for them?"

The president picked up the question.

"Everything that can be, General. Most of the ten thousand U.S. citizens in the area have already been alerted and arrangements are presently in hand to effect their air lift."

"Mr. President . . ."

The President relaxed into the leather of the chair and allowed his mind to drift back to his own hometown. The hubbub of voices ran around his mind and he heard himself responding automatically while he thought of the peace and quiet he had left behind.

The military mind versus the political mind. None of them had looked at the wider canvas as he had. None had wrestled with the problems over long, sleepless nights.

Yes, the deaths were reaching horrendous proportions and that would continue until an answer could be found. But of equal importance was the damage area which would be caused following the departure of the locusts from any given area. The breakdown of law and order would rank high on the list of things which had to be repaired.

The famine that would spread over any country which depended on the importation of food; the famine in countries which had suffered an initial onslaught. People would want only to protect themselves and their families. No thought would be spared for the maintenance of factories or the continuation of communications or travel.

Half those places could grind to a halt, leaving anarchy, terror and bestiality to stand side by side with the horror of the insects themselves.

The man who hid in the basement with his stockpile of food would have to come out one day. What sort of monstrous environment would he find when he did at last emerge?

The voices drifted further away and the president wondered if he would live through it all. He was so tired, so very tired. And there was the numbness creeping through his limbs. The only thing he really wanted now was sleep.

The SS *Island Princess* was almost at the end of her Mediterranean cruise as she steamed on the last leg of her journey from Cyprus to Liverpool via Sardinia.

Six hundred suntanned, happy passengers and crew had enjoyed the pleasures of their last stopover on the island. Now, some ten hours later, they were heading for the Strait of Gibraltar in preparation for their final run up the Portuguese coast, and home.

Feelings were mixed about the end of the voyage. Some were glad that home and a return to normal were close at hand, while others, perhaps the majority, wished they could go on sailing for the rest of their lives.

Stewards made their customary visits to the occupants of the cabins which had been under their wing during the trip. As they were more than practiced in the art, attempts at extracting final tokens of appreciation from the passengers for services rendered were successful.

Bartenders hurried back and forth faster than at any time on the voyage to make sure they creamed their own maximum profit from an ever-enthusiastic clientele. All in all, for everyone concerned, it had been a most satisfying affair.

The swimming pool was crowded with tanned, and in some cases lithe, bodies rejoicing in a last moment of expensively-bought sunshine.

The captain and officers were relaxing on the bridge in their summer issue clothing. For them also it had been a good cruise. Only one death (an older gentleman who had suffered a heart attack while sampling the bountiful delights of a Sicilian prostitute), one rape of a passenger by a crew member, who swore that he had been encouraged and who would have the chance to tell the Liverpool police all about it, and three cases of card sharping.

Junior Officer Terry Stebbings looked lazily around the mass of oiled bodies on the deck below him and decided this outing had been well up to par. He had scored with eleven women of various shapes, sizes, and appetites during the voyage and one widow, of undoubted income, had even suggested he might profit from leaving the sea and moving to settle in Lancashire with her. He'd stick to the sea.

Stebbings looked around the clear blue sky and luxuriated in the feeling of freedom he felt out here. His gaze wandered to the south, toward where Africa would be, and a puzzled frown creased his brow. Fine weather had been forecast for the next twenty-four hours, and yet here on the horizon was the largest thunderhead he had ever seen.

He drew the phenomenon to the attention of the officer of the day, who studied it briefly through his binoculars before moving inside the bridge to alert the captain.

Captain Thadeus Nelson called for a weather report and upon hearing the initial prediction confirmed, took up his own high-powered glasses and studied the cloud for several moments.

"It's moving fast, gentlemen, whatever it is. Sparks, contact the French authorities at Bordeaux and ask them about it, will you?"

The officers continued to watch the spreading shape as it moved over the gentle swell toward them. At length, the radio operator reported back. "Captain, I couldn't raise anybody at Palma," his voice trembled, "but the naval base in Gibraltar answered the call. They wanted to know what the hell we were doing here. After I explained who we were they asked why we were ignoring the warning to stay out of this sector and if we were aware that locusts—maneaters—are swarming all over it."

The Captain looked in disbelief at the operator. "You have got to be putting me on, Sparks," he said scornfully. "Maneating locusts? It's got to be some radio ham pulling your leg." The officers on the bridge laughed together at the radio man's discomfort.

"Sir," persisted the hapless technician, "I don't think so. He sounded too genuine, too concerned. He also said not just shipping had been warned to stay away, but everything."

"Have you received any such message?"

"No, sir, I haven't, but my relief might have done," replied the operator obstinately. He prided himself on knowing whether messages on the air were false or genuine. Too often some kid would get bored with talking to a radio freak half-way around the world and send a Mayday. But he had always been able to tell the phony ones.

The captain turned and rang the crew quarters on the intercom. In moments he was talking to the night relief operator who had been roused from his sleep. Captain Nelson listened briefly and then slammed the receiver back into its cradle.

"Mr. Stebbings," he roared. The junior officer entered the wheel house and looked quizzically at his fellow officers before facing the captain.

"Sir?"

"You were on duty last night?"

"Yes, sir, dog watch."

"All night?"

Stebbings looked fleetingly around. How much did the captain know? He had slipped off at three o'clock to have a last piece of that gorgeous chick from Southport. O'Reilly had promised to sound the alert if a senior officer came looking for him. No alert meant no one had come. Or had O'Reilly double-crossed him?

"Er, yes sir," lied the officer.

"Bullshit, Stebbings. You probably slunk off to screw one of the passengers in the middle of the shift. But that can wait. I hear that O'Reilly took an 'Eyes of the Captain Only' message last night and that he gave it to you to bring to me. I also understand the message was classified 'Immediate' even if it meant waking me. You haven't given me that message yet, Mr. Stebbings. I'm still waiting for it, am I not?"

Stebbings' heart hit his feet. He had indeed been given the message and wondered why the company was using code which, although not unusual, more often than not signified trouble for someone.

He had meant to go first to the captain's suite, but the thought of Lorraine had made him forget all about it. He could feel the folded message now, like a ton weight in the right-hand pocket of his shorts. He groaned and reached for it.

"Sorry, sir, I forgot," was all he managed to say before his mouth clammed shut under the captain's withering glare.

Nelson tore the paper open and cast a practiced eye over the sequence of numbers and letters that had been radioed with such urgency from London the night before. After several heartbeats he whirled around to the helmsman. "Hard-a-starboard, bring her about one hundred eighty degrees, mister, and fast." He swung back to his officers. "Sparks was right, the message was a warning. The bastards are in this area and we're right in their way." Nelson turned again to the helmsman. "Full speed ahead."

Stebbings looked in horror at the captain and then out through the window and back toward the African coast. The blackness was growing ever larger, its shadows lengthening toward the stern. Through his fear he could hear the murmurings of the passengers below, who by now had realized the ship was turning back the way it had come. Laughter broke out as someone suggested the crew must have mutinied and they were sailing to Mauritius.

Ten minutes later nobody was laughing as the locusts caught up and boarded the comparatively slow-moving ship. The lovely Lorraine ran to her young lover with blood pouring from her beautiful body and insects hanging from her skin. Stebbings couldn't help her; he was dying himself.

The Royal Air Force 737 carrying Mark and Stephanie back to London was over Corsica when the red warning light started flashing impatiently above the copilot's seat.

The Captain checked the source of the problem and then, unbuckling his safety harness, walked through the door which separated the flight deck from the passenger cabin.

"We have a problem. Oil pressure is dropping in the port engine. Corsica is our nearest available airport. We'll be landing as soon as possible."

Holland frowned. "Corsica? I don't think much of that, Captain, we could be stuck there for days before the RAF gets mechanics out. Nice isn't far away, is it?"

"Fifteen minutes on reduced power—why?"

"Can we make Nice?"

"We could, but I am under standing orders to land at the nearest airport in cases of emergency. If we lose the other engine—"

"I know that, but we have to be mobile. Corsica isn't any good. Please, head for Nice!"

The captain studied Holland for a long moment. In any case of emergency it was up to him to make the decision. Under no circumstances should he, or would he, be influenced by outside forces. But there was something about this man, something in the eyes that brooked no opposition to his request. And while they had been on the ground at Tunis, they talked with the air traffic controllers. He had heard about the locust swarms, what they could do.

There had also been the attack on the plane, the hundreds of terrified people who had swarmed across the runway. That could be repeated on a small island like Corsica.

"Nice it is then," he said.


By contrast to the bedlam of the airport at Tunis, it was like landing on another planet.

Gendarmes nodded politely and grasped hands with their colleagues in the French manner of greeting, cars raced along the wide boulevards and along the sea front, not in panic, but in their normal frantic haste to get from here to there in the shortest possible time.

A cursory inspection of the port engine revealed one of the fuel lines had been fractured. A mechanic extracted a large lump of flattened lead and handed it to the captain with a quizzical look. The Air Force captain grunted. The machine-gun bullet could have killed them all long after the weapon's owner had died.

The airport police arranged for rooms at the Imperial for six and sped them there in two black Citroen cars.

Stephanie had the room next to Mark's. He showered quickly, luxuriating in the feel of the water against his skin. As he toweled himself dry he looked out across the busy sea front, his gaze drawn irresistibly toward the horizon. But the sky remained a mocking blue, and because the windows shut out all external sounds, he suddenly felt a great distance from his surroundings, as if this whole thing were happening to someone else. Then he heard the connecting door open, and the whisper of cotton as she came to lean against him.

"It's all crazy, isn't it?" she whispered. "It's not happening to us, it can't . . ."

He looked down and saw tears begin to glisten. She had tied her hair back, drawing it tightly to the nape of her neck. Somehow, it emphasized the untold pain that lingered in her eyes.

"Mark," she said.

"Yes?"

"Love me."

# CHAPTER SIX

THEY PASSED THE NIGHT IN AN EXHAUSTED, COMA-LIKE SLEEP, their bodies drawing strength from the cool darkness.

The telephone jangled, causing Holland to snap awake. Reaching for the offending instrument as he sat up in the king-sized bed, he could see the sunlight streaming in through a gap in the curtains. It must be close to ten o'clock.

"Holland! It's Volk." The urgent tone in Volk's voice caused Mark to sit fully upright.

"What's the matter?"

Volk almost groaned, his voice sounding raw with what Holland imagined was a night without sleep and irritated by too many cigarettes. "Everything. The locusts have joined up in one almighty swarm and no one really seems to know what to do next. The advice and the ideas are flying about like chaff in a wind storm. To add to all the problems the president had a heart attack last night and the fear is the Russians might decide now is a pretty good time to attack the West. Your aircraft is ready, get out to the airport. You can be in London in just under three hours."

Stephanie stirred and snuggled back into the warmth of his

body. He shook her and she, grudgingly, opened her eyes before struggling into an upright position, allowing the sheets to fall away from her. Her skin seemed to glow in the morning sun. He reached for his pack of cigarettes and spoke deliberately into the telephone. "What do you mean the locusts have joined forces?"

The question was more for Stephanie's benefit than anything else and the sudden, wide-awake look on her face told him it had registered. She leaned on his shoulder so she could hear Volk too.

"They didn't rest during the night as we anticipated. They just kept right on. The Saudi swarms joined up again in the northwest corner of the country. They just flew straight out over the Mediterranean. The North African swarm left Tunisia, Libya and northeast Algeria at about the same time, heading in the same direction.

"Starling has plotted the course and it looks as though, if maintained, they will all meet up."

"Where?"

Volk's uncharacteristic chuckle sounded ominous. Was Volk cracking up? "Believe it or not, right where you are now, the south coast of France. But that's only the head. The tail covers the toe of Italy, Sicily, Sardinia, Corsica, Crete and even Corfu to the north. It's a massive cloud.

"And they'll be hungry when they get there! Starling says they are not following normal habits. Instead of eating their way across, they appear to be flying until hungry and then settling down to eat.

"Incidentally, you knew the Saudi king didn't you?"

"I met him once or twice. Why?"

"He's believed to be dead. Word just came from Mecca. A real nasty mess. Anyway, I want you and Dr. Caine to get moving as soon as you can. I presume you can pass on the message." His sarcasm was ill-concealed.

The sound of sirens in the street outside reached their ears and soon the clamor of police, army, fire trucks and ambulances racing along the coast road made hearing difficult.

"I can hear that, Holland. The French are a bit more organized than normal. We judge you have two hours before the swarm hits your area. See you in London."

Holland replaced the receiver quickly and sprang out of bed. "We don't have much time."

Stephanie stayed where she was. Holland turned as he realized she hadn't moved.

"What's the matter?"

"I was just thinking—all we are doing is running ahead of them. Sooner or later they will catch up with us and then there will be nowhere else to run."

Holland moved back to the bed. "Stephanie," he said softly, "we'll worry about that when it happens. Right now you can do more good by hightailing it back to London and helping to work on the research than sitting here getting paranoid."

She looked into the level blue eyes and smiled. "You're right. I suppose it's the sense of family guilt. I'll get ready."

She threw back the covers and Holland aimed a playful slap at her naked backside. "That's better. I'll call the others."

Fifteen minutes later they had left the hotel. The RAF crew had checked out some two hours before. The taxi sped along the sea road toward the airport and Stephanie sat close to Holland, glad now of the strength of the man. She stared across at the Mediterranean. Somewhere out there . . . The sandy beaches were crowded with sunbathers, oblivious of the screaming sirens which now filled the road in both directions.

Stephanie wondered how the people could ignore the broadcasted warnings in favor of working on their tans. She gazed back out toward the horizon and gasped involuntarily.

She gripped Mark's arm and pointed south. A cloud, irregularly shaped, seemed to be flowing across the sky like oil running down steps.

Mark nodded, then glanced at the crowded beaches. He leaned across to the driver.

*"Arretez, monsieur, s'il vous plait."*

The bored driver shrugged and pulled over to the side of the street.

"Stay here," Holland shouted as he dashed from the cab. He didn't know if he could do anything, but he had to try. He raced to a set of steps leading to the beach and quickly ran down them. She ignored his command, and followed.

People stretched along the golden expanse as far as the eye could see. It would be an impossible job to move them all, but perhaps some would listen. It was the only hope. Holland stood on a block of concrete that stood above the level of the sand. Taking a deep breath, he shouted through cupped hands.

"Listen to me. You are all in danger. Clear the beach, the locusts are swarming toward this area now. Clear the beach!"

Someone laughed and another jeered. He glanced around quickly and saw several people avert their eyes in embarrassment at his supposed madness. Stephanie came up to join him.

"Goddam it, you are in danger. Clear the beach!" she repeated, angry and frustrated by their indifference.

"Are they crazy, Daddy," sang out a child's voice. Holland turned with blazing eyes. A family of four was sitting nearby and his sudden turn caused the woman to draw her two children closer to her as though to protect them. He ran over to her.

"Listen to me. Unless you want those kids dead within the next half hour you'd better get off this beach."

One of the children began to cry.

The father scrambled indignantly to his feet. "Now look what you've done, you madman. Get the hell away from here before I—"

Holland didn't let him finish. He grabbed him by the shoulders and swung him around to face out to sea.

"See that?" he shouted. *"That's* the reason you have to get away from here. *That's* why you have to take those poor kids undercover. Those sirens up on the road—do you think it's all a joke?"

The man looked out to sea, uncomprehending, then turned back to Holland. "We're on vacation. . . ." he said helplessly.

The woman scrambled to her feet. "Joe, I'm scared. Something is going on. I think we ought to get the children back to the hotel."

Joe remained where he was, feeling the situation slipping away from him.

"Stay in one room and make sure that the shutters and

windows are closed," Mark ordered. "If any of them get in make sure you kill them right away."

The cloud was nearer. They looked around the beach. Others who had been sitting nearby and had heard his conversation were also starting to move.

Two dozen or so people were now running toward the road, intent on getting back to their hotel rooms and the relative safety which they offered. The excitement caused would now spread, more would leave the packed beaches. But Holland knew inevitably still more would stay.

Reaching the taxi, he fell inside, then turned to Stephanie. "Why wouldn't they listen?"

She shook her head.

The taxi raced along the road, continuing its journey. Darkness seemed to be falling and the driver looked constantly through the windshield at the huge cloud that grew ever larger, ever nearer. He muttered softly to himself and finally slowed the car to a stop ten miles from the airport. He turned to Holland.

"I do not like this. I go no further!" he stated in flat Gallic tones.

Holland smiled and rested the long nose of the Colt .45 on the back of the man's neck. "All the way, buddy," he growled.

The driver jerked back, outraged at the sight of the weapon. "I do not like what is happening. I have family, I go now to them."

"*After* we've been to the airport." Holland waved the gun to indicate they should get moving.

The Frenchman looked at him, then toward the gun, before shrugging and turning back to the wheel.

At that moment, the hailing began—beating a rythmic tattoo on the metal roof of the car. Holland reached across Stephanie and proceeded to wind the window up on her side, calling to the driver to do likewise.

Marcel Beauchamp was not a coward and he recognized that the American was more interested in winding the windows up than he was in Marcel. Cat-like, he reached out and swept the Colt aside with his right hand while opening the driver's door with his left. He was not going to sit in the same car with a crazy American who played around with guns. Marcel had been raised in Algeria and knew all about locusts. They couldn't hurt you. The crazy American could!

Marcel bounded away from the car and Holland scrambled frantically over the seat to pull the door shut.

The tattoo increased to a frenzy and the road itself appeared to be alive as the locusts landed, exhausted and hungry from their flight.

He slammed the door and quickly wound up the window. Stephanie screamed and pointed through the glass. Marcel was frantically slapping at his shoulders and face as he fought to stop the locusts from shredding his skin.

Four locusts crawled through the right quarter window and Holland reached over and opened the glove compartment before scooping the intruders up and shoving them into it. He clicked the compartment shut. "You've got your samples," he muttered.

Then he started the Fiat and slipped it into gear. Marcel had now fallen to the ground, covered with the clicking insects. Holland could see movement and he hoped they would not be too late.

He drove the car straight toward the taxi driver and leapt from it, scattering insects from the body. Marcel was still breathing, but Mark felt sickened by the sight of the man's torn and bloody face. An eye socket gaped emptily at him.

Stephanie quickly opened the back door and helped pull him inside, covering her suit with blood. Mark slammed the rear door and felt a searing pain on his neck. He slapped hard and felt the cold body of the locust that was tearing at his skin. Another sharp pain, and then another and finally he was in the car.

The pain slashed its way across his face. Stephanie reached out to pull one of the locusts from his cheek. The soft flesh stretched like molten cheese as the body of the insect was pulled away, but the teeth maintained their hold.

Mark fished into his jacket pocket and handed her his cigarette lighter. "Burn them off."

She fired the flame and held it under the one nearest his ear. His hair caught fire briefly, then the locust crackled and released its hold. It smelled like decomposing meat. She quickly repeated the exercise with the other two on his face and the one on his neck.

He turned, blood running down onto his shirt as she finished. Two of the insects were attacking her bare forearms. He grabbed the lighter from her trembling hand and stabbed at them with the flame.

"For Christ's sake," he shouted in rage, "why didn't you say—"

Marcel groaned. "Mark, he needs help. We haven't got anything to patch him up with; he needs a doctor."

Holland put the car in gear and drove off. The nearest medical aid would be at the airport.

Cars slithered and crashed into one another as drivers fought unsuccessfully to steer over the insect bodies that carpeted the road surface. The stench was overpowering. Mark drove as though the road were covered in black ice and after a torturous forty minutes he suddenly found the way ahead was clear. The locusts had concentrated on the busier areas of the town.

He pulled the cab to a halt outside the small, red-brick police station and raced inside. In moments, three police officers were hauling Marcel out of the back and placing him on a stretcher. He was more dead than alive.

A police inspector escorted Stephanie and Holland to a car and drove them across the field to the waiting Boeing. Its engines were already idling in anxious readiness for an immediate take-off.

"*Capitaine* Holland, Londres requested we give you every assistance. Your flight is ready for immediate departure, but I think you and Madame should see a doctor?"

Holland quickly shook the inspector's hand as they got out of the car. "No thanks. Madame can patch us up with the first aid kit on board." Then he asked, "How bad is it, Inspector?"

"Terrible. They came faster than we thought. We did not have time to warn everybody."

Holland nodded and slammed the door. Stephanie was already halfway up the steps to the aircraft, clutching the tin box the police had given her. It contained the specimens they'd trapped in the glove compartment. She listened for a moment to the beating of their wings against the metal.

As the door to their aircraft slammed, locking into position, the man Mark had told to hide with his family in a shuttered room was busy shoving pieces of newspaper and bed linen into cracks under the door of the children's bedroom.

Joe and his wife had manhandled the children, unceremoniously, across the wide street which separated Nice's major hotels from the beach, dodging and darting to miss, and be missed, by screaming vehicles which drove at full speed, sirens blaring, impervious to the scuttling, crab-like figures of the tourists now pouring from the beach.

At the entrance to the hotel Joe and his wife had stopped and turned to look back at the advancing cloud. Still unconvinced, they fully expected to walk sheepishly back across the road and resume their places on the rented beach mats in an area designated strictly for patrons of the Montpeleier Hotel. Though the man and woman who had screamed the warning seemed sincere enough, Joe was convinced it was either a case of stupid trickery or, more likely, a matter of overreaction.

The cloud had reached the beach area now. He could hear several screams drifting toward him over the roar of the speeding emergency vehicles. He watched with drawn breath as an ambulance sped around the slight curve to the left of the hotel and wobbled slightly. Joe had seen the carpet of locusts covering the road being squashed quickly by the tires of other vehicles which, in turn, had difficulty gaining traction on the now oily surface of the hot road. The ambulance was in difficulty and, as a bus driver, he knew the lock on the wheels was all wrong if the driver hoped to avoid skidding uncontrollably when he hit the straighter part of the road.

The ambulance slid sideways for what seemed an eternity as the driver fought for control, and then, inexorably, toward a group of people frantically waiting to cross the road. Joe and his wife saw the horrified looks on the frozen faces and then the blue and white ambulance smashed into them before jamming itself against one of the familiar palm trees which lined this beautiful avenue.

Then they saw that the locusts really were a bigger threat than they had imagined. A pair of scantily-clad young women rushed into the road intent on reaching the safety of the hotel, swatting and screaming at the insects as they flew around their heads and ripped at the bronzed, oiled skins. Joe watched in horror as one of the girls suddenly threw a hand to a torn and bleeding cheek while the second collapsed to the ground and was quickly covered with a crawling carpet of snapping, tearing insects.

All this happened in less than a heartbeat, but to Joe it was as though all the horrors of a lifetime had passed before his eyes. He gripped his wife anxiously by the arm and almost in a whisper urged her to move. "They were right, Moira, these things are maneaters. Get the kids upstairs, quick!"

The children's room was before theirs on the second floor and they raced headlong up the wide staircase, pushed and shoved by others intent on securing a safe haven, and pushing and shoving in turn those weaker than they.

They almost fell into the room. Moira screamed at the sight of half a dozen of the insects settling already on the window sill. The locusts raised their heads slightly at the noise, and inquisitive antenna twirled in the air to locate the succulent vibrations of human meat tainted with that most delicious of all scents, fear. Joe rushed forward and with one hand swept the insects from the ledge, slamming the large French windows shut.

The two children sat huddled at the corner of the bed, holding each other in total bewilderment. Gradually they began to sob as their father screamed at his wife to plug the gaps under the door to the room while he tore strips of bedding to wedge between the cracks of the window. And then the main body of locusts arrived!

They rattled against the glass and Joe held his family close to him as they watched in terror the thousands of bodies slam-

ming against the fragile glass panes. Moira looked to her husband with an unspoken question and he smiled weakly,
understanding her concern. "The glass should hold out OK. I
don't know if they are flying blind or really know we are in
here."

The room was darkening rapidly because of the mass blocking the daylight. They sat together listening to the cacophony
of wings and bodies against the glass and the shrill squeaking
which emitted from millions of tiny throats. From the hallway
they heard a sudden scream of anguish and terror as a woman
pleaded with a husband to help her. An unseen door slammed
as the husband saved himself; gradually his wife's screams
turned to moans and then they heard nothing.

At length, daylight seemed to creep up the walls and almost
imperceptibly the assault on the window panes slowed. Except
for the occasional lone locust appearing they could see nothing
but a slimy yellow liquid oozing down the glass to testify to
the suicidal determination of the little bodies.

Joe walked carefully over to the window as though he were
afraid that if they saw him they would renew the attack on his
family. He sidled around the window frame glancing outward.
Several dozen injured and dead locusts lay on the small balcony,
crushed by their fellows in the onslaught on the room. Joe
thought briefly of saying a prayer in thanks at the family's
salvation. He strained to peer over the rim of the metal railing
which surrounded the balcony and at last he was able to see a
portion of the street below. It teemed with locusts. He watched
in an almost hypnotic state as they swayed this way and that,
exploring the bodies of his fellow vacationers, tearing hungrily
at the exposed flesh. He glanced at his watch; fifteen minutes
was all the time that had passed and yet it seemed like a lifetime.
He turned away from the window and looked steadily at his
wife.

"They don't seem to be interested in us anymore; there's
plenty for them outside." He moved back to the bed and sat
down beside his wife and draped a comforting arm around the
children.

"Look, we don't know how long it'll be until we can go outside, but they didn't get in the first time and I honestly don't think we have too much to worry about. I'll ring downstairs and see what we should do next. OK?"

Moira nodded silently and was only vaguely aware that her little boy was tugging at her sleeve. Finally she looked at him and smiled. "Yes, Christopher, what is it, dear?"

"I wanna go the toilet," explained the six-year-old.

Moira nodded absently as she watched her husband walk to the table and lift the receiver. He jiggled it a few times and then turned toward her with an exasperated look. A puzzled look crossed his face as he saw his wife and daughter. Where was Christopher? He glanced wildly around the large room and saw the boy opening the door to the toilet.

As Christopher pushed open the door into the bathroom he froze rigid with fear at the same time as his father shouted the warning, "NO!" He dropped the telephone and stepped forward, afraid that his son's immobility indicated just what he had feared when he saw the door to the bathroom. Nobody had checked the window in there!

He reached the boy and placed a hand on his shoulder to reassure him. As he did so, he glanced inside the room to confirm what he knew he would see, had known by the look of sheer horror on the boy's face.

Inside, locusts hung and sat from every available surface, like catkins on a tree waiting for the slightest breeze to send them scurrying here and there to propagate the earth. They sat on the edge of the open window, in the bathtub, on the sink, around the toilet, glaring at the intruders.

Joe held his breath as he extended his reach for the door handle aware of the malevolence in the staring eyes. The silence was ominous and he felt the bile rising in his throat as he pulled gently on his son's shoulder to move him back into the room so that he could close the door fully. The boy couldn't move. He remained frozen to the spot incapable of following his father's insistent pulling, mesmerized by the sight of the creatures staring with such longing.

Joe broke the spell. "Step back, son," he muttered, "I've got to close the door."

Moira was awakened from her transfixed stare by the sound of his voice and she screamed for her son to come to her.

The locusts awoke at the same instant, swarming for the open door. Joe pulled the boy roughly back and dragged the door toward him. As Christopher felt himself yanked backwards he also felt one of his sandals fly off his foot with the exertion of being pulled so unceremoniously. The door suddenly stopped and Joe howled as he saw the obstructive sandal wedged strategically to allow safe passage to the locusts.

"Outside, quick!" he yelled even as the insects bit through his skin, tasting the rich blood. Moira lunged for the door to the hall and sobbed loudly when it refused to open. They had done a good job of wedging newspaper into the cracks. The heavy wooden door was jammed.

The woman fell on her daughter in a vain attempt to protect her and she felt the presence of her son struggling to get underneath her and away from the snapping creatures. She was vaguely aware that her husband was falling to the floor covered with locusts. Then her son screamed with pain as an exposed ankle provided more nourishment.

At length the children ceased screaming and through bloodied eyes she watched with detached interest as the locusts fed on her children and on Joe. She had reached and passed her own threshold of pain and she studied with curiosity her own legs as they were torn to the very bone.

And then she, too, died.

# Book Three

# GETHSEMANE

*And the locusts went up over all the
land of Egypt, and rested in all the
coasts of Egypt . . . before them there
were no such locusts as they.
For they covered the face of the whole
earth, so that the whole land was
darkened; and they did eat every herb
of the land and all the fruit of the
trees and there remained not any green
thing through all the land of Egypt.*

Exodus 10

# CHAPTER ONE

*IT WAS GOOD. THE STRENGTH HAD RETURNED, THEY WERE GATH-*
*ered again as one.*

*Thirty million eyes watched, and waited.*

*The long flight over the water had been taxing, but had*
*served to cull the swarm of its weakest members. Now, the*
*most powerful, the most resilient remained to embark on the*
*longer journey still to come.*

*They understood that they must not delay too long. The first*
*abdomens were beginning to swell with eggs. Soon, others of*
*their breed would join them. They knew the others were coming,*
*they felt them. Then they would be truly ready.*

"My dear Lord, look at the state of you both!"

Dr. Starling bustled forward solicitously as they entered the
control room deep below the American embassy in London.

They had been given a police escort from the RAF airport
at Northolt to Grosvenor Square. All the officers carried side-
arms. Nowhere but in England could the sight be more dis-
turbing.

They joined the heavy traffic on the North Circular Road

and crawled past the deserted parking lots and factories that stretched along the industrial corridor around London. Military vehicles raced along the highway, truckloads of soldiers scything their way toward the business areas. Automatic rifles between their knees boded ill for anyone found guilty of riots and looting.

Ambulances, both civil and military, scurried like frenzied ants to predesignated stations in preparation for the expected assault. Their driver told them radio and television stations had been full of the news of the locust attack on the French Riviera and a provisional state of emergency was in force throughout Great Britain.

As far as the population seemed to be concerned, the full emergency was already with them. Lines formed outside bakeries, arguments raged at supermarkets, liquor stores ran empty of stock, hardware stores enjoyed a boom in the sale of everything from reinforced glass to chicken wire, lumber yards realized they couldn't get more wood and the chance of a quick fortune was quickly realized, quickly taken. Gun shops ignored the law and sold shotguns, handguns and hunting knives until the police moved in and impounded their stocks. Everywhere it was the same. No class distinction now. Titled ladies fought with former servants over items they both thought would either protect them against the initial attack or be valuable afterwards.

Afterwards! The feeling of doomsday was everywhere. This was the Armageddon the Bible had predicted. Not the nuclear holocaust every politician and armchair statesman had forecast. Insects! Rotten, lousy little cabbage-eating bugs had suddenly come to teach mankind the danger of extremes—extremes in nuclear tests, air pollution, sea pollution, the birth control pill, aerosol sprays and drinking too much. With the philosophy of one who spent most of his working life breathing other people's carbon monoxide fumes, the driver appreciated the irony.

They had looked on at the scenes of panic, sensing the impending violence that permeated the air. The car stopped at the signal from a military policeman, allowing a south-bound convoy to cross the intersection. The occupants of the Humber watched with horror as three youths beat a man to the ground.

It was robbery in daylight, but they weren't after the victim's wallet. The large bag of groceries he had been carrying was swiftly spirited away by his assailants, leaving the man on the ground spitting useless teeth into the gutter.

"Happening all the time now," explained the driver. "White against black, black against yellow, black against black. No more of this 'brother' crap. Everyone's looking out for number one and it's going to get a damn sight worse before it's finished.

"I hear there's riots in the Midlands. Half of Birmingham's been set on fire . . . s'pose that can't be bad though, eh?"

And it had all happened so quickly. Three short hours ago they had lifted off from Nice to fly to a London quickly taking on the appearance of a city under siege.

"Started to happen last night," reported the driver. "Notting Hill suddenly flared up. Seems the Muslim community started to preach the Big Man was coming back and they should all get ready. Course, everyone knew about the trouble out in the Middle East and it only needed some smartasses to let on they were heading this way and you had yourself a full-fledged riot."

"Many hurt?"

"Hundreds. Maybe even thousands, who knows? The paratroop regiment collected forty bodies this morning—half of them with knife wounds. It looks like a lot of people used the riot as a chance to settle old scores. The army shot about a dozen or so who wouldn't stop chucking Molotov cocktails and generally behaved like bad lads.

"Anyway, that really set things going. Little, bordering on *no* chance at the moment of stopping the sort of thing we just saw. We had a couple of officers early this morning torn to pieces by looters. The idea is to seal the city, you know, occupy all the strategic points, and then clear up later."

Stephanie glanced at Mark. "Do you mean *after* the locusts have attacked London, officer?"

The policeman looked uneasily at her reflection in the rearview mirror. "What do you think, Miss?" he said.

Grosvenor Square was sealed off to traffic. The police driver was forced to maneuver through two checkpoints, manned by capable looking Red Berets, before they were able to pull into the wide square and drive around to the United States embassy.

The block-long building stood forlorn among the wreckage of a siege. Broken glass still littered the sidewalk and sooty marks blossoming darkly on the facade testified to the use of gasoline bombs. Holland looked to the police officer for an explanation.

"One of those 'Better Red than Dead' groups. Hell of a battle, but unfortunately for some of them they broke through the main doors. Your marines were in no mood to tolerate Communists charging a U.S. embassy."

The statement had been flat and devoid of emotion and Holland got the impression this guy had himself been through a rough night. He acknowledged the officer's salute and stared back at the front of the building. It looked more like a rundown shack in a banana republic. He could just imagine the grim smiles on the faces of the marines on guard inside as the protesters surged into the building. A year ago—hell, two days ago—it would have been unthinkable for them to open fire.

"We're fine, Doctor, really."

"My dear girl, you do not *look* fine," muttered Starling anxiously. He turned to Holland. "I thought the idea was that you were going along to take care of her?"

Stephanie stepped in quickly. "Doctor, I'm a big girl now, really."

Reluctantly, Starling changed the subject. "I understand from Mr. Volk you have some samples to show us after all."

She handed the scientist the metal box she had nursed on the trip from France. "Be careful," she said wryly, favoring her cuts. "They bite!"

Starling patted her arm. "Well done, my dear. These are the best live specimens we have been able to get our hands on." He turned to leave the room and then, remembering Holland, turned back. "Oh, Captain, thank you."

"You two look terrible," Volk observed. They found the CIA agent in the situation room and both were struck by his gaunt condition.

"You don't look so hot, either," retorted Holland.

"Yeah, sleepless nights don't do a lot for a guy's appearance, do they? On top of everything else, my ulcer is starting to act up."

A medic walked purposefully into the room. After looking around, he marched toward Holland and Stephanie. "Roll your sleeves up, please!"

"What for?"

"Tetanus. Those bites could turn nasty."

Holland surrendered his bare arm to the marine who swiftly administered the drug. He repeated the operation on Stephanie before bustling self-importantly away.

"How's the president, Volk?"

"He was taken to Walter Reed right after the attack and he seems fine at the moment. As a matter of fact, he's discharging himself from there just about now, against all advice from the doctors. Typical ex-navy man, wants to be a hero. His heart attack couldn't have come at a worse time from the public relations viewpoint. You've seen what's happening in London. Well, I just hope the situation doesn't repeat itself. Those guys have screwed it up all along the line."

"That sounds kind of cynical."

Volk glared at Mark through red, tired eyes. "Does it? Well maybe it's time for a little cynicism. God alone knows how many have died already and how many more are going to because the president and his liberal friends were afraid to take action. We should have blasted them in Saudi Arabia while we had the chance."

He pointed across the room to a large illuminated screen that showed the land mass from Iran to England. The screen was operated by computer feedout which constantly updated the information, displaying it in visual form.

"The shaded areas are locusts, not where they hit, but where they still are. Thin on the ground in Algeria, heavy in Tunisia, Libya and Egypt. Black as night over the Mediterranean, southern Italy and the Riviera between Monaco and Toulon. You can see the lines starting to move north toward Grenoble and west toward Montpellier."

Volk wiped a hand over his forehead. "There was no need for this to happen. If we'd only taken the initiative we could have stopped them out in the desert."

"The 'if only' could also apply to you guys," replied Holland testily. "If only the CIA hadn't tried to screw around with nature this would never have happened. You and your agency are as much to blame for this nightmare as anyone."

Volk glared at Holland with a look that bordered on hatred.

"Blame, Holland? What is blame? If you want to start laying this at someone's doorstep, then be a little more specific when you start dispensing blame. Put part of it with the U.S. government because they don't know enough about what agencies like mine are doing, part with the CIA for wanting to ensure biological experimentations continued so we wouldn't fall behind the Russians and the mad dictators in the world who want to swallow it with their lust for power. Put part with the greedy Arabs who are not satisfied with a reasonable price and hold the West for ransom with their oil, part with the scientists who want to constantly stretch the barriers of human understanding. And then put a part with the driver who wants to run his car and his central heating, the manufacturer who needs oil and petroleum byproducts to keep his factories in production and give the average guy a job so he can go into the market place as a consumer.

"Blame? You wouldn't know where to begin putting it, Holland, even if you really knew what it was. It's only when something like this happens the public starts to get a glimpse of what is going on in the *real* world. They're shaken out of their apathy and forced to take a look at what's going on in their name. Then they scream. All the bleeding hearts start saying 'this is terrible, it must stop and never be allowed to happen again.' But tell them they have to walk to work because there's no more gasoline for their big cars, or tell them to turn the thermostat down ten degrees to save oil and they say 'you must do something.'

"Blame? Bullshit, Holland. We're *all* to blame!"

Volk wiped a trace of spittle from his lips and slumped

down into his chair. After a moment he looked up and smiled sheepishly.

"Sorry about the outburst. I guess I'm a little strung out at the moment."

Mark and Stephanie sat down. She had just come into the room wanting to murder Volk for his part in what they had just experienced. Now, for the first time, she sensed he needed help.

Volk was silent for a while, then he looked up. "I guess I'd better bring you up to date. The British government is preparing to declare martial law, as are most of the other European countries. France has already done so. Key personnel are being moved to safe areas to ensure continuity of government after any attack."

Holland couldn't forget the locusts on the road, the sight, the sound, the smell or the image of the taxi driver's torn and bloody face.

"For what? The way things are going there won't be a damn thing to govern in a month!"

"We all have to work on the assumption that this situation will not become a terminal program. There is a good chance this problem will not overescalate before we can find the solution. On that premise we have to prepare for as smooth a transition back to normality as possible."

Volk suddenly changed the subject. "Well, what do you think of our Eagle's Lair, Holland? You should feel honored, it's not everyone who gets the chance to visit this facility."

Holland looked around the large room. Banks of sophisticated equipment were monitored constantly by white-coated technicians who hurried, wordlessly, around the metal machines like so many worker bees in supplication to the queen, in this case the huge IBM computer spread along one entire wall.

Overshadowing the whole, the huge screen, the eye with which the technicians could see any part of the world and monitor anything they chose from Russian nuclear submarines to tribal warfare in Zaire. Now it was an invaluable aid in plotting the progress of the locust swarms. While they had been talking, the lines on the screen had grown.

"They've reached Montpellier and Grenoble," Volk said quietly.

The screen showed a solid black band stretching across the triangle formed between Monaco, Grenoble and Montpellier with lighter gray areas along the coast towards the Pyrenees. The Mediterranean was almost clear. The bulk of both swarms was now over European soil.

Even as they watched, the lines darted further out from the triangle. The new arrivals were moving into virgin territory.

A telephone jangled and Volk swore. He took a small key from his pocket and swiftly opened a drawer in the desk in front of him. He pulled out a red telephone and using another key released the security lock that prevented unauthorized use. He lifted the receiver to his ear, taking a deep breath as he did so. "Yes . . . no, we don't . . . no. Well, sir, put him on."

Volk listened to the voice from Washington for a moment longer, then leaned over the telephone to punch a sequence of buttons on the desk console. The room speakers came alive with a crackle as Volk addressed the president.

"You can now be heard by everyone in this position, Mr. President."

Activity stopped on the floor below as all heads turned toward the wall speakers. The cultivated accent, made familiar by radio and television, purred across the command center.

"Ladies and gentlemen, I have to say we here in America are very concerned that a solution so far has not been found to this very grave problem. As you are aware, the world scientific community is pooling all its talents, all its resources, and all its spirit in the search for a responsible solution to this situation.

"I just wanted all of you there in London to know how very much we value your contribution to this fight. But I must also say to you that we believe it is of paramount importance to the continental United States that you maintain your posts, in order that we can know on a minute-by-minute basis just what the overall picture is.

"I know that we can count on you in this fight. God bless you all, and with His help we shall overcome."

The speaker crackled once more and then went dead as Volk cut the connection.

Holland had only half listened to the president's morale-boosting chat to the men in the trenches. He had been watching the lines spreading and merging on the big screen like waves on a beach.

He leaned forward, puzzled at what he thought he was seeing. At length, he caught Volk's attention.

"Look at the way those things are spreading."

Volk studied the map for a moment, then asked irritably, "So?"

Mark pointed with his finger. "No activity north of the town of Grenoble, right? Yet you can see them moving west toward the Rhône River. In the south they are moving toward Toulouse—again, that's west. They are as far as Monaco and then they stop. Northern Italy is clear yet you would assume they would flood into that region, since it's very fertile. And Spain is completely clear of any activity. The locusts have stayed on the north side of the mountains, on the French side, but wouldn't it have been easier for the ones that came from Algeria to have flown directly to Spain? It's the nearest available land, but instead they flew straight to France, to join up with the others. Why?"

Volk stood, barely able to conceal his excitement. "You're right, Holland. Doctor, any ideas?"

Stephanie studied the screen for a long moment. "Yes, but it really doesn't quite add up. Locusts herd together like this when they have become mature adults preparing to lay their eggs. But in order to become mature they must pass through five molting periods, known as instars, and then through a period as immature adults before reaching maturity. Once maturity is attained they copulate and lay their eggs, but this stage is reached only after several weeks of immaturity. The time frame is all wrong if, in fact, they are gathering to mate and lay eggs."

Starling leaned forward. "Yet surely you would agree,

Stephanie, if the locusts who escaped from the plane mated with the unsullied desert locust the offspring would carry the same genetic defect as the parent, who had carried the original impurity?"

"Of course, but . . ."

"And we know that instead of five instars those in the Niah Valley only went through two or possibly three instars before reaching immaturity."

Stephanie nodded thoughtfully. "I see what you mean, Doctor. The mutants went through the same cycle as unaffected insects only heightened and more accelerated."

"Precisely. Mr. Volk, I think that's your answer. Their growth rate is accelerated and they have settled in a fertile area which offers ample moisture for the young when they hatch out of the eggs."

Volk looked to Stephanie for confirmation. She nodded. "Yes. Yes that must be it. After all, they are rewriting the text books just by being carnivorous so why wouldn't they have different life-cycle habits? They are preparing to copulate and lay the next generation of insects and they will be just as daunting as these, but with, perhaps, the added ingredient of the knowledge their parents have gained."

Volk turned back to the drawer and its direct telephone line and in moments was apprising the White House of the latest developments.

# CHAPTER TWO

"MR. PRESIDENT, VOLK IS RIGHT. WE HAVE TO HIT THOSE bugs while they are on the ground. We have to hit them with everything the SAC and the Russians can get into the air. We have to obliterate the Bordeaux Corridor."

The insects had spread past Toulouse toward Bordeaux but had still not passed Grenoble. They were confined to an area that stretched across southern France. Confined as they were, with the high Pyrenees to the south, the vast Atlantic to the west and the Mediterranean to the southeast, the opportunity to attack was greedily grabbed at by the military. The enemy was boxed in and there might not be another chance.

"No, General, that will not do at all. The French are not prepared to allow a blitz against them in that area. It would, among other things, completely destroy the wine industry—"

"Jesus, Mr. President, you can't feed *Mouton Cadet* to a dead man!"

The president held up a hand to still the outraged chief of staff.

"The French are prepared to delay for the moment to see what happens. Under no circumstances are they prepared to allow a strike right now. If the insects move north, into the heart of France, then, and only then, will they permit a strike on French soil."

"They are taking a hell of a gamble, Mr. President," observed General Carthy. "What happens if the locusts split up and go in different directions? They could even end up here, for Christ's sake!"

The president rubbed his chest. The tightness had returned and he felt for a moment as though he were going to suffer another attack.

"I think it unlikely, General. We're protected by over three thousand miles of ocean."

The president rose and walked to the windows of his office. He looked out onto the sumptuous White House lawns. He was deeply troubled. The general spoke again, cutting into the president's thoughts. "If I may say so, sir, the rest of the friggin' world can go to hell as far as I'm concerned. We should clobber the sons-of-bitches right now and worry about the repercussions later!"

He turned angrily on the man. "You have your orders, Tom, that's all."

Carthy glowered at the president for a long moment before wheeling around and stalking from the office. The president returned to his desk and sat down shakily.

For the thousandth time since this all started, he wished he hadn't run for his second term of office.

"Captain Holland, Captain Holland, sir." The insistent shaking and the urgency of the voice finally penetrated through to the unconscious man and he allowed one eyelid to flicker open. It was difficult to focus so the other was brought in to assist.

The marine sergeant stopped shaking Holland and stood back slightly to allow him space in which to sit up on the cot.

"Mr. Volk's compliments, sir, and would you join him in the situation room as soon as possible?"

"What's wrong?" Mark was now fully awake.

"I really don't know, Captain," replied the sergeant. "I was just told to wake you and pass on the message, but something's wrong, that's for damn sure. People moving in and out of that room like beavers."

Holland knew he needed to shower. He felt dirty and the dried blood on his face and neck itched. He had intended washing after he had left Volk earlier, but exhaustion had swept over him as soon as he entered the room.

Now there was no time. He splashed his face at the metal wash basin, glad of the sharpness of the cold water, and looked down at his clothes. Their crumpled appearance testified to the events of the last hours. He grimaced at the thought of wearing them any longer than necessary. He glanced around and his eyes fell on the USAF issue flight coveralls that lay draped over the back of the single armchair.

Mark stripped quickly, climbing into the outfit and then smiling as he noticed the disposable razor and box of band-aids that lay on the seat. Volk and the crisis would have to wait a few minutes, he decided.

"I see you found the gear we put in your room," said Volk as Holland joined the small knot of people around the console.

"What's happening?"

Volk pointed toward the board. A wide, black band spread from a point some sixty miles west of the northern Spanish town of La Coruna into the Atlantic and the Bay of Biscay. The tail of the cloud stretched back to the mainland of France, over the ancient seaport of Bordeaux and into the world-famous wine-growing region. Even as they watched, the forward edge of the swarm inched further and further out into the wide expanse of water.

"They're swarming out over the Atlantic," Volk muttered unnecessarily to the small group around him.

The general mood of the situation room was one of quiet euphoria, like that of men, who having lost all hope in a battle, suddenly and inexplicably see their enemy turn about and march away.

"I must be slow, but I don't understand what's going on."

Starling laughed softly at Mark's incomprehension. "We are

cautiously optimistic, Mark, because the swarm is heading out into a hostile environment. There is nothing out there for them to feed on, or, more importantly, to rest upon."

"Except the North American continent," observed Mark dryly.

Starling nodded in unhurried agreement. "Granted, but that is a very long way off and so far they have only flown relatively short distances. While we can not say at this juncture that this is definitely the end of them the general consensus—the hope— is that nature has taken matters into her own hands."

Holland was confused, his tired mind and body unable to grasp what the scientist was driving at. He asked for clarification in a tone which indicated exasperation, directed as much at himself as at Starling.

"You are familiar, no doubt, with the phenomena of the lemmings," Starling began patiently. "Once there are too many of them nature runs them over a cliff in the form of mass suicide. We think that is what is happening here, a mass exodus which can only, we fervently hope, culminate in mass suicide.

"It's not really surprising though, you know. Our preliminary examination of the mutants indicated that they were developing in a very rapid manner.

"Their whole genetic structure has been altered. The ones you and Stephanie brought back from Nice are larger than the normal desert locust. They are stronger physically and their whole metabolism has changed.

"Imagine what future generations of these creatures would look like. Perhaps five or six times bigger than the ones you captured; stronger in the body; able to fly greater and greater distances. It would be like having a breed of flying cannibals plaguing the world. Once the warm-blooded creatures were gone they would probably revert to the foliage in order to survive. The world would become stripped of every living thing, animal and vegetable.

"Without plants to reproduce the oxygen, ultimately the land surfaces of this planet would perish, leaving only the seas and their life forms. Then the locusts would also die.

"No, Mark. Nature wouldn't, couldn't let that happen. She

gets rid of those which do not fit into the overall scheme of creation by moving them out over a wasteland in order that they can be destroyed.

"Nature corrects her mistakes, Mark. And thank God for us she still cares enough about this planet to do so.

"We are not sure that this is what is happening, of course. It could be that they will swing back toward land and start the whole nightmare over again, but this latest activity, taking them away from nutrition, is so far removed from their normal, instinctive pattern that even ordinarily cautious scientists are forced to the conclusion that this could be the death knell for the mutants."

Volk shook his head slowly. "And we came close to obliterating the Bordeaux Corridor. Thank God the president held back."

"The BBC will start broadcasting the news once we are sure there is no danger of them turning back toward land. I imagine a lot of people are going to be feeling pretty guilty over the way they handled themselves.

"But as we do seem to have room for optimism, I suggest we freshen up and meet in the private dining room for a decent meal and a couple of bottles of good wine. There's nothing more to be done here for the moment."

As they left the room, Mark glanced back at the huge screen. The lines that plotted the westward movement of the locusts continued to inch forward. His stomach ached momentarily before Stephanie yanked impatiently at his arm.

The white-coated mess stewards cleared away the remnants of the meal from the table and Volk poured himself a liberal amount of five-star brandy before passing the decanter to Holland.

The mess corporal placed a box of cigars on the table before signaling to the two other stewards that they should leave the private dining room.

"Well, I hope you enjoyed the meal," said Volk amiably, resuming his role of sophisticated government servant.

A telephone on a side table immediately behind Volk's chair

trilled and, excusing himself, he turned and listened briefly to the voice on the other end. Gradually a smile broke across his face and with a word of thanks he replaced the receiver.

"Operations reports the locusts are now completely off any land surface. They are well out over the Atlantic.

"Apparently the news is spreading fast upstairs. The streets are crowded with jubilant people celebrating. I guess they have good reason to."

Starling was grim, however, as he said, "Of course, they could always swing around and head due south towards Morocco or the Sahara region of North Africa." He chuckled at the rapidity with which Volk's grin faded before adding, "But I don't think so. I really believe they are finished. And good riddance!"

Three glasses were lifted in unison at the toast, but Holland ignored it and reached for a cigarette.

Volk frowned at him. "Is something wrong, Mr. Holland?"

Mark looked steadily back at Volk and then toward Stephanie. "I don't know," he sighed. "Perhaps I'm just being negative, but it still seems to be too damn simple."

Volk relaxed visibly. "You worry too much, Holland. Dr. Starling is right when he says nature takes care of its mistakes. I sometimes wish it would take care of ours." He leaned across the table, adopting the tone of a patient parent to a recalcitrant child.

"There is nothing out in the Atlantic for them to land on, other than a couple of very small rocks. No food at all. They must be finished. Look, we're following them with satellites and Nimrods. The leaders are now eight hundred miles out. The longest flight of locusts is recorded at . . . what was it, Dr. Starling?"

"Sixteen hundred miles, from the Canaries to Britain in 1954," replied the scientist firmly. "Even these characters have not managed to get as far as that without resting. As I said before, we can be cautiously optimistic that they will not be able to make land by proceeding on their present course."

"So," continued Volk, "if you take that as the yardstick they are almost half way there now. If they turned back right now, they would equal or just pass that record, but soon, very soon, they should reach the point of no return."

"Providing they don't carry straight on, I guess I can accept that. Maybe I *want* to accept that the only ones left will be those we brought back." Mark tapped his cigarette ash into the silver ashtray.

Volk glanced at Starling before replying. "No, we have others which have been collected all along the path which they took. It was necessary for us to be able to monitor their growth in relation to normal locust development patterns."

"But it's all over now, you don't need them, right?"

"Well, the opportunity does, of course, now present itself for us to study the mutants in greater depth. Isolate the bacterium which caused the growth and so on. We may be able to use the knowledge for—"

Holland was incredulous. "Good God, haven't you learned anything from the past week? Those things are dangerous. If we have another accident with the ones you've got caged up it's going to start all over again—"

Starling intervened.

"We know that, Captain, but you must recognize this accident was caused because proper control factors were not adopted. Mr. Volk is quite correct when he says we have the greatest opportunity to learn from them. We do. There won't be a next time, I assure you.

"It might be possible to discover an important biological factor which could be used to curtail *all* breeds and strains of insect pests. If we ensure proper safeguards are taken, there shouldn't be any problem."

"That's what Steiner thought," Mark exploded. "Those creatures are unlike anything any of us had to deal with before. It's like a science fiction horror story come true and all you can do is get ready to start a sequel."

Volk held up a placating hand. "It's not that simple. The Russians are bound to have collected their own samples and will be trying to isolate the strain as well. We can't let them get a hold of the bacterium alone. We have to—"

Holland threw up his hands in disgust, cutting Volk short.

He pushed the chair back from the table as he stood. "That's typical of the sort of crap that got us into this mess in the first place. Them against us. You guys won't be happy until the whole world is destroyed."

Mark stormed from the room and Stephanie hesitated, then headed after him. As she reached the door she turned and fixed Volk with a withering glare. "You know something? He's got one hell of a point!" She slammed the door shut behind her and the two men sat at the table in silence.

Finally Volk reached out for the decanter. "More brandy, Doctor?" he inquired.

She found him in the situation room. The swarm was about eight hundred and fifty miles out to sea. He touched a button on the console by his seat, switching to the television feed from the police video cameras dotted around central London. The silent pictures changed constantly as the police operator switched to different locations: Oxford Street, Piccadilly Circus, The Mall and the traditional point of celebration, Buckingham Palace, with the royal standard fluttering from the staff.

The picture changed to the looted and ruined shops of Bond Street. In front of many of the fashionable stores the pavement was littered with goods. Furs, dresses, jewelry, discarded as worthless to the roving mob that had sacked the area.

Broken glass lay everywhere like a thin covering of snow, and a curl of smoke rose from one gutted interior. There was a quick glimpse of a window dresser's dummy, a silent witness lying in the gutter, before the image shifted back to Buckingham Palace.

Crowds milled and danced around each other on the screen. She placed a hand on his shoulder and he looked up at her.

"Hi."

"Look at them, Stephanie. Those are the same people who a few hours ago would have torn your heart out for the clothing on your back. Now they dance, shout and congratulate themselves on having beaten the enemy."

"It looks like the films of VE Day. You can't blame them

for wanting to survive, to make sure they live, even if it's at others' expense. We're not that sophisticated after all, are we?"

Mark took her hand. "No, I suppose not. I remember thinking back in Nice I ought to leave that cab driver and just concentrate on getting us away. If you hadn't thrown the back door of the car open I might have done just that."

She squeezed his hand and changed the tone of her voice to try to lift him out of his depression. "Listen, we can't do anything more here, even if they do turn back."

She knelt in front of him and brushed her fingers lightly over the bandage on his cheek.

"Mark," she said. "Take me home."

# CHAPTER THREE

—

As Mark and Stephanie crossed London in the black embassy Cadillac, a fleet of aircraft was taking off from airports all over Europe. A similar squadron of transports was also taking off from military airports along the southern border of Russia near Turkey, Iran and Afghanistan.

The aircraft lifted high into the sky, their cargo holds jammed with equipment and supplies—not the arms of war which they had been built to carry, but equipment needed to ease the suffering and pain of countries ravaged by the mutant insects.

Blankets, food, medical supplies, fuel. All were needed desperately in countries as diverse in their lifestyles as Sudanese salt is from the grapes of the French vineyards.

Bordeaux had been attacked mercilessly by the creatures. Civil order had degenerated almost immediately after the warnings, received too late, had been broadcast. A part of the population had fled the city only to be caught in the open countryside. Some had hidden in deep cellars and survived. Others had taken to the open water in the first boat that had come along. A profusion of smallcraft drifted aimlessly, the corpses of their crews lying in mute testimony to the futility of their flight.

The problem was much the same everywhere that had been visited by the Messengers of Allah. Death, breakdown of public order, destruction of food reserves, fires raging uncontrollably. It would require, agreed the United Nations, a concerted effort by all countries to aid in the restoration of services and to help heal the deep rents in the fabric of their existence.

Apportionment of blame could wait until after the healing was completed.

Doctors and nurses flew to Europe from across America and Canada, from Australia and India, from China and New Zealand, from Russia and Chile, from the smallest village to the largest city. An unending stream of aid poured into the command points in central Europe. From there, the Red Cross and United Nations officials sent them to the areas most in need.

And the Saudis finally called for help, understanding at last that their God would need more than blind faith to save the lives of those whose souls He had so vigorously cleansed. The country lay in ruins with more than half its leadership dead beside the king at Mecca.

But it was long since the massacre at the Islamic holy city and the hot sun beating down upon the bodies had begun to work their evil upon the rotting, fetid corpses. Flies, attracted by the pungent, decaying flesh had hastened to the city, breeding by the millions. Uncounted and uncountable hordes of filth-ridden insects were free to travel wherever carrion beckoned.

The flies finished their work and spread out to Jidda and across the Red Sea in plague-bearing hordes to Egypt and Sudan. They moved north to Jordan and east to Iraq, taking with them the legacy that they had collected from the dead.

The first volunteers to arrive in the infected areas saw people stagger and fall, saw others lying in the dust with large purple spots upon their skin. Occasionally, screams of delirium broke through the stillness.

Typhus raged.

Engineers flew to the Suez Canal with salvage operators and experienced seamen in an attempt to clear away the confusion of wrecked shipping that now blocked the vital water route.

Crews had been trapped aboard some two dozen vessels along its length. Trapped by water and desert all around them, they had made an easy meal. Incapable of flight, the ships were left scattered like dodgem cars in a madman's amusement park.

The Seventh Fleet worked with Russian warships in the sweep through the Mediterranean for drifting vessels which would cause a hazard to relief suppliers.

The Portuguese, Spanish and British warships and cruisers handled the North Atlantic and Mediterranean area in a vain attempt to locate those ships which were reported missing or from whom no word had been received.

The warship *Taurus* discovered the SS *Island Princess* and took her into tow. The only survivor among the six hundred passengers and crew was the ship's cat.

Rescuers reached the island of Sardinia and found a land stripped of its lush vegetation and human habitation. Crowded beaches were covered with chaotically-strewn cadavers. The only sound the advance party heard as they landed on the golden sands were the incessant hum of flies. The only movement, that of bones shifting, ever so slightly, as maggots wriggled amongst the suppurating flesh.

On a vacation island, people don't stay indoors. They lie in postures of nakedness to soak up the unfamiliar sun. Or, when they have had enough, they go to sit in the shade of a cafe and drink tall, exotic-sounding cocktails. Whatever it is vacationers do, they do it in the open, so that others can see just how much they are enjoying themselves.

Thousands wished they had stayed in when the locusts swept out of the cloudless sky, to enjoy the beaches and cafes with them.

And then, incredibly, two old ladies wandered down the street of Cagliari, looking from left to right in shocked bewilderment, horrified at the sight of the dead and mutilated bodies.

Frightened at the sight of rescuers, in the white sterile suits with oxygen masks, running awkwardly toward them. Two old ladies, who had suffered from heatstroke and gone to bed in dark rooms, the shutters closed and drapes drawn.

Two old ladies who would pass their twilight years gazing fearfully at the Oxfordshire sky from padded cells.

And London. Dear London that had survived the Great Plague, the Great Fire, the might and fury of the Luftwaffe, fell to the onslaught of its frightened natives.

The people had rushed to and fro like bewildered mice, kicking and screaming, killing and stealing. How much worse could it have been if the locusts had reached the capital? Now, the threat was over and the perpetrators returned to their homes in shame.

Their shame was equaled only by that felt by the population of Paris and Brussels, in Madrid and Rome. Equaled indeed by the population of Europe as the deadly threat to them and their way of life receded beyond their seaswept shores.

Many hundreds had died in the self-inflicted terror, fed by the flames of fear. Even those countries untouched by the mutants required help in the restoration of order.

On a city street in Leeds, a Norwegian soldier shot two men who were raping a thirteen-year-old girl in the city center. International cooperation had taken on a new and deadly meaning.

# CHAPTER FOUR

SEA FOG IS NOT AN UNUSUAL OCCURRENCE TO THE HARDY people of the area known as the Maritimes.

The east coast of Canada is well used to the dense blanket sweeping rapidly in from the Atlantic or down from the Labrador Sea. It comes in swiftly and without warning, catching both the amateur sailor and professional fisherman unaware.

The people of Prince Edward Island, tucked offshore the sister provinces of New Brunswick and Nova Scotia, almost welcome its clammy coldness. When it descends the cry goes up, "the mainland is cut off again," and the island settles back to a peaceful, tourist-free existence.

Although unusual in its density for the time of year, the gray fog that now descended over their paradise held no fears for those who had lived and breathed it through the years. Fishing fleets at sea dropped anchor and the watch was increased to make sure the larger freighters and passenger liners heading into the mouth of the St. Lawrence didn't run them down while they settled to await the winds that would drive the fog away.

At the U.S. Coast Guard station in Bangor, Maine, the on-duty officer noted its sudden arrival in his log and called to ships in that sector. At length, he located an East German cargo ship bound homeward from Brazil with a full load of coffee. The German had sailed through the bank fifteen minutes before and, allowing for the vessel's speed, the officer was able to make an accurate estimation of its density.

He whistled softly to himself and then reached for the telephone.

She woke in the early evening of the second day and lay there, comforted by the soft light and the feel of the linen against her skin. Then she turned and watched him sleep on, his chest rising and falling as he breathed.

The strain of the last days had lifted from them both during the hours they had been alone together, but there were still lines of tension on his brow, even as he rested. She wondered if he would ever tell her about the past, about the scars across his body that she often saw reflected in his eyes.

"Mark Holland," she whispered. "Don't go away too soon."

They had not talked much, just been content in each other's company, perhaps discussing the likes and dislikes that joined lovers—books, music, food, sex. She slipped out from under the quilt and walked naked to the stereo. Gradually the first sad strains of the slow movement from Mahler's *Fifth* crept into the room. She was pleased that despite all that had happened she could still be an incurable romantic.

When she returned to the bed he stirred, and she reached to touch him, peeling away the band-aids from his face and neck. The wounds were healing well, with no signs of bruising left around the tattoos of dried blood.

As the music ebbed and flowed she led him to the shower and they embraced under the warmth of the cascading water. Then she began to soap his body, examining and exploring with sensitive fingers and unspoken questions as he leaned back against the wall of the cubicle, eyes closed, tension swirling away with the water.

Then he came forward and took the soap from her, rubbing

it across her shoulders and breasts, teasing the nipples into life. She pushed hair from her eyes and opened her legs wider as he touched her thighs, moving gently up to the tenderness that lay between them. He moved against her there and she moaned softly, arching her back. Waves of soothing ecstasy washed from her clitoris across every nerve end in her body and she knew that if she did not have him now, she would die. Gripping the flesh of his buttocks, she guided him slowly, deep inside her and cried out with pleasure as he pressed her to him.

Neither noticed the blood that began to well once more from the gash on his cheek as he kissed her, before it was washed quickly away.

"Mmm," Stephanie said as Holland seared the steaks. "I feel positively decadent." She padded around the kitchen in bare feet, dressed in a loose shirt that didn't quite make it to the tops of her thighs.

They ate the meal and drank the full-bodied wine and tried to hold the lightness of their mood. At last, Mark pushed back his chair and stacked the dishes. The table clean, he sat down and fished into the bathrobe for his cigarettes and lighter. Blue smoke streamed from his lungs toward the ceiling and Stephanie felt saddened at the expression on his face.

The time that she had dreaded was here.

"Thank you," he said, picking his way carefully toward what he knew he must say.

"And now it's time for you to get going, right?"

Mark looked at the woman across the table and nodded his head. "Yes. It's time for me to go."

"Oh Mark, why? What are you going to do? Go back to work, flying junk-heap planes full of ignorant oilmen?"

He shook his head, understanding the way she felt.

"I have to go, because I still have some unfinished business." He paused. "Trans-Global blew up that plane, somebody must have ordered it. I have to settle that score, Stephanie. Once that's done, this whole business will be over and perhaps then I can start thinking of putting my life back together."

"Do you *really* believe Kate would want you to look for revenge to settle the score? Do you?"

"No, she wouldn't, but that's not the point either. I know she was murdered by a company who cared more about its precious oil rights than it did about sixteen lives. Those sixteen have escalated to hundreds of thousands. Whether whoever authorized it acted alone doesn't matter. He's first and if he got his orders from someone higher up then I'll get him too. And I'll keep going until they get me, or I finish the job."

She looked pityingly at him, for the first time really seeing and understanding the hate, the driving hate, he felt which drove him constantly toward his inevitable self-destruction. She wanted to scream at him, "Why stop there? Why not go after all the people who covered up the Fong Lee raid and who nearly ruined you and would have except the court-martial felt a conviction would be unsafe?" She wanted to and nearly did, except a warning bell in the back of her anguished mind reminded her that as far as he was concerned she didn't know anything about that part of his life.

Stephanie sighed and leaned forward across the table. As she was about to speak the telephone rang and she ran to the hall, grateful for the interruption. The call lasted several minutes and Mark refilled his coffee cup and stood looking through the kitchen window, thinking back over the events which had led them along the same path.

The kitchen door flew open and she appeared, pulling a sweater over her head. "Mark, that was Volk. They've lost them."

His face went gray.

"The Nimrods tracked them most of the way across the Atlantic and then they flew into a fog bank. The infrared reading is very faint."

"They have to be at the end of their strength now, surely,"

She shook her head. "Satellite pictures showed millions of them dropping into the sea, but a large body made it well over the halfway point. Mark, the fog bank stretches from the east coast of Canada out nearly eight hundred miles. It's possible some of them will make it to land."

He stripped off his robe and got dressed. In five minutes they walked into the quiet street and hailed a cab.

The mood in the situation room was now very different. Volk, dressed casually in slacks and sports shirt, sat at his command console and spoke rapidly into a bank of telephones, lifting first this receiver and then that, at times talking into two at the same time.

He didn't look up when Mark and Stephanie joined him. "Jesus Christ," he said to no one in particular, "it's still going on!"

"How? How did it happen?"

"How did what happen?" mimicked Volk sarcastically. "The bloody things just kept right on going, that's how. Jesus!"

Stephanie moved in to question him. "How many dropped into the sea?"

"Millions."

"And that fog bank is eight hundred miles wide, right?"

"Right."

"Speed?"

"Now that's the killer, Dr. Caine. Those things picked up speed and are now, or were when we last logged their air speed, flying at up to seventy miles an hour."

Holland said, "How long ago did they enter the fog?"

For the first time, Volk turned and looked at him. "That's the most pertinent question of them all, Captain Holland. Just over eight hours ago."

Mark calculated swiftly. "Landfall should be two hours from now."

"Two point six, to be exact." Volk pressed a sequence of buttons on the desk console. The screen changed images and the projected point of the locusts' flight registered on the board.

"That's where they are right now, to the best of our British friends' knowledge. There's so much down there that's hotter than a bunch of flying locusts that the infrareds can hardly see a thing."

They looked at the image of the Eastern Seaboard and the

dark lines that inched their way toward the Canadian coast. Nova Scotia lay directly in their path.

"We have no way of knowing just how many are left. The satellites can't penetrate effectively through the soup, either."

Holland studied the image on the screen and traced a mental picture back toward the east, the Bay of Biscay and Bordeaux. "If you haven't already done so, I think you'd better warn the Canadian authorities they are about to be attacked."

Volk lifted his head. "OK, wise guy—so you've just become an expert."

Holland ignored him and pointed to the screen. "They took off from Bordeaux, that's on the forty-five degree latitude. You last spotted them eight hundred miles out, still on the forty-five degree latitude. Novia Scotia is right on the forty-five degree line. Volk, I've just given up believing in coincidences. I suggest you project west along forty-five degrees and see what comes up."

Volk stared at him. "Do you know what will?"

"I think so. But you'll have to see it for yourself." Buttons were punched rapidly and the projected map section started changing as the computer scanned across its memory. The picture of Nova Scotia was replaced by a series of landscapes obligingly identified in the top right hand corner of the screen as BANGOR, MAINE.

This too was quickly replaced by Ottawa, Lake Huron, Mackinaw City, Lake Michigan, Illinois and the twin cities of St. Paul and Minneapolis. On and on scanned the computer, across wide stretches of land that the billion-dollar brain identified as the midwestern part of the United States.

Then another name was projected and Volk immediately stabbed a button to freeze the image. The picture seemed to swell and Volk rose slowly from his seat, unable to tear his eyes away from the legend in the top right hand corner.

"It's not possible," he said. "My God, *it's not possible!*"

Mark nodded. "Dr. Starling said the other day that lemmings run off those Scandinavian cliffs to commit suicide. What he didn't say was there is another train of thought on that subject.

That the lemmings aren't committing suicide, but trying to cross a land mass that used to be there. A memory chromosome triggers them into charging right across where they remember land should be, but isn't. They are simply trying to go home."

The image stayed as the people in the room looked in horrified fascination at the sequence of letters that had appeared at the edge of the huge screen.

GRASSHOPPER GLACIER, MONTANA.

The president turned angrily on the man. The vote-catching lilt had disappeared from his voice. "Damn it all to *hell*, Tom, that's the most naive thing I've ever heard from you and I've heard a lot of stupid remarks come out of that mouth of yours. Do you think I like the thought of even a low-yield nuclear attack on U.S. soil?"

The president stormed to his desk and grabbed the white telephone. "Get me the Secretary General of the United Nations," he barked. To the general he said, "And I suggest, Tom, you start preparing your men for a strike against those locusts at Grasshopper. It looks like that's where they will end up. Jerry, you better alert the governor of Montana I need to talk to him in fifteen minutes. You can tell him to put out a general alert for the National Guard to go on Ready status. That's all, gentlemen."

As the men left the room, the President of the United States looked over at an old rocking chair that had been used by John F. Kennedy and now took pride of place beside his desk. He whispered quietly to it, as though expecting the ghost of the long-dead leader to help him. "What would you have done, Jack? *What in hell would you have done?*"

"Cyrus, you and I go back a long way. We've seen a lot of changes in this town and we weathered a few storms together. But if this frigging wheat farmer does what he says he ought to do, then we got ourselves a whole mess of trouble coming."

"Tom, you're a military man and I'm a politician—"

"You're the Senate Majority Leader, Cyrus."

"That may be, Tom. That may be. But I'm still a politician

and if the president decides the best way of handling this problem is to blast those bastards then I've just got to support that decision. You, surely, can see that?"

"Cyrus, if the president pushes the button, we drop nukes on American soil. Do you have any idea what will happen to this country? There'll be civil war at worst, and that's the truth. As far as what'll happen at best, you can bet your ass in the next election you and all the other old guard will be booted out. You can't let him do it. In God's name you can't."

Cyrus Whittaker looked at his old friend and comrade. It was true, they did go back a long way. West Point and World War II had welded the two men into firm friends and allies in the harder theater of Washington politics. They knew, each of them, where the other had buried his skeletons, and each owed the other unswerving loyalty for past favors.

"Leave it to me, Tom, I'll see what can be done. OK?"

The general stood and offered the man his hand.

"Many thanks, Cyrus. I knew you'd see things the right way. So long for now. See you at the club tomorrow night."

Cyrus Whittaker slapped the general amiably on the back and chuckled. "You can bet your ass on that, old buddy. You and your cronies took three hundred dollars off me last week in that crooked game."

Once the general had left his office, the senator returned to his desk and dialed a number on his private line. In moments the call was answered. Whittaker cleared his throat and talked quickly to rid himself of the distasteful but necessary thing he had to do. "Mr. President, Cyrus Whittaker here. You were right, he came hotfooting it over to me as soon as he left your office. Wanted me to start lobbying around the Hill to stop you ordering the strike. Made some sense too, Mr. President. He pointed out that come the election all us old timers on both sides of the Congress would probably lose our tickets. Guess I figure that maybe it wouldn't be such a bad thing, seeing as how it was us who supported this type of operation in the first place. Anyhow it's up to you now, Mr. President. I would suggest you immediately relieve Tom of his command citing health reasons. I assure you even the opposition will be with you in that. We feel this drastic situation requires a drastic solution."

Cyrus listened for a moment to the president's reply, then, "I agree, sir, it is a damn shame that the only time we all pull together is when we are in trouble. But maybe, after this . . . Anyway, sir, I am at your disposal should you need me."

The conference room was crowded with personnel and diplomatic staff from the embassy. Smoke was eagerly sucked at by the air conditioners and the low hum of urgent conversation continued as Volk rapped on the table.

Stephanie, Starling and Holland sat with him at the main table, along with the ambassador and his aides. Other seats were taken up by the senior of the embassy staff. All those in the room had top security clearance.

"Ladies and gentlemen, we'll get right to it, if you'll please be quiet." Volk's familiar clipped accent was there, but without the normal courtesy of tone.

"The ambassador and the president have been in communication and we have now been authorized to release to you the latest information on the locust swarm. Before I continue, I must remind you that this information is classified Top Secret and must not be discussed outside this room.

"The situation at present is that we have not had a visual sighting of the locusts for . . ."—he checked his watch— "nine hours. They entered a bank of fog off the Canadian coast."

"Our original belief was they would not be able to cross three thousand miles of open water. It now seems there is every likelihood that they will. That they will be on North American soil in one and a half hours."

A gasp ran through the assembly and Volk allowed it to dissipate before carrying on.

"They followed the forty-five degree latitude right across the Atlantic from Bordeaux to the point where we lost sight of them. If they keep on that meridian, they will end up in Montana."

Volk took a drink from the glass on the table and looked

around the room. "The most likely theory is that memory chromosomes passed on to this new generation are urging them forward. They are going home. The ambassador notified the president as soon as we developed this theory and five minutes ago we received this message from him. I quote:

FROM COMMANDER IN CHIEF TO ALL COMMAND CENTERS.

INSTRUCTIONS HAVE BEEN GIVEN FOR CLEARING GRASSHOPPER GLACIER IF ANALYSIS FROM LONDON PROVES CORRECT. EVACUATION OF WIDEST AREA NOW UNDERWAY.

IMPERATIVE NO WORD OR DISCUSSION BE CONDUCTED WITH UNAUTHORIZED PERSONNEL.

CODE NAME IS OPERATION ICEMELT.

MAJOR GENERAL THOMAS CARTHY HAS BEEN RELIEVED OF COMMAND.

LIEUTENANT GENERAL ARTHER B. GAINES ASSUMES POST OF ACTING COMMANDER IN CHIEF, SAC.

Volk continued, "Before anybody asks, we estimate that if they carry on flying they will reach Grasshopper in forty-nine hours. However, the likelihood of that is remote. They will be tired and hungry after their flight. There can be little doubt they will need to replenish their strength before moving on. Any questions?"

"Yes, sir, what sort of strike is envisioned against them at the glacier?"

"Conventional. Any other questions?"

"Excuse me, sir," insisted the same questioner, "but Grasshopper Glacier is at an elevation of three thousand feet. The combined altitude and mass make conventional bombing difficult, if not impossible."

Volk stared hard at the young man. "What's your name?"

"Trapper, sir. Transferred from State last month."

"Occupation?"

"Statistician, sir."

"You would be. Right, that's all for the moment. We will keep you informed of developments."

The room cleared and Stephanie and Mark rose to leave. Volk glanced quickly up. "Please stay, we'd like to ask you something, Doctor."

She sat and Volk crossed the room and closed the door. He looked to the ambassador, who nodded saying, "Let's get on with it, Mr. Volk, please."

"Yes sir. Doctor, that was a lie about conventional bombing. We are dropping a nuclear device on the mountain. However, the bomb will only be dropped after a small survey team has collected samples of the locusts which make it all the way across to Montana. We must have samples of these creatures to evaluate the final degree of their evolutionary abilities. I have agreed to allow you to join the team if you want to."

Stephanie did not hesitate, "Yes, I do."

The ambassador straightened in the chair. "In that case, Doctor, I am instructed by the president to tell you that under no circumstances can the United States accept any responsibility for your safety and to require you to sign a waiver of responsibility and a pledge of secrecy."

Stephanie quickly signed the document placed in front of her.

Holland moved back to the table. "I'm going, too."

The ambassador smiled. "Captain, I wouldn't dream of trying to stop you. Your papers from your Air Force days still hold you to secrecy. Happy hunting to both of you."

An hour later, they took off from Heathrow Airport and were speeding across the Atlantic. At the same time, the first of the locusts was turning into the wind and dropping silently toward the town of Truro, Nova Scotia.

# CHAPTER FIVE

*THE INSECTS ROSE HIGHER INTO THE AIR. HIGHER INTO THE FA-vorable tradewinds that swept across the surface of the earth. The cooling winds, the warming winds. The winds that swept across the oceans, rippling the waters, and roared across the prairies, bringing life to the wheat stalks and grasses.*

*The locusts stretched their wings and as one body rose and fell with the currents of the air, speeding on their way to the other side of the world. To the land they knew was there, waiting for them to return.*

*They used the elements to good advantage. Many hours later the lead locusts sensed land. They knew that after their long journey they were once more near food.*

The Canadian government had ordered a mass evacuation of the land that lay in the hungry insects' path, but Nova Scotia, Newfoundland and New Brunswick would never be the same again.

The island portion of Newfoundland, so carefully tended by generations of immigrants, would be deprived of crops for years to come, contaminated by insect effluence as far north as St. Anthony.

The locusts wheeled and turned, as though undecided about

which direction they should move in first to sample the fruits of the Canadian provinces. The incredibly beautiful landscape of Prince Edward Island bowed and was broken by the immense weight of the collective mass of insects. It would be long before the world-famous Charlottetown Festival was held again for the enjoyment of thousands of Canadian and American tourists.

New Brunswick suffered to the same degree. Huge numbers of livestock and the few humans that had not heeded the warnings to evacuate died violently within hours after the first locusts had been sighted.

The twin islands of St. Pierre and Miquelon, situated off the coast of Newfoundland, had been forgotton by their masters in Paris and the French-owned islands suffered horribly under the creatures' inexorable advance. The islands had been overlooked in the evacuation plans. Hadn't the late President de Gaulle stated often enough that the islands' sovereignty should be maintained at all costs by the French? The cost was high.

At length, the locusts settled to recover their strength after the arduous Atlantic crossing. The advance guard of the monstrous army came down west of Ottawa in the lush farmlands of eastern Ontario. The Canadian government moved hurriedly away from the center of danger to the nuclear attack shelter near Barrie, some one hour's drive from Toronto.

After a full day of resting and feeding, the swarm swayed and rippled in its unseemly dance and rose steadily into the bright Canadian sunshine to continue their flight west. Across Lakes Huron and Michigan they flew. On toward the midwestern states with their rich, fertile soil and crops, on toward the homecoming that had been so long delayed.

The Air Force jet from London landed with a squeal of tires and taxied across to the special VIP area. It had made excellent time across the Atlantic, leaving in the afternoon and arriving as rays of early evening sunshine slanted across the capital city of the richest nation on earth.

They had passed well to the south of the now-thinning fog bank, and the radio technicians had kept the passengers updated on the locusts' progress.

They heard of the dreadful massacre at Truro as evacuees and rescuers alike were trapped by the hungry insects. Starved to the point of madness, the creatures had proved that their jaws were capable of tearing through the wooden Canadian houses like a chainsaw in order to reach the edible morsels that cowered within for shelter.

Stephanie and her companions knew the locusts were being driven forward at greater and greater speed. The swarm was staying in an area only long enough to feed before again taking to the air.

The aircraft remained on the ground to refuel and take on more passengers for the scientific side of the expedition, then headed west toward Denver and the helicopters that would lift them on to Livingston.

The city of Toronto lay spread along the shore of Lake Ontario, one and a half hours' drive from the border town of Buffalo, New York. As the major urban center in English-speaking Canada, Toronto was the commercial pulse, heartbeat and brain of the nation. It was also the capital of Ontario, the richest of all the provinces.

The locusts spread out along the forty-five degree meridian, often veering to the more populated south. The smell of the city attracted scouts and they hurried back to the main body to report the abundance of food.

It was early evening as the hordes swept in low over the waters of Lake Ontario. The tallest structure in the city, The Canadian National Tower, seemed to act as a landmark to the millions that hastened their flight as the musky odor of human flesh reached their senses.

The locusts flew into a city that was outdoors. An entire population playing, relaxing, and trying not to think about the deadly menace that was supposed to be hundreds of miles to the north.

The evening disc jockey, perched on the very top floor of the Toronto Star building, right on the edge of the lake, spotted them first as a huge black cloud coming in from the American shore. At first he smiled, relieved at the promise of rain and sanctuary from the heatwave, but when the cloud separated he knew what it was.

The DJ didn't wait to get approval from the station manager—there wasn't time. He flipped the needle off the Anne Murray record which was playing for the tenth time that day and broadcast the warning to the city.

Very few heard it and those that did wasted precious minutes trying to call friends and relatives to make sure they had also heard the broadcast.

The locusts first attacked and smothered those enjoying the Toronto Islands, driving screaming, panic-stricken men, women and children into the quickly bloody waters of Lake Ontario. Hot dogs burnt to a crisp on hundreds of untended barbeque grills and half-eaten suppers were dropped and scattered. Children cried for lost mothers, mothers screamed for lost children as the locusts came to supper.

The main body swarmed onto the mainland, unhindered and unstoppable. Driving hard against the windshields of cars, obscuring the view of drivers racing along at seventy miles an hour. Settling on the hot concrete surface of the MacDonald Cartier Freeway and Don Valley Parkway. Thousands of locusts squashed by the hurtling cars, creating a film of grease on the highways which made driving impossible and the thoroughfares smell like open drains.

On the MacDonald Cartier Freeway, Gordon Harrison sped away from the city with an ease born of many years handling huge tractor trailers. He had one thing in mind, and it was nothing to do with the surrounding traffic. The girl in the passenger seat shuddered with pleasure as his right hand left the gear lever once more and buried itself in the wetness between her mini-skirted thighs.

Suddenly, his vision was obscured as the insects smashed into the windshield. Splattered bodies spread their oily fluid across the glass. His windshield wipers jammed with the sheer weight and volume of the locusts. The girl screamed and he realized with terror that the huge vehicle was losing traction on the road surface as the sixteen wheels fought to get traction through the locusts that now blanketed the roadway.

Please God, he prayed, I *was* going to make it up to Ethel, perhaps take her out west, away from this . . . He felt the trailer whip around and then, with the slow inevitability of a train entering a tunnel, saw the guardrail loom in front of him as for a moment the windshield cleared. The restraining metal burst with the impact and they were falling, trapped in the cabin, toward Lakeshore Boulevard beneath. The trailer smashed into a gasoline tanker and the full load ignited with a roar under the force of impact.

The fireball rolled along the highway, igniting cars and trucks. Within three minutes, one hundred and fifty-three vehicles were blazing. They would never establish how many died in the inferno.

At city hall, the crowds were trapped by the surrounding buildings, like wild horses into a box canyon. Rolls of paper and hats were used as futile weapons to swat them off, but for the most part there could be no escape from the unthinkable omnivores.

The DJ watched with horror through the high-power binoculars that he kept in the studio. They normally provided a backup to the two traffic helicopters that buzzed around the city during rush hour. If the helicopters were away from the immediate area, the announcer could monitor the traffic to the west of the city. On a good day, he could see almost to Mississauga. They were also great for sunsets across the lake and pretty girls in nearby office buildings.

Now, the DJ scanned the streets, watching with uncomprehending eyes the dreadful scenes unfolding far beneath him. Road surfaces seemed to be swelling, flowing, and it took a conscious effort on his part to recognize that the blacktop was not melting—that he was seeing thousands of millions of insects rippling in waves toward their source of nourishment.

They followed the well-laid-out road system. North–south arteries became clogged first, then they fanned out to cover those that ran from east to west.

He watched the pall of smoke rise from the western end of Lakeshore Boulevard and moments later the windows of his studio rattled as the sound of the explosion hit the building.

He panned quickly and recognized the signs of a multiple collision. He couldn't know his wife and child had just died in the fire.

A streetcar full of people intent on traveling from the crowded Italian quarter of the city raced carelessly along Queen Street. He followed its progress with the glasses. It disappeared behind a building and then reappeared for a moment before ducking out of sight behind another.

He could see the panic-stricken passengers waving frantic hands over their heads to ward the locusts off and he watched with detached interest as the car slammed violently into the back of a stationary bus. The bus was also crowded, but the driver had obviously ordered all the windows to be closed as a protection against the marauding insects. In other circumstances, they would probably have been able to survive unscathed.

The shock of the collision forced the old-fashioned trolley car to rise into the air. The rods that took the power from the overhead cables became snagged in the live wires. As the streetcar crashed back to the tracks, the weight of it ripped the wires down onto its metal roof. Death by electrocution was immediate for all within.

The DJ watched for another two hours before turning slowly back to the abandoned turntable. His mind cracking, it was easier to imagine that what he had witnessed in the streets below simply hadn't happened.

He picked up his script of cues, spot announcements and commercials, adopting the silk-smooth voice of the professional announcer.

". . . Anne Murray and her first big hit, 'Snowbird.' Now, a word about a really *great* furniture sale this week at K-Mart. Did you know . . ."

# CHAPTER SIX

Bo Phillips and his girl, Sue Ellen, had pulled the camper truck off the road and settled down for three idyllic days in the open air. "Roughing it," Bo had called it. "Suffering," Sue Ellen had replied testily.

Sue Ellen would have much preferred the drive to Minneapolis to this stupid camping trip into the Oahe Reservation on the Missouri River. Apart from loving the bright city lights—of which there was a considerable lack in the town of Aberdeen—she knew that if the Indian police caught them on reservation land they would face a hefty fine.

She remembered, with a slight thrill, the story she had been told in high school about a group who had gone camping on the reservation back in '78. The Indian police had caught them and had taken their turn in raping the girls. The story went they had planned a two-day trip and had been held for four. Apparently the girls had been subjected to the most outrageous positions, had been forced to perform all those things they only dared to read about.

Mind you, Sue Ellen was no prude. She figured she could give the best hand job in the school. Wasn't it a fact the boys on the football team were all anxious to date her?

She looked across at Bo. Quite a guy by any standards. Best quarterback the team had ever had. Rumor had it the Green Bay Packers' scouts had their eyes on him. Now he would be quite something to catch as a husband. Ma would be real pleased if she could trap a real live football player. Maybe she ought to pretend she was pregnant. She knew that worked because her sister had managed to get that snot-nosed creep John to marry her after only one session in the back of his car. Now he owned the general store in Aberdeen, as well as the gas station and coffee shop.

Sue Ellen decided her best bet was to give Bo the best blow he'd ever had in his life. That'd clinch it. Guys always like the big treatment. Maybe this trip wouldn't be so bad after all!

"Come on, Sue Ellen," called Bo. "Help me get this crap out of the camper." He pointed toward a flat patch of land away from scrubland and rocks. "That's gotta be the best spot. We won't be bothered by snakes or scorpions over there. They like to stick near the rocks to make sure of plenty of shade!"

Sue Ellen shuddered. Scorpions and snakes. Who needed them? Why the hell they couldn't sleep in the camper was beyond her.

They cleared away an area of stones in the place Bo had indicated and while Sue Ellen carried equipment from the camper, Bo started to gather materials for a fire. At last he was happy with the store he had layed in, and coaxed the brushwood into flame.

"What the hell are you doing that for in this heat, Bo?" whined the girl, looking up incredulously as the searing ball of fire hung there in the sky.

"That's your problem, Sue Ellen, you're too used to central heating that clicks on automatically as the temperature outside drops a degree at a time. Out here, the sun goes down and the cold snaps in. Just like turning off a light. Without a fire, you'd freeze that lovely little ass of yours, and we wouldn't want that to happen, would we?"

Bo reached for the girl and fondled her backside with one hand while he pressed his groin into hers. His free hand roamed over the ample breasts.

She pulled away in mock resistance. "Come on, you horny ballplayer, why don't you get some food cooking before I'm too weak to do anything?"

Bo grinned and reached for the cooler, slapping her on the rump as he did so. Within five minutes, the aroma of steak cooking on the open fire wafted toward Sue Ellen and she decided this open air routine had a lot going for it. She was feeling very wet for Bo right now and after they had finished the steaks, she decided they would have a long session in the sack.

As the two busied themselves with their campfire, a small insect settled on an outcrop of rock two hundred yards away from the sputtering fire. After a few moments of sampling the vibrations in the air with its antennae, the creature clattered its wings and lifted off into the declining sunshine. As Sue Ellen was digging into her first mouthful of delicious meat, the scout had made its report and a larger body of locusts was swirling into the air to advance upon the unsuspecting pair.

Sue Ellen finished her steak and looked sneakily around the bush. "I guess there's nobody for miles, Bo. Right?"

Bo grinned at her. "Sure is, Sue Ellen, what you got in mind?"

Sue Ellen unbuttoned her halter top and slipped it off her shoulders, allowing her breasts to tumble free. "I guess I might as well get a good tan while we're out here," she said, stretching her arms back over her head to lift her bosom.

Bo felt a stirring in his jeans. "Why don't we get an all-over tan, then," he said, peeling off his shirt and pants in one fluid motion.

Sue Ellen affected her expression of mock surprise for the briefest of moments until Bo peeled off his jockey shorts and threw them onto the pile of clothing near the fire. He was big and that excited her. The girl unzipped her cut-off jeans with a laugh that rippled around the surrounding rocks. She hadn't bothered with underwear and the sight of the naked girl standing in the sunlight quickened Bo's pulse as he moved toward her.

With a high-pitched squeal, Sue Ellen ran away from his outstretched hands and, breasts bouncing, darted between the rocks. She was eager for him but understood well enough that it was important for him to catch her first—to play the game as long as possible before she allowed him to take her.

After darting and dodging for several minutes, she allowed herself to make an apparently fatal mistake by taking the wrong turning and running straight into him. His lips slavered across hers and she thrust back with her tongue, probing deeper and deeper into his mouth. She felt his hand caress her wetness and she willingly sank to the warm, reaching for his extended manhood.

As they coupled furiously, the first of the locusts rose into the air from the rocks where they had been watching and flew lazily toward the writhing bodies on the floor of the secluded canyon.

Sue Ellen groaned loudly and dug her nails into Bo's back and Bo grinned to himself at the pleasure he was able to give. Best lay in school they had said, and by Christ they hadn't been wrong! Pain coursed through his buttocks and momentarily he thought he ought to tell her to be careful. Then she screamed and he realized the pain he had felt first on his backside had now moved down his thighs.

They became aware of the locusts almost at the same time. Hopping insects jumped onto Bo's back and ripped, shredding their way through to his nerve centers. Sue Ellen brushed wildly at them, crying loudly when the hungry horde clamped and chewed at her breasts. She jumped to her feet, scattering many of them, and waved her hands in panic for Bo to remove a locust hanging, like a hungry babe, from her right nipple. When Bo ignored her she ripped at the insect leaving a glistening crater at the center of her breast. Blood gushed onto the sand, causing renewed frenzy amongst their attackers. Sue Ellen screamed, and tasted the bittersweet fluid that poured into her mouth from shredded lips.

Bo slapped at the insects vainly and screamed to Sue Ellen to help him. Tears streamed down his face and he rose and fell in a gesture of futility, hoping that the action would dislodge his tormentors. He babbled, screamed and cursed the girl for not coming to his aid.

Numbed by the network of welling lacerations that criss-crossed her body, Sue Ellen lay stretched out on the sandy rock, submitting to the crawling, probing insects that violated her flesh. She tried to smile at the sight of the tough football player crying like a baby and in that last, pain-filled moment she realized she had Bo all to herself throughout eternity.

"Nice to see you again, Hank—or is it Harvey?" Mark offered his hand to the hotel keeper.

Hank chuckled deeply and his eyes crinkled into a smile. "Howdy, son. Sorry about the little down-home deception last time you were here, but I figure you're clued in enough to know it was necessary. Howdy, ma'am, good to see you again."

He suddenly became serious and dropped the posture of the backwoods hotel keeper. "Washington has done a good job in setting up a projection and flight path, but then I guess you know all about that, Doc. We swung a satellite around from its orbit to give us a true trajectory of the bastards' flight across the country. They are still holding roughly to the forty-five degree line, right across the midwest. The head is in the Rapid City area—incidentally, any town or populated area fifty miles either side of the line has been evacuated, just in case. The tail stretches back to Minneapolis and St. Paul."

Hank rolled a cigarette before proceeding. "There was a real disaster in the Twin Cities, so I hear. We won't know what the death toll is until it's safe to go back in, but it's going to be big. Real big."

Hank accepted a light from Holland and blew a steady stream of smoke from his lungs into the clear mountain air. "Then they had trouble with looters and such like, of course. What they call a breakdown in civil obedience. Anyway, the locusts are expected to be here within the next six to seven hours. The end of the column should settle over the next twenty-four. That's about it. Assuming, of course, they really are coming home to roost."

Stephanie looked worriedly at the sky as if she expected to see the insects' vanguard at any moment.

Holland cleared his throat. "What about the Air Force—are they ready?"

Hank nodded, indicating a nearby officer talking rapidly into a field telephone. "Yonder's the liaison officer, Major Chuck Bellows. Told me a little while ago that the nuke is armed and loaded and standing by at Brookings Base. All we gotta do is give him the word, the bird takes off and drops it right down their throats."

Holland looked around sharply. "*We* give the word?" he asked incredulously. "Why not decide when the computer says they are all on site?"

Major Bellows had finished his conversation and was striding toward the front steps of the hotel. "I think I can answer that," he offered as he reached the group. "The computer could quite easily determine the optimum moment for the nuke's release from the aircraft, but we couldn't be sure of getting them all. The satellite picks up the mass of the swarm, not individual groupings. So, in order to ensure a wipeout situation, we have to rely on eyeball verification. That's my job. The second reason is, of course, the scientific team want to take their samples. As I understand it, that entails taking not just the leaders of the swarm, but samples of insects from the varying stages of arrival. Wouldn't do to drop the bomb while they are still shoving the little bitches into jars, would it?"

"How the devil do they collect the samples from the middle of the swarm without getting themselves eaten alive?" Holland asked.

"Quite simple, really," answered the officer. "The space program does a lot more than put men on the moon. During the course of the Apollo launches we had to develop new materials that could withstand the heat of the sun, radiation and small particles of meteorites—dust really, but capable of puncturing the suit of a man working outside his ship.

"Anyway, one of the problems was the astronaut also had to be able to function with this supersuit on. The answer was found in a substance called Tri-X 87, a material that allows a person to operate at ease, yet is heat resistant and can withstand terrific punishment for quite a while without hurting the occupant. We think it'll withstand an attack by locusts for as long as it takes to collect samples."

"I hope you're right, Major," replied Holland. "But as you, presumably, won't be wearing one of these up on the glacier, I imagine your interest is purely academic." Holland continued to study the liaison officer until the man shifted uncomfortably.

"No, I won't be wearing one. There aren't enough to go around. But I shall be down here along with my men and I imagine that some of the locusts will wander into town. We'll be a damn sight more exposed than the scientists up there!"

Holland smiled at the major's defensive attitude. "Touché, Major, I apologize for any unseemly inference. But let me ask you this—what's the backup?"

The major looked to Hank, who nodded imperceptibly.

"One of my men will be with the team on the face of the glacier and if he finds the suits aren't working he will advise me by radio. In that eventuality, my orders are to presuppose the party will be lost before any rescue team can go in and I am to advise the president that the scientific expedition is a failure."

"And the president will order the attack forthwith?"

"In essence, that's about it. We will have time to evacuate the remaining personnel from the town by helicopter to a safe distance, but the orders are quite plain—once the job is deemed successful or unsuccessful, the attack commences to ensure the swarm does not have the opportunity or the desire to move on from this point."

"So there is *no* contingency plan?"

"You mean regarding the personnel on the glacier, Captain? No, there is none. Nor would any be needed. If the suits are penetrated we will have to assume that the personnel are expended."

"You mean, Major, the personnel are expendable, don't you?"

"Captain, you are being at best argumentative and at worst obstructive," retorted the officer quickly. "I have my orders and I intend to carry them through. That doesn't mean to say, if, and I repeat *if,* I decide action on the field is required I will not carry it out. Including, I might say, the rescue and recovery of personnel on the glacier. But the decision will be mine. Do we understand each other?"

Holland looked at the man and thought how little things had changed. A military mind with a military singlemindedness. Precisely the same as he would have been—how long ago? Twenty years?

"We understand each other, Major, and I'm sure that General Gaines will give you all his support, if you are successful. But let's hope you are not called upon to make those decisions, eh?"

"Aye, aye, to that, Captain," replied the major seriously. Holland closed his eyes, thinking of the sunny day when a pilot in his wing had called virtually those same words cheerily over the radio. "Aye, aye, Captain, turning now. Chop chop, you little yellow buggers, here comes papa with eggs to make you cry. Turning now, skipper . . ."

Then Gaines was there, along with the image of shrieking jets and blossoming earth as the bombs smacked into the fertile soil. The woman with clothes alight came screaming silently toward him and he shuddered.

After they had put their overnight bags into the two rooms Hank had kept aside for them, Stephanie and Mark returned to the porch and watched the bustling activity.

Army jeeps and trucks were driving in steady procession toward the former top secret establishment at the base of the glacier. The noise of revving and changing gears was almost deafening. Military police directed traffic and stood guard at intervals along Livingston's one main street. There were, by now, no civilians left in the area, but there was still the danger of looting. Signs of their rapid departure lay all around, a gas range unceremoniously abandoned when the owner realized his truck was overloaded, a dressing-table mirror lying smashed against a privet fence.

Mobile command posts were put up in the street opposite Sinclair's Grain and Feed Store and men hastened up and down the steps of the caravans with grim, determined faces.

Further to the right, toward the end of the town, row upon row of temporary housing units had been erected on the small baseball pitch. These units housed the officers, scientists, government officials, press corps, doctors and security forces of the FBI and CIA.

It was a mammoth operation, swung into action with little advance warning. If anything, mused Holland as he took the scene in, it proved America really was one step away from military government. The speed and efficiency of the machine gave rise to terrors of its own.

"It doesn't look like the same town, does it?"

Mark looked fondly at her. "No, it doesn't. I was just thinking how unbelievably fast these guys can move when they have to. This operation must be costing a fortune. If only they'd spent that sort of money on securing . . ."

His words trailed off. There was no point in talking about the if onlys.

"Stephanie, do you think this will work?"

She shrugged. "What other option is available? A nuclear bomb will certainly ensure a high degree of destruction, to the ones that come here, at least. Then we have the problem of getting rid of the eggs that have been laid."

Holland flipped the lighter and lit the crumpled cigarette he had pulled from an equally crumpled pack. "So how do you manage that?"

She moved to the porch rail and propped herself against it, watching the troop movement on the street as she continued.

"Locate the ground where the eggs were laid and turn the soil over. The eggs become exposed and we take care of the rest with a lot of help from birds."

They lapsed into silence. Both involved in their own thoughts. Neither really wanting to talk. They sat, aimlessly, watching the road for a full, silent five minutes before Stephanie spoke again.

"It really makes you feel insignificant, doesn't it?"

"What does?"

"This! All these people moving for one purpose. What the hell could these guys do if they turned against *us?*" Then the smile she had tried to build collapsed, her attempt at levity replaced by a gray and tearful trembling.

Mark slipped an arm around her shoulder. She was starting to feel the full impact of the last few days. It wouldn't take much for her to break completely. He recognized the first indications of what used to be called battle fatigue. Waiting here, ahead of the swarm, could prove to be the final stroke. He pulled her tightly to him, cursing himself for not having noticed the building tension in her sooner. He had been too preoccupied all along with his own suspicions and hatred.

Stephanie stiffened. "The major's running this way. He looks excited."

Bellows ran lightly up the steps and joined them. "I've got good news for you. Message from your Dr. Starling in London. The mutants haven't laid their eggs yet."

Stephanie looked at the major in undisguised puzzlement. "That's crazy," she said finally.

Holland interrupted the exchange. "Why?"

Stephanie turned. "Normal mature locusts can last for anything up to two weeks before dying. During that time they complete their life cycle—which includes laying their eggs. These locusts must be infertile."

The major held up a hand. "Not so lucky, Doctor. Apparently the mature ones you and the captain took to London were around thirteen days old, as near as Dr. Starling can determine. That was four days ago and they are still alive. Starling says the females are fertile, but not about to drop their eggs. He postulates that—"

"That the genetic structure has been altered so much the life cycle has been lengthened," finished Stephanie as her mind raced along the avenues of possibilities.

"That's right."

"So we don't have to worry about a mass outbreak of mutated locusts because the main swarm hasn't yet laid any eggs, right?"

The major nodded, the grin spreading across his face. "Certainly not in the States or Europe. There are two or three locations in the Gulf which already have discovered egg depositories from the earlier breed and a program will be getting underway as soon as possible to destroy them." He stopped talking suddenly as Stephanie lowered her head in thought. Mark and the major glanced at each other.

"Dr. Caine, have you just thought of something?" asked the major.

She nodded. "I think I have, yes. Look, the locusts heading this way haven't stopped long enough to lay since the Atlantic. They seem to be bent on only one thing—returning to the mountain. I think they are coming *here* to lay their eggs!"

"So what's the problem? We get rid of the whole lot in one go—eggs and all!"

Stephanie shook her head. "If they lay the eggs in the earth around the glacier before the bomb is dropped, there is every chance we will have this problem repeated.

"The atom bomb obliterated Hiroshima and Nagasaki and yet, within days, insects were hatching normally from eggs, ones laid before the bomb destroyed the cities. In Viet Nam, the U.S. Air Force embarked on a program of defoliation of the forests, in order to deprive the Viet Cong of hiding places. They dropped millions upon millions of gallons of powerful insecticides and poisons on the forest which stripped the trees and shrubbery. It also killed all the livestock, birds, humans and poisoned the soil. It's still poisoned and can't be used for agriculture. Yet, despite this heavy assault, which went on for months, the first creatures back in the ravaged area were ants. And they hatched from eggs left in formicaries by parents long since dead. The poison didn't kill the eggs. Just as the radiation from the bombs didn't kill the eggs in Japan. And just as the bomb on the mountain will not kill those which will be laid when the mutants arrive. If anything, the radiation in the soil might further mutate the newborn insects."

The major looked hard at her. It made sense. But before he called Washington he had to have an alternative plan. "So how do we make sure we get them all, Doc?"

Stephanie looked at the major and then to Mark for help.

She looked at his drawn, craggy face, at the strong chin, at the ugly bite marks, and she felt instinctively for the welts on her own arms.

"Fire!" she exclaimed suddenly. "That's how." She looked eagerly at Mark. "Remember in the cab in Nice, we got those locusts off our bodies by holding a flame from your lighter under them. They reacted by trying to curl away from the heat. They didn't try to fly away. Fire must be the answer!"

Removing his hat the major wiped a hand over his thinning hair. "But that doesn't get rid of the *eggs*, does it?"

"Yes, it does. Look, first we burn the locusts themselves—which gets rid of the ones that haven't laid. Even if eggs have been laid, a strong enough heat will cook them up to six inches into the earth. The ones in the earth are the real problem. Locusts lay up to three lots of eggs so we shall get most of them before they are even laid. Before they leave the female. The laid eggs will be no deeper than four to five inches in the soil and I think we can get to those by *baking* them in the ground."

"I don't know, Doctor, it seems like the nuke is still the best bet."

Stephanie threw up her hands. "Do you know *anything* at all about locusts?"

"Not much, but—"

"But you're learning, right? Well, by the time you realize what I'm telling you is correct, it'll be too late. The simple fact is your precious nuclear device will not get the eggs that were laid prior to the explosion. You'll get ninety percent but it's the other ten percent that will cause the problem later on. Use fire and you get the eggs buried in the first laying as well. Do you see now?"

The officer nodded. "It's gotta be a hell of a fire to incinerate a whole damn mountain all at once. And hot, it's gotta be hot. The fire has to be able to seep into all the nooks and crannies . . ."

"Napalm," muttered Mark softly. "Napalm the area, that'll do it."

"How? Jesus Christ, that mountain is three thousand feet high!"

Mark thought for a moment. "If the fire starts below the mountain, the locusts above will fly away. Start it at the top so the air above is too hot for them and you trap them in an inversion. Sequential charges, spread across the mountain and the area around the glacier, looped all the way down at intervals, say every hundred feet, the delay between charges igniting at the top and those at the base no more than twelve seconds apart and you have an instant burn that creates heat in a cyclonic fashion. Intense heat. Nothing could survive."

"Like Dresden in the war, eh?"

Holland inclined his head in agreement. That was exactly what would happen. The Allies had bombed Dresden mercilessly and the fires that were started burned so fiercely that cyclones of fire columns raged, sucking the air out of the city. Those who didn't die by the bombs and fire, died because the massive fires sucked the air away, leaving a furnace-like vacuum.

"Right, I'll call Washington right away. General Gaines will have to talk with the president about this."

Holland snorted. If Gaines followed true to form, he would pass the buck until it was too late to act.

They watched Bellows race back to his trailer and Mark placed his arm around Stephanie's shoulder again.

# CHAPTER SEVEN

"ALL PERSONNEL ARE NOW ON-SITE, MR. PRESIDENT. SCIEN-tific team will be airlifted to the glacier as soon as the locusts settle."

The president nodded in understanding and turned back to the screen in the Pentagon's war room. The global map showed there was heavy activity going on in the Soviet Union and the Red Alert signal flashed its grim warning.

As expected, the Soviets had put their huge Tupolevs into the air. They would be fully armed with nuclear capability. Despite SALT neither side trusted the other, and the military members of the Politburo had persuaded their chairman they must take steps to protect themselves in case the Americans used the chaos as a cover for a sneak attack.

So the Russians put their armada into the air and the Americans had been forced to put the Strategic Air Command on Red Alert.

And so it went on. Around and around, each side suspicious of the other. Shaking his head sadly, the president turned from the board and addressed the uniformed general sitting nearby. "Show me the present position of Ice Melter."

The general had been asked a dozen times in the last hour to punch up the sequence of numbers that would show the location of the aircraft carrying the bomb. He did it for the thirteenth.

The map changed on the screen and instead of the multiple flashing dots that had shown on the previous picture, this carried only one. "There he is, Mr. President. Still in a holding pattern over Butte. We shall have the device in the air, ready at all times for your authorization to bomb the mountain."

"Thank you, General Gaines. You're a very patient man."

Gaines smiled at the self-deprecating remark. "Mr. President, you can ask a hundred times. What we have to do is scary enough without worrying about how often the president wants to be reassured."

The president smiled back. "You'd make a good politician, Arthur."

"With respect, no, sir. I have enough trouble in the Air Force without taking on the bears on the Hill."

"I know what you mean, General." The president glanced again at the board. Once he gave the command, that dot would cease flashing and speed to the east to deliver its lethal cargo.

With a shudder, he turned back to the general. "You know this guy at the glacier, don't you, General?"

"Yes, sir. Holland. He was a captain in my command in Korea. Good pilot, but got shook up and went to pieces. We managed to cover it up as much as possible, but he was finished. Resigned his commission after a court-martial found against him."

The president listened, as though hearing this for the first time. He knew the real story, having been fully briefed on the background of all participants in the operation. As he listened to Gaines lying through his teeth, the president decided he wouldn't offer Gaines' name to Congress to replace Tom Carthy after all.

The colonel supervising the communications link with Livingston called to Gaines that he was needed. "Channel two, General. It's Major Bellows."

The president indicated that Bellows should be put onto the open speaker and Gaines punched the appropriate buttons.

"General Gaines here, Major. What is it?"

In Livingston, the major took a deep breath. This could well be the end of the line.

"General, request that you stop Ice Melter."

"What did you say?" roared the president. "Would you be good enough to explain?"

Bellows groaned audibly at the familiar sound of the president's voice. This *was* it!

"Sir, Dr. Caine has pointed out that as the locusts haven't laid their eggs, they are probably going to wait to do so when they arrive. She advises that it will be impossible for us to destroy the entire swarm prior to them laying a batch around the mountain. The doctor also advises that a nuke will not affect the eggs substantially to terminate an ongoing problem."

"Can she supply proof of that?"

"Yes, Mr. President. She points out that after we blasted Japan, insects hatched from their eggs quite normally. Neither the blast nor the radiation killed them off. She also says after the defoliation in Nam the ants were first back on the scene, again from eggs that had been under the contaminated soil. It didn't have any effect on them, and she says we will have the same result here."

"Hold for a moment, Major." He nodded to Gaines who placed Bellows on hold. "What do you think, General?"

"Sounds like bull to me, sir. Nothing could live through a nuclear strike. But nothing!"

The president rubbed momentarily at tired eyes. "I am not so sure, General. After the tests on Christmas Island they found many insects had survived. Bikini Atoll was the same. I think there is a chance that this Dr. Caine might be right. Contact our own people in Washington and see what they think. Also check with London and the Leningrad Institute to see what they make of the theory. Put Bellows back on."

Gained punched the speaker back to life before moving to the communications officer and issuing terse instructions.

"Major, any suggestions as to what method should be used?"

He glanced at the clock. "According to the time schedule there appears to be about five hours before they start arriving."

"Mr. President, Mark Holland, he's one of—"

"I know who he is. Go on."

"Yes, sir. Holland suggests that we use napalm. Virtually encircle the mountain with the stuff. Set the charges off at the top first to prevent them flying upward and then the lower charges blow, trapping them in the middle of a conflagration. Holland says we can create a vacuum like at Dresden in WWII. We either incinerate them or suffocate them and bake the eggs under the surface."

"Do you think it will work?"

"Mr. President, I don't know. But after listening to Dr. Caine, I think it's a better bet than a nuke—for a lot of reasons."

"How long will it take you to organize delivery of napalm in sufficient quantities?"

Bellows hesitated. "I have already started, sir. I put out the word before I called."

The president smiled at that. Then a thought occurred to him.

"Major, how could you get ordinance to gather that much napalm? It's against executive orders to stockpile the sort of quantities you envision in one place."

In Livingston, Bellows looked to Holland, his face stricken. He groaned again.

"I told them you had ordered it, Mr. President," he admitted quietly.

The president looked at the speaker, trying to imagine what sort of a body was wrapped around the distant voice.

"Did you indeed, Major? I want to see you at the White House as soon as this is over. Do you understand?" The voice came across frosty, but there was a trace of an appreciative smile in the president's eyes. He was going to enjoy meeting this officer who acted by instinct.

"I then assume you have already started to ring the mountain with the stuff?"

"That is correct, sir, yes. I'm interspersing the drums of napalm with drums of oil—it'll burn better."

"And if I disagree with your scheme, what happens then, Major?"

There was a long silence during which the president scanned the message that Gaines handed to him. At length the speaker crackled as Bellows replied.

"I guess a court-martial, the stockade and booted out of the service, sir."

"That may still happen, Major, but you will be pleased to learn the experts agree in theory with Dr. Caine. We will call off Ice Melter. I hope it works, Major, for all our sakes."

*"Yes, sir."*

Gaines clicked off the speaker and glanced at the president. After a while the president looked up.

"Maintain Ice Melter, General. If that boy's idea doesn't work, then we'll have to order the plane in, immediately."

"Sir." Neither of them mentioned the ground crews caught in the open. There was no need.

"You'll have to arrange for a spotter to monitor the fire. If the locusts look like they're getting away from the area, we send the nuke in. You'd also better move the aircraft up closer once they seem to be arriving at the glacier."

The general moved away again to relay the latest orders to the communications officer as the president stared deeply at the silent speaker. He hoped it would work.

If not, he would never get to meet the major who had the courage to issue orders in the president's name.

*The Other Place. They had returned.*

*Recognition had swept through the mass as they arrived at the mountain, understanding, acceptance, that their journey was now over.*

*Many had been lost, but there would be more generations to come once the families had laid their eggs. Eggs that even now, as the first of them settled, were ready to burst from the swollen bodies.*

*The pungent smell of the rich glacial earth assailed their sensory glands, then their antennae began twitching as another familiar odor was detected in the evening air.*

*The locusts watched the strangely-clad humans moving awkwardly across the rough terrain and their instinct told them there was no danger from these creatures. For the moment, they were prepared to allow a mutual cohabitation of their home.*

*Thousands settled on the oil drums that encircled the mountain, spiraling from top to bottom. Thousands more upon the huge canisters of napalm. Inquisitive jaws investigated the hard, cold metal and then, promptly, forgot about them when nothing in the way of nourishment came forth.*

*The miles of piping that housed the electric wiring which ran between the oil and the napalm charges was also examined and similarly rejected when the casing was found to be too tough to penetrate.*

*The locusts would concentrate on the softer flesh of humans when they felt again the need to eat. But, first, the eggs had to be safely deposited.*

"The important thing to remember," the Major had repeated, "is if you feel a locust getting through the fabric, you mustn't panic. Do you understand?"

"What the hell are we supposed to do—pray?" muttered Holland, his voice was distorted through the voice box in the front of his suit.

The major made a correction in the setting of the volume by adjusting the balance of the twin speakers. He grinned at the face peering out through the thick face mask.

"No, Captain, I don't think that would do much good. Do just what you were briefed to do, let out a holler and one of the support troops will hose you down with a flamethrower."

"It better work, Major, otherwise you're liable to have a few barbequed scientists on your hands!"

"It should work. After all, the heat of the sun up close is many times stronger than a flamethrower and this material helps to protect our men in space. I'm not worried about that."

"Why should you be?" retorted Holland. "You're not going up there."

Bellows grinned again and slapped Holland on the back to indicate he was ready to go. The reports from the mountain had shown that the numbers of locusts arriving were steadily decreasing. The scientific survey team which was monitoring the arrival had concluded that no more than an hour remained before the last would settle.

Stephanie had been scheduled to fly to the breeding ground with the final shift. Mark had been assigned to assist her, carrying one of the cumbersome sample boxes that, by the time they returned to Livingston, would contain hundreds of locusts from varying locations on the face.

They had been told they had exactly one hour to collect their samples from the time they were deposited inside the compound at the Bug Hutch. Bellows had told the hushed roomful of scientists and support staff that in precisely one and a half hours the mountain would be ignited. Any who did not make it back to the rendezvous point in time to be airlifted back to the town would be assumed dead.

There was no room, or time, for independent activity. They were told they had to operate according to the strict rules laid down by the army, that the safety of the majority would always take precedence over the individual.

Hank finished checking Stephanie's equipment and after satisfying himself she was secure, gave her an encouraging pat on the arm and a quick thumbs-up signal. Mark helped her across the street to the waiting helicopter and the rest of the group which would be involved in the final sortie.

Hank and Major Bellows shielded their eyes as the Chinook lifted off in a cloud of dust whipped up from the street. They watched as the helicopter circled once before turning to the south, heading at full power to the point where the nightmare had started and where all hoped it would now finally end.

Holland peered through the small window in the doorway of the huge machine. It was difficult to see through the awkward, claustrophobic helmet, but at last he could make out the small figures on the street below. He was reminded of the morning he had left Sadallah's mountain encampment. And of the day his own nightmare had started, long before.

He moved closer to Stephanie and reached for her arm with his heavily-gloved hand. She turned and smiled at him and in that moment he made the decision. He moved his helmeted head closer to hers so that she could hear him better.

"I love you, Stephanie. When we got back I'm going to marry you."

Stephanie heard his words echoing through the electronic voice pack and groaned silently to herself. She cared for the man, of that there was no doubt. But marriage! After studying his character analysis she had concluded that Holland was basically a weak man living his own role-playing fantasy. The sort of man who, on paper at least, was easily manipulated.

The emergency had disproved much of the so called expert analysis. While he did have many character flaws, she had found him to be capable of sensitive, warm emotions, and more than dependable in a tight spot. Although she was forced to agree with Fort Langley's analysis that Holland could be manipulated successfully, Stephanie knew Holland's decision to marry her was made genuinely, without coercion or psychological blackmail being applied on her part.

Stephanie suddenly felt angry—at herself, at the system, at Holland and everyone connected with the disaster. It wasn't fair to place her in this position—Stephanie suddenly stopped her random thoughts as she realized Holland would be expecting a response.

"That's got to be the most romantic proposal any woman ever had," she said huskily leaning against him and relaxing her guard enough to allow a sigh to escape from her lips.

Ahead of them, the last of the locusts settled on the mountain to join the seething mass which covered it like a shroud.


"Red team, you are moving too high for safety. Return nearer the Green point." The disembodied voice crackled over Mark's speaker and he glanced awkwardly upward. High above him he could see the ghostly figures of three of the team designated Red moving slowly among a wave of insects disturbed at the intrusion.

"Green Team, do you have any problems?" Mark clicked

his transmit button and spoke slowly, allowing the throat microphone to pick up his words. "That's negative, Command. How long do we have?"

"Twenty minutes. No more."

"Roger."

"Godammit, Red Team, I told you, you are too far up the face. Begin descent. *Now!*"

Holland grinned to himself at the young officer's annoyance. He glanced upward again and saw the team climbing even higher into the mass of locusts. If they ran into trouble at that height, they would be beyond the reach of the soldiers with flamethrowers circulating at different levels on the lower face. The idea had been that each of the six teams would stay in clearly defined areas to enable at least one of the flamethrowers to reach them quickly if they did have trouble. The Red Team leader obviously decided that discretion was the better part of valor and, as Mark watched, the three men started their ponderous descent.

Mark felt a tug at his elbow and turned. Stephanie handed him a sealed sample jar containing half a dozen insects. He nodded and opened the case, placing the bottle in one of the spaces along the extendible shelves, marking on the map the position from which it had been taken.

When they had all alighted from the helicopter, they had been shown a series of relief maps of the mountain pinned to a large board. Each shift had been allocated an area from which they could collect samples and make other observations. The final shift, theirs, had been allocated to the east face.

Mark's experience showed him immediately that this would be a dangerous spot to be caught in if the locusts decided to attack in force. Sharp crags intermingled with deep holes, and crevasses pitted the entire eastern flank.

Although, so far, the locusts hadn't seriously bothered the other teams that had moved among the scores of females laying in the glacial earth, Holland knew the first waves had arrived on the east, and would now have finished depositing their eggs. They would be hungry.

As the team emerged into the clearing beneath the mountain,

a hushed gasp went up from the throats of the expedition. The entire skyline seemed to be alive.

The noise of the insects was almost deafening as they moved into the midst of the sea of dark-brown creatures. As they climbed higher and higher up the face, it sounded like they were treading on wet gravel. Almost immediately, the insects began to cover their suits.

Those that came behind cursed as they gripped their ropes and scrambled for a foothold as they slipped on the crushed bodies and oozing liquid that spurted over the rocks.

At last, they had reached their allotted areas. Under the watchful eyes of their guards, they had gone to work with a curiosity and eagerness that testified to the scientists' urge to get a firsthand look at the creatures. To them now it mattered little what the Bible and Koran predicted, what misery they had seen. What mattered was that a new species had evolved, and now they too were given the chance to investigate, to probe, to evaluate.

Sample after sample disappeared into the bottles of liquid. There would only be a few taken alive for the laboratories. The president had agreed to the expedition taking place only on the condition that live samples were not collected. There could never be the risk of the mutants escaping to cause havoc again. In time, the president would hear of these in laboratories in England and France, and pressure would be brought to destroy them . . . after the locusts had given up their genetic secrets.

The third member of the Green Team, an excitable professor from Harvard, seemed to be on the collecting spree of his life as he bobbed up and down among the agitated insects.

Mark brushed a sleeve across his face plate to clear the locusts that had covered it, but in moments they alighted more densely than before. It was really only now that he saw them right up close, their eyes glinting, their abdomens curling grotesquely against the glass, that he realized how ugly they were. This had been the hardest part, moving among them—the swarms thickly covering every available inch of the suited bodies.

A feeling of impending suffocation made it necessary to fight off panic by closing one's eyes and trying to breathe normally. The internal air packs automatically started operating when the air intake, through the metal vents, fell below an acceptable level. The only danger would be if someone wandered too far away from help, unable to clear the vents himself, thereby stopping the flow of air which supplemented the internal air course.

Stephanie waded into the mass of bodies once more. Mark thought he recognized her need to be a part of this expedition, to be in at the death of the creatures that those close to her had created. It was a form of atonement.

"All teams, this is Command. Return to rendezvous point. I repeat, return to rendezvous point."

Allowing for the time needed to descend to the base of the mountain and the flight back to Livingston before the mountain was cleared, they would have spent one half hour collecting their specimens.

To the intrigued scientists, it was too short. To Holland and the rest of the supporting network of men, it was plenty long enough. He cleared his face plate again and glanced above him to see other team members gradually working their way down the face in obedience to the command.

A locust hung upside down from his helmet and peered back at Holland through the glass. It bobbed its head and studied the face within through red, liquid eyes, the small jaws opening and closing in a gesture that left Mark in no doubt as to what the thing desired. Holland raised a gloved hand and squashed the insect against the plate and a rivulet of yellow liquid smeared the glass.

Sample boxes were lowered gingerly from level to level and then the team members themselves started the perilous journey to the base. Experienced rock climbers helped lower the scientists, to clear everybody off in the quickest possible time. When the inexperienced were safely down, the marines would quickly cross the face, making the evacuation complete.

Mark lowered the last of the sample boxes to the two men

fifty feet below him and then turned to help Stephanie as she struggled to untangle herself from one of the climbing ropes which had snarled itself around her foot. Mark could see, even at the distance he was from her that she was starting to panic.

The woman's thrashing movements were agitating the locusts. "Stay calm," he ordered through his communicator. "I'm coming, just stand still!"

A cloud of locusts flew straight into her face plate and Mark heard her shriek in fright at the sudden movement.

She stumbled and fell backward, unable to regain her balance in the clumsy suit. Mark watched with horror as she fell toward a sharp boulder that jutted outward and upward from the rocky ground.

The edge of the boulder snagged into the material beside her breast and with the sudden arresting pull of the granite on the fabric, Stephanie was thrown further off balance, falling heavily into the heaving mass on the ground.

Mark heard the ripping of the cloth over the intercom and screamed to a nearby marine. "She's in trouble, give me a hand! Quick!"

The man hoisted his flamethrower to his shoulder and moved as swiftly as he could. Mark reached the point where the marine's path intersected his and they both heard Stephanie scream with pain. "Oh God, Mark, they've got into the suit. Help me!"

Inside the suit, Stephanie felt an uncontrollable surge of panic. The heat of the material and its claustrophobic closeness made her sweat fiercely. Now the insects had found the rip, and she was terrified. There was no way she could defend herself against the insects that were becoming more excited as they sensed the fear and tasted the sweaty meat. She felt as though she were being cut to pieces with razor blades. They tore away the skin from her stomach and thighs.

The marine was several steps ahead of him when Mark realized with horror that the man was bringing the flamethrower into the firing position as Stephanie struggled to her feet. The suit was ripped the full length of her side, from just below the armpit to the knee. She was covered from head to foot with a blanket of ravenous creatures. The inside of her suit seethed with them and the sound of her incessant cries cut through his head like a high speed drill.

"God, No. *Don't fire,*" yelled Mark.

The burning tongue licked hungrily outward from the long barrel and swallowed Stephanie in a sheet of flame. She raised her hands as her body arched in pain and for several frozen seconds resembled a fiery cross.

His mind flashed back across the years and saw at once the image of the Korean woman, the child burning with napalm as she ran toward him. The only difference from the scene he'd visualized so many times in his nightmares was that now he could hear the screams. They reverberated through his earphones and through his head. And the woman had Stephanie's tortured face. He could see her face. He could see where the flames had found the tear in the suit, where the napalm had reached through to scorch and burn flesh that already hung in strands from naked bone. He had to get to her, to help her.

Just as he reached her, she stumbled again blindly and rolled away towards the crevasse. He stumbled after her, stretching out with his hand to give her support. Stephanie tried to grip it, but the weight of her burning body and the cumbersome suit took her over the edge. Mark knew she wouldn't have the strength to hang on, so he flipped his hand around and gripped the material near her extended right glove.

"For Christ's sake, help me," yelled Mark into his communicator. "I can't hold her for long."

He looked down into her visor and saw the brown eyes pleading. "I'm so sorry, Mark," she whispered through the pain. "So very sorry." Then she vomited into her helmet as a group of insects sought sanctuary in her throat from the smoldering flesh.

She lapsed into unconsciousness and he felt his hand and arm tear apart with the exertion of trying to hold her weight. He could hear the labored breathing of the marine in his earpiece and knew that help was coming. Then he knew it was too late.

With a howl of anguish, Mark felt his fingers, injured by

the thug in London, give way, and he watched Stephanie's body hurtle into the crevasse.

Sadallah motioned his visitor to sit on the couch opposite him and, as he did so, scrutinized him carefully. Mustapha had informed him, by radio, that one of their southernmost bases had stopped two Land Rovers carrying five men on the torturous track which led high into the mountains. That they should be on this route at all indicated a prior knowledge of what they would find at its end as, to the casual observer, the track looked capable of supporting nothing heavier than the occasional mountain goat.

The rebel chieftain had listened to the brief radio report and its cryptic message, deliberately kept short of habit to avoid detection by government monitoring vehicles but now an unnecessary precaution as the government was in almost total disarray. He decided that for once he would allow the party to proceed into his encampment.

"For the one who is supposed to be the Mahdi," he began softly, "you have arrived with very few followers."

Ishmail Khalkali winced at the jibe and glowered back at Sadallah. Over the last few days the self-styled Prophet of God had convinced himself that at last his time and the time of his people had arrived. Wherever he had gone he had been welcomed as the savior of Islam enjoying the reverence bestowed upon him both by kings and common men alike. A retort sprang to his lips and was as just quickly stemmed by Khalkali. There must be accord between the two of them—for the moment at least, until the rebirth of Islam was completed.

"My brother," he said instead, "I have come to you because Allah has directed me to do so. Allah has need of your soldiers to rid this land of those who deny Him. The need is—"

Sadallah held one hand up to stem the Mahdi's speech. "First," he said leaning forward in the chair, "you are not my brother. Second, if Allah has appointed you to lead a crusade against the infidel then I should be very much surprised. You are an extremist and extremists are unwelcome in my country

and in my own battle to reunite this unhappy country into one
cohesive and contented country. A theocracy of the type you
envision would rapidly become as oppressive as the one which
has plagued our brothers in Iran. You wish only to replace
serfdom with slavery. There can be no unity between you and
me."

Khalkali rose slightly. "Then I must warn you, our people
are ready to follow me. You and your men will, by your refusal,
be considered to be against Allah. That can only lead you to
eventual defeat by the hands of the very people you say you
wish to help."

Sadallah smiled his careful smile and leaned back in the
chair. He had heard reports that this man could be a persuasive,
almost hypnotic speaker, yet the image presented to him now
was one of a messianic and tired mortal. Hardly the type to
have been selected by Allah for the greatest mission on earth.
The fact remained, however, that Khalkali *could* draw the people to him now. The entire Middle East was in turmoil following
the locusts' attack and as a battle-hardened commander he knew
that now was the time to strike.

The fact that the so called Messengers of Allah had exacted
a toll on Islamic people as well as Christians was beside the
point. It wouldn't take much to convince the people that those
who had died had been unworthy to witness the coming of
Allah.

"By the way, we thought you had perished at Mecca. How
did you escape?"

The Mahdi smiled crookedly. "Allah himself plucked me
to his bosom and carried us away. The unworthy perished."

Sadallah nodded thoughtfully. That would certainly convince the ignorant peasant who would make up the bulk of this
madman's army and it would ensure Khalkali's status as Mahdi
was not challenged. In reality Sadallah knew that under Mecca
was a labyrinth of tunnels designed to hold an army which
would emerge to protect the city in case of war. Although built
many centuries ago, the tunnels were maintained and, undoubtedly, a great many of them would exit far from the city

in the desert in order that the protective army could launch a sneak attack from an enemy's rear. The Mahdi and the remnants of his followers would have used this method to escape from the city and in so doing create the myth of his escape by divine intervention.

He decided his course of action and stood. "I shall consider what you have said. You will be escorted to another of our encampments further down the mountain and I ask that you wait there one day longer for my decision. If my answer is a final no, then you may leave to begin your jihad. May Allah go with you."

The Mahdi moved forward and kissed Sadallah on both cheeks. "I trust you will change your mind and join with us. If not..." the rest was unsaid, but the threat was implicit in his voice. Without further word he turned and walked through the door of Sadallah's bungalow. As he did so, Ziad caught Mustapha's eye and the man walked across to the carpeted room and stood before him.

"Mustapha, I want you to do something for me, for the cause. You know that part of the road where it narrows so badly that unless you use extreme care even a goat would fall into the valley below."

"Where the tree stump still bears blossom in the spring? Yes, I know the place."

"Kill the Mahdi and his men and throw them and their vehicles into the ravine. Use men who will never talk of this. But it must be done if we are to prevent a splitting of loyalties amongst our people."

Mustapha looked carefully at his commander. "Is that wise? What of those who know the Mahdi is alive and has come here? They will spread the word that you killed him and turn against you surely?"

Sadallah shook his head. "I doubt that our friend the Mahdi had told anyone he needs to ask us for help. The messenger of Allah should not need outside help after all. Nor would he be prepared to reveal that he escaped from Mecca just yet. Better to wait until the people are sure he is dead and present himself again, much more theatrical and impressive. No, I think he has come to us quietly and as far as the world is concerned he died at Mecca. Let it be so!"

Mustapha turned with a slight nod and walked toward the door. As he pulled it open, Sadallah called to him. "One other thing, Mustapha. Let us keep this between ourselves—don't bother to inform your friends in the CIA." Mustapha glanced sharply at his friend, relieved to see the familiar, warm smile crease the man's face as he added, "I have known of your relationship for many years; don't look so startled. It has also served my purpose in the past to have the Americans know things which I couldn't tell them directly. Get on with your task."

Mustapha shook his head in admiration, walking through the door with a jauntiness in his step.

# CHAPTER EIGHT

WILLING HANDS HELPED MARK HOLLAND FROM THE CHINOOK and he stepped dazedly into the swirling dust of Livingston's main street.

Frantically they had grabbed at him, pulling him back up over the edge of Stephanie's tomb, stopping him from scrambling after her down the precipice. The faceless hands had restrained him and the distant voices had shouted again and again that it was no use.

He had a vague recollection of being half dragged to the waiting helicopter, and of the brief flight back to the town— a vision of averted glances and sorrowful looks, sympathetic touches and a feeling of misery deep within him that he knew he would never outlive.

He staggered drunkenly against the metal of the helicopter and quick hands sought to help him regain his balance. Other hands released the locking bolts on his helmet and lifted it over his head. Instinctively, he reached out and took the helmet from the technician. He needed to have something in his hands and he turned it this way and that, as though examining it for possible flaws. All the while, a churning anger ate away at him.

Hank and Major Bellows walked toward him and wordlessly took an arm each to walk him slowly to the steps of the nearest trailer.

Holland slumped down onto the stairs and leaned his head against the door frame, eyes closed.

"I'm really sorry things turned out this way, son."

Mark opened his eyes slowly and looked into the distraught face of the hotel owner. He nodded his head slowly, several times. "Yeah, me too, Hank." He slammed his fist hard against the door frame, splitting the skin and smearing the wood with his blood. "What a dumb thing to happen. Jesus, Jesus, Jesus . . ."

Bellows reached forward, placing a hand on the slumped shoulder.

"I know it's not much comfort, Captain Holland, but the marine didn't realize the rip in her suit was so bad. He was following standard procedure in hosing down somebody who was in trouble. I'm sorry . . ."

Bellows' words trailed off as Holland glared at him. "Christ, I told him not to fire. If that sonofabitch had waited we might have been able to save her."

Holland leaned back again and closed his eyes. There was little point in ranting against an inexperienced marine who had done what he thought was the best thing. There had been no choice for the soldier. No way of calling on past experience. There was trouble and he had reacted as he had been told.

Mark's mind started numbly to accept the inevitable. It had been that way after sorties against the Communists in the hills of North Korea. Attack and kill, every man for himself and then back to the safety of the airfield and count the losses. "Sorry, Captain Holland, Billy didn't make it. Saw him go down—no parachute!" The moment of sad reflection, then the reply, "That's too bad, he was a good kid. I'll write to his folks. How about a beer?"

There had been no time to think too long about the loss of another nineteen-year-old pilot. Or to wonder what his family and friends would think when they heard that Billy, or John, or Paul would not be coming back. You'd never be able to get back in the air if you did. Never be able to carry on living and watching for the planes coming at you out of the sun.

Stephanie had known the risks, just like those kids in Korea, and she had accepted them willingly, almost eagerly perhaps. And she had been another casualty of the war.

Tears trickled slowly through the closed eyelids and ran down dusty cheeks before Holland sat upright and wiped them away. "Oh, shit!"

He looked up. Hank was still standing there with the concerned look on his face. He smiled weakly at him.

"I'm all right, Hank. When's detonation?"

Hank turned and indicated Bellows standing in deep discussion with several other officers. "Anytime now I guess, son. They're just making sure everybody's away from the area—"

He glanced quickly back to Holland who smiled tightly at him. "Everybody who's coming, anyway, eh?"

Hank averted his eyes and Holland pushed himself upright. "Come on, Hank, let's go and see the button pushed on those bastards!"

As they joined the small knot of officers a low droning noise reached them and all heads turned toward the west to locate its source.

High above them, a long con trail stretched across the crystal clear blue sky. As they watched, the aircraft started turning on a flight path that would center it right over the mountain that now lay in the distance to the south of town.

Bellows smiled grimly. "The president is obviously keeping an ace up his sleeve. That's got to be Ice Melter, on the spot in case our operation isn't successful."

Hank looked at Bellows. "You mean that thing's loaded? Christ, we won't have time to get clear!"

Bellows nodded. "That's right. There's a low yield nuke on board and if the observers decide the bomb should be dropped, then they'll drop it."

He turned back to the officers. "Right, you know what to do, but make sure you detonate in the correct sequence or . . ." he glanced skyward again, ". . . they'll do it for you. Get going!"

The officers turned and moved to the detonation trailer. Bellows studied Holland.

"You want to watch this, Captain?"

Holland nodded, barely perceptibly. He understood the major's concern. It was never pleasant attending funerals and this one, this cremation, was going to be hard to take.

Bellows checked his watch. "Thirty seconds."

As though instinctively, activity stopped among the soldiers and airmen on the ground. Everyone turned toward the mountain. At fifteen seconds the speaker on top of the firing wagon crackled into life. "Fifteen, fourteen, thirteen . . ."

A soldier scratched his backside absentmindedly and a dog clattered the lid from a garbage can in search of scraps of food, obliviously happy in its quest.

"Twelve, eleven, ten . . ."

Holland accepted a cigarette from Hank, gratefully sucking the harsh smoke into his lungs. He saw an almost complete circle of vapor from the huge jet as it positioned itself to jetison its load.

"Nine, eight, seven . . ."

The dog pulled a piece of meat out of a bag and started to chew it noisily. An airman flicked a stone and the animal scurried away with the prize dangling from its jaws.

"Six, five, four . . ."

Mark glowered at the mountain that had claimed Stephanie as a toll for its invasion, for the obscenity man had created and sent back to its slopes. Holland almost hoped it wouldn't work. That the plane would drop its device and kill them all. He hated this mountain. He wanted to see it totally and irrevocably destroyed.

"Three, two, one."

They stared at it. Nothing. For an eternity, nothing happened. Bellows held his hand up to stem the inquiry forming on Hank's lips. "It takes a moment for the signal to reach the relay station and then pulse forward."

Then, high up at the peak, there was a cloud of smoke rushing skyward, followed by another and another. Smoke mingled with smoke as the silent explosions erupted in well-ordered chains across and down the face. Red and yellow tongues of fire leaped and scurried, searching for fuel to satisfy their insatiable appetite. Fire roared like ocean waves and was then obliterated instantly by more smoke, black and oily as it enveloped the mountain and the glacier.

Then the sound of the detonations reached them and shouts of euphoria went up from the troops as they clapped each other on the back and the mountain turned like a huge funeral pyre.

The fire raged and secondary explosions could be heard as the remains of the ice buckled under the intense heat, exploding skyward. The bodies of the original Rocky Mountain locusts, entombed so long ago, provided added fuel.

At length, the speaker at the firing station crackled into life and they heard General Gaines' voice.

"I have a report from Ice Melter One. Congratulations, it looks as though they are not needed. They shall maintain position until advised by the president to return to base. Out."

Bellows turned with a grin. "They should know. They'll be linked into the satellite scan of the area. If they say we got them, then by Christ we did!"

Holland stared blankly at the officers before looking again toward the burning mountain. All around him, activity resumed as the unessential equipment was stacked away into the huge trucks that had carried it to Livingston. The military machine would just as quickly transport it all away, leaving only a small amount of equipment to handle the mopping-up operation.

Now that the main threat had been taken care of, the secondary attack would begin. More napalm would be dropped for miles around to kill any locusts that might not yet have reached the target. The humans would have to rebuild their nests elsewhere.

Fire breaks would be dug and the National Guard would assist in ensuring the flames that would rage did not spread too far into the national parkland. That they would spread was beyond doubt. That they would destroy millions of acres of prime trees was unavoidable. But the fight against the locusts must end here. That had to be assured.

Even as they stood watching the acrid smoke snaking toward

the sky, a massive follow-up program was moving into position, readying itself for the protracted sweep that had to be undertaken along every inch of ground over which the mutant swarms had flown, searching and probing to ensure any maturing adult eggs were found and destroyed along with mutant survivors in Europe who had been too weak to make the long trek back to the glacier.

The horror experienced by individuals and nations would ensure the massive funding needed would be made available, and for once the United Nations would live up to its name and purpose by ensuring that the cleansing of the earth was thorough and coordinated.

The one thing the United Nations could not stop, however, would be the quite natural wish of the public to put the entire episode behind them, to lock the horror away in an attempt to forget that such a thing could ever have happened in the first place. This would be the main danger to those scientists who would counsel continuation of the program after it appeared the danger of a second outbreak had passed.

Mark lost all track of time as he stood watching the death of the mountain and at length Hank touched his arm. "They want your suit, son," he said gently.

Holland looked vacantly at the man and then started to climb out of the equipment. Hank handed it to a sergeant, tossing the helmet to another non-com, before turning his attention back to Holland.

"Don't know if you're planning to take off right away or not. But if you want to stay around for a while, there's plenty of room inside."

Holland tried to put together a smile of thanks, then glanced back at the column of smoke. He seemed unable to tear his mind away, could almost hear the crackling, popping of the locust bodies as they were consumed by the flames. And somewhere up there, Stephanie . . .

He shivered. The old man still stood solicitously by his side.

The black, oily cloud spread into Livingston, tainting the air with the smell and taste of death. The mountain was obscured completely from sight and suddenly Holland felt old, and very alone.

"I am tired, Hank, maybe I'll take you up on that offer for tonight, eh?"

Hank steered toward the steps of the hotel.

"As long as you like, son. As long as you like."

# EPILOGUE

THE HEAD OF THE NATIONAL SECURITY COUNCIL EASED HIM-
self into the deep leather chair at the head of the oval table and
fished into a jacket pocket for the briar pipe and pouch of
aromatic tobacco.

He studied the other members of the council as he tamped
the tobacco into the bowl and applied a match. The Director
of the CIA, gaunt and vulture-like in appearance, meticulously
set out his papers, notepad and soft lead pencils; Army Security
sat upright, as though afraid to relax; Navy sat relaxed and
grinning as though the whole thing were really one big game.
Air Force looked worried, but then the Air Force Security
representative always did; the Director of the FBI sat with quiet
confidence, probably generated as a result of the files that had
been passed down for years—J. Edgar Hoover's legacy lived
on. The buried skeletons of a nation's leaders were in his mind,
brought out only when a favor was needed or pressure was
required to change a senator's mind.

The NSC head lit the pipe, thinking briefly of the awesome
power each of these men could wield if they so desired. The
taste of power was a delicious aphrodisiac, needing constant

replenishment. And he knew that each, himself included, made full use of the powers available to him.

He sighed and straightened himself in the chair, hopeful this month's meeting would not last as long as normal. He had much to do before the day was out, it was his granddaughter's birthday. He coughed gently, immediately the low hum of conversation died and all faces turned in expectation.

"Good morning, gentlemen. We have a heavy schedule, so I suggest that we attempt to get through the agenda as rapidly as possible."

He turned a page of the minutes of the preceding meeting and wondered how many corrections would be required this time. It was inevitable there would be some. There always were.

"The minutes of the last meeting, may we approve?" He waited for the objections he knew would come.

"I move the minutes," intoned Navy.

"Seconded," replied FBI.

The National Security head blinked in surprise. "All those in favor?"

He noted the unanimous acceptance of the committee on his pad and smiled. He might make Lucy's birthday party after all!

"Item one on your agendas, gentlemen, Operation Ice Melt. FBI first, please."

The FBI Director cleared his throat, perched his half moon spectacles on the end of his nose and peered at his notes.

"We experienced thirteen bank robberies during the emergency, quite low considering the opportunities available; one hundred twenty murders; one thousand reported rapes; auto thefts at the moment number five thousand and still climbing. Looting was extensive and some thirty persons were shot."

The director leaned back slightly in the chair and removed the glasses. There were no questions for him, as normal. Rarely did anybody question the Director of the Federal Bureau of Investigation.

"Thank you, Mr. Director. OK, let's get to the CIA."

The Director of the CIA smiled his tight little smile and repositioned an already perfectly placed pencil on the highly-polished surface of the table.

"We are sure, at this stage, Ice Melt has cleared away our mutual problems. Your dockets list the number of casualties experienced along the flight path of the mutants, therefore I see no point in going over these figures verbally. Suffice it to say that losses were very large, although perhaps not as large as we had prepared for from an emergency on the scale just experienced.

"The military will, undoubtedly, be reporting on their aspects, but CIA would like to point out that the emergency provided an excellent theater for testing our mobilization capability and an equally excellent opportunity for establishing Russian contingency plans. We evaluate that, in a similar emergency situation, the Russians would not be able to move to a ready situation as quickly as ourselves.

"Indeed, there is every indication that the Russians did not give any thought at all to civilian casualties. They preferred concentrating their energies solely on troop movements. I needn't tell you how beneficial this information will be to us in time of war.

"In the Mideast, we have been able to make considerable inroads in the oil producing areas. The Saudis, and most other Arab countries, are looking to us for aid and military support and this is already en route, despite Russian protests. Another most encouraging result of the crisis is the Yemeni situation.

"We are now ready to allow an insurrection in this region. There can be no doubt at all that the government is in a state of considerable disarray, following the worldwide emergency. Many of the Yemeni leaders left the country at the first sign of trouble. We have," he added wryly, "been successful in ensuring they have difficulty in returning."

The CIA director drank from a tumbler of water and then continued.

"Aid to the freedom fighters will be ferried through Saudi Arabia to the mountains. Sadallah is ready to launch his coup."

"All in all, gentlemen, despite the trouble the locusts caused, I feel the United States is poised to come out of it all rather better off than before, just as soon as one or two minor details are sorted out."

A slight murmur ran around the room at the mention of an insurrection in the sensitive Mideast. Most of the men remembered the Bay of Pigs fiasco and none of them wanted to be involved in a similar debacle.

The council leader coughed gently and silence returned. He re-lit his pipe before looking back to the CIA chief.

"And what are those 'one or two minor details,' Mr. Director?"

The CIA chief returned the penetrating gaze unflinchingly and replied, "There are several people who remain in possession of information that could reverse the situation entirely."

"How do you intend to remedy this?"

The director smiled.

"We have been taking steps for some time now to ensure that our name is not too closely associated with what has occurred, in the public eye. And we have in our possession a swift, easy, risk-free solution to the problem posed by our friends at Trans-Global."

The national security head leaned forward. "And what exactly have you arranged?"

"I'd rather not reveal that," replied the director.

"We would rather you did," the FBI man was quick to answer. "May I remind you this council is structured to ensure the fullest possible cooperation between the various security agencies of this country. It is also structured to ensure the best possible advice is given to the president concerning security matters. We can not give that advice if we do not all have the full picture."

The National Security head glowered. There had always been acrimony between these two and doubtless there always would.

CIA sat silently for a moment and observed the slight smile of pleasure which crossed the FBI director's face.

"Very well," he conceded. "Fort Langley determined that a potential answer to the situation lay with a former Air Force captain by the name of Holland. He was court-martialed in

Korea and given a reprimand, resigned his commission and spent the intervening years up to the emergency as a pilot flying for a variety of companies in an even wider variety of locations.

"Holland graduated with an engineering degree after his service in Korea, but didn't employ it. From that time, until we picked him up, he was really a shell of a man. Going through an identity crisis. Our psychiatrists evaluated that the rot in Holland's mind started with his war service when he questioned the validity of U.S. action in that theater and was further heightened by his court-martial. Later factors which contributed were the death of his mother and the immediate rejection of him by his father. The rejection factor of the two entities he cared most about—service and family—attacked the very fabric of his psyche.

"Outwardly, of course, the subject was the epitome of the macho stereotype and this is why Holland was so ideal as a control subject. His inner torment was never allowed to rise to the surface, he could not expurgate himself of the sense of guilt and inadequacy which he felt. Guilt over his mission in Korea, which subsequently led to his court-martial. Inadequacy over his failure to both heal the rift between himself and his father before the latter's death and his inability to come to terms with all these factors. This left his mental door wide open for subconscious control.

"Langley determined that reverse psychology would enable us to walk through that door. Agent Volk was established as the antagonist on the premise, the successful premise, that Holland would do what he was told not to do in order to prove to the oppressive father figure, Volk, that he was his own man and not subject to paternal influence.

"Holland's own pathetic inadequacies and mental state made this method of subject control both desirable and relatively easy. He fell in with us every step of the way, never once not believing that the courses of action he embarked on were anything but his own wishes and intentions.

"Holland was of no interest at all, until we discovered that his fiancée was one of those killed on board the Trans-Global airplane. Now, we knew that Holland wouldn't do anything to help us willingly, and could do quite a lot of damage. We needed to ensure that his interest was maintained along the right lines regarding the crash, so we could manipulate him into a position where he would both obscure our present machinations and safeguard our future.

"One of our agents was instructed to carry out the brief, and did so most successfully. Holland now is in a situation whereby he had lost two women he loved deeply. He is a man who considers himself outside the mainstream of society and is, without doubt, a man who will act according to his instincts.

"In short, the ideal subject for unconscious control."

The Air Force security chief looked at the CIA director with considerable distaste. "You said, two women, Mr. Director. I thought he only lost his fiancée."

The man looked at the Air Force officer with amusement. *"Only* lost his fiancée, Colonel? I should have thought that was enough, wouldn't you?"

The colonel blushed. "I meant—"

"I know what you meant. The second woman was Dr. Stephanie Caine. Albert Steiner's niece. She suffered a most unfortunate accident on the glacier. She had become very close to Holland during the days prior to the final solution."

The colonel flipped through the red leather folder in front of him. "I'm confused, sir. Where did this agent of yours come in to keep the interest going?"

Again the tight little smile. "They were one and the same. Caine belonged to us."

"How does Holland fit in now?"

"Perhaps most importantly. We can't allow Trans-Global executives to tell what they know about the mutants. Politically, it would be suicide.

"Action is needed now, gentlemen. We cannot use CIA operatives, so it has to be a private individual. Somebody with a big ax to grind. That's where Holland comes in. Given enough room to maneuver, he will exact his revenge and the ends we require, doing it quickly enough to ensure silence. After all, he thinks Trans-Global has been trying to kill him as well as having murdered his girlfriend."

"Political murder," muttered Navy.

"Perhaps so," agreed CIA, "but one which will ensure this country's credibility and oil supply for the next several decades."

"How many will Holland hit?" asked Army.

"There were three who were involved in the orders for the destruction of the aircraft, as he suspects. What he doesn't know, of course, is that these men were also our operatives. He'll learn their names this evening. We also want him to take care of a couple of others who are an embarrassment to us. Five in all. I think we can be assured that all the skeletons will again be back in their appropriate cupboard!"

The National Security head spoke again. "You say he will learn their names this evening. How?"

"Holland has spent the last week at a motel in Livingston and this indicates to us, even more, that he needs a mission to become motivated again. After the operation was completed he just hung around the town, visiting the mountain every day. He's a broken man. One of our operatives runs the hotel. Tonight, he will inform Holland of the names and lead him deeper into the conclusion that it has all been a Trans-Global operation. Of course, by the time he finds out, if he ever does, that T.G. is blameless it will be much too late for him."

Navy ground his cigarette viciously into the ashtray. "The man has been . . . programmed, for Christ's sake!" he spluttered angrily.

The Director of the CIA looked up in surprise. "Hardly. He will be operating because he wants to. We have simply supplied the stimulus, the motivating factors. Now Holland's own psyche takes over."

At length, the meeting adjourned for lunch. None of the men felt particularly elated at the report, but equally, none felt particularly depressed. It was all part of the world they had come to accept.

The National Security head buttoned his pants. He had resisted his tailor's demands that he should insert zip flies. He wanted at least one old-fashioned concept to remain steadfast.

The Director of the CIA stepped away from the urinal and moved to the washbasins. The chairman finished soaping his hands and passed the bar to the director.

"None of the bright boys bothered to ask you, then?" he said dryly.

"What's that?"

"About the girl—what was her name?"

"Dr. Caine?"

"Caine. Yes, that's the one. You said he'd lost the two women in his life, but nobody bothered to ask you exactly how Dr. Caine died."

"Neither did you."

"Perhaps I don't care to know."

The National Security head washed his hands again as though to remove some more unseen dirt. The director cleaned his fingernails with a file, examining the result with great care.

"How did she die? Planned or accidental?"

"I thought you didn't want to know."

"I changed my mind."

"Let's just say that her death would and did provide that extra and vital stimulus for Mr. Holland."

"You murdered her?"

The director shrugged. "It seems she was issued with a sub-standard suit which ripped and the locusts penetrated. A flame-thrower operator thought he was doing the best by hosing her down. Unfortunately . . ." He left the rest unsaid.

"Sub-standard suit, flamethrower. I suppose the operator was one of your men?" The National Security leader shook his head angrily. "No, don't tell me any more, it'll spoil my lunch. You and Volk certainly seem to have made the best of a bad job."

"Thank you, sir," the director said, ignoring the sarcasm. Then he smiled and decided he would spoil the politician's lunch after all.

"Of course, Volk hasn't exactly escaped scot-free for his part in the screw up. Nor should he; after all, his man killed the journalist, Sandy Howard, with a lousy shot."

"Hasn't he? I don't understand."

The director looked apologetic. "Oh, I'm sorry, I thought you knew. Dr. Caine and he—"

"What about them?"

"They were married."


Mark Holland tossed the suitcase into the back of the station wagon and turned back to Hank, who now sat on the third step of the porch.

"Goodbye, Hank, thanks for letting me stay."

"So long, son. You take care of yourself."

Mark smiled. He would certainly do that. At least until he had completed what he had to do. He had the names and the hate had surged uncontrollably through his veins the evening before as Hank had finally admitted all that he knew.

He drove out of town toward Butte. When he was high in the mountains he pulled the station wagon into the side, got out and looked back just once more at the shape that stood solid on the horizon.

He stared at it for several minutes without thought of Kate or Stephanie. Just the mountain in his mind. Then, abruptly, he wheeled around and returned to the car.

A movement beside the litter basket on the side of the road caught his attention. The discarded remains of a picnic lunch seemed suddenly to come alive. After a moment he saw and recognized them for what they were.

A low chuckle started from his throat. As he slipped the gearstick into drive and headed onto the road his hysterical laughter echoed across the valley.

The sun climbed higher into the clear morning sky as they devoured the remains of the chicken carcass. Then, as one, they lifted into the air in search of more.

# Acknowledgments

*The author would like to acknowledge and applaud the efforts being made constantly on our behalf by the Centre for Overseas Pest Control and Research. I also wish to acknowledge C. F. Hemmings' fine work, The Locust Menace, which puts the tremendous problem of locusts and the fight against them into understandable layman's language.*

*I should also like to extend thanks to the staff of the reference library at the United States embassy in London, who helped tremendously and readily, almost making research a pleasure, as well as to my official editor, Liza Dawson, for her patience and suggestions and my unofficial one, Kathryn Marriott, for helping to spot the traps and pitfalls which are so easy to fall into.*

*Lastly, my gratitude to the Central Intelligence Agency which takes the necessary steps to ensure the continuance of our society.*

*J. H.*
*Ditchling, England*